Cover Photo © 2013 O'Neil De Noux

# GRIM REAPER

## O'NEIL DE NOUX

# FOR Buddy

*GRIM REAPER* is a work of fiction. The incidents and characters described herein are a product of the author's imagination and are used fictitiously. Any resemblance to actual persons living or dead, business establishments, events, or locales is entirely coincidental.

Author Web Site: http://www.oneildenoux.net
Twitter: ONeilDeNoux

*Published by*
Big Kiss Productions
New Orleans

First Printing 1988
Second Printing 1991
Third Printing 2013

# GRIM REAPER

## *Chapters*

# THIS IS NEW ORLEANS
# 1981

*Chapter 1*
Dauphine Street

The first murder occurred on a cool spring night on a street named Dauphine in the old French Quarter. A soft breeze flowed down the narrow street, filtering between the timeworn buildings and the lacework iron balconies as Marie Sumner strolled toward Esplanade Avenue. Marie was heading back to her car parked at the edge of the Quarter. She was thinking about where she would go next because it was still early for New Orleans night life. Things were just getting started around eleven at night, especially on a Friday night. And after two drinks in two boring lounges in the Quarter, Marie was looking for something more lively. She did not notice the man following her as she crossed Ursulines Street.

The breeze made Marie's light blue dress swish as she walked, revealing more of her legs than usual. It felt good on her legs and especially nice as it flowed through her long dark hair. As she walked, she listened to the soft sound of the wind. It was quiet at the edge of the Quarter, unlike the noise of Bourbon Street. Near Esplanade the buildings were houses instead of the bars and shops of Bourbon and Royal Streets. Marie glanced up at the full moon and thought how pretty the night was.

That was when she heard something else, something behind her. She turned and saw the man right behind her.

"Oh!" she jumped. "You scared me." she moved back instinctively.

The man stopped and smiled at her, in a shy way. He made no movement toward her and looked away from her stare, as if he were embarrassed, as if he suddenly had been caught doing something he wasn't supposed to do. He was a pudgy man, wore a plaid shirt and looked plain, looked ordinary.

Marie gave him a stern look, a don't-bother-me-look that she kept in reserve for weirdoes and jerks. then she turned and walked away without a backward glance. She did not hear him following and she was not about to look back. She just stopped up her pace and fumbled in her purse for the spray can of mace she kept in case of – whatever.

She crossed Barracks Street and closed in on Esplanade when she realized that she had seen that face before. She had seen that shy smile, that pudgy face before, that very night, in one of the bars. She walked faster and strained to listen for anything behind her. She did not hear a thing.

Marie didn't even feel him strike her from behind. She just felt the sidewalk slam against her face and then a deep burning sting in her back. She tried to scream but the burning ripped deeply through her as she felt something sharp and hot in her back. The last sound she heard was the sound of plunging.

•

He had her. He had her down and the knife was sinking deep in her again and again...he could not catch his breath and his arms felt like rubber as he sank the long-bladed knife into her...and his hands were on fire as he struck...and he continued until the seething frenzy in his chest gave way in one gasping exhalation of air...he leaned back away from the warm wetness of the object beneath him.

He knelt back and tried to catch his breath as he looked down at all the blood on the light blue dress. He was shaking. His arms quivered in tense spasms. He felt as if he arms were about to fall off, as if he were about to collapse, to pass out because there was not enough oxygen in the air for him to breathe. He was exhausted.

But there was something else. There was something inside him that fought the exhaustion, that gave him strength. It returned power to his arms, power to his body, power to his mind. It was an inner strength, a rush of energy, the same rush he felt when he overpowered her. It was an elated feeling of overpowering a weakness – first the weakness of the girl, then the weakness in himself.

He sucked in another deep gulp of air, reached over and withdrew the knife, wiping it on one of the legs next to him before he put the knife back in his belt. Then he went back to work. He rolled the body over and began to quickly pull the dress off. He yanked it down past the legs. Then he pulled off the stockings ad panties, tossing them inside. He spread the legs wide and left them that way. He lifted the severed bra and stuffed it into his pocket.

He looked at the face one more time before moving his mouth down over the exposed breasts. Then he leaned down and bit the left nipple as hard as he could.

The phone was answered promptly after the first ring by the newest detective in the Homicide Division.

"Homicide – LaStanza," I said as I put the receiver to my ear.

"Detective LaStanza?" asked the voice at the other end.

"That's what I said," I came right back, still not used to the title of detective, but it sounded good to me.

"This is Headquarters. We got a good one for you." It was the voce of the Communications Supervisor. He spoke in that quick, typical, police-staccato voice, "Got a Signal Thirty working. First District. 1300 block of Dauphine Street. Need a Homicide team."

I reached over, picked up a pen from my newly assigned, worn-metal desk and started jotting notes:

"Date: Friday, 3/12/81. Time: 11:22 p.m. Signal: 30. 1300 Dauphine."

After a few more quick questions I completed my notes.

"White female. 34C (Cutting). Perpetrator Unknown."

I hung up the phone and looked across the squad room at my partner, who was busy attempting to type a report. He was a lousy typist and wasn't having much success. I picked up my notes and started across the room. "Mark," I called out, "we got a Thirty. A whodunit."

"Are you fuckin' kiddin' me?" My partner looked up from the typewriter, his mouth falling open. He glanced at his watch and bellowed, "Half hour from knocking off and we get nailed with a murder and a whodunit to boot!"

I nodded.

"Fuck!" Mark yelled as he jumped back from the typewriter. He glared at the machine with teeth gritted.

"Come over here!" He shouted to me, "Come here and show me where the goddamn *p* is hiding on his worthless machine." He pointed to the typewriter as if he were accusing it of murder or whatever. He huffed loudly.

My new partner, Detective Mark Land, looked like a grizzly bear when he huffed. Hell, he looked like a grizzly bear even when he didn't huff. He *was* a grizzly at 5 feet 10 inches and two hundred plus pounds, none of it fat. He had a large black moustache, the kind Brando had in *Viva Zapata*, and unruly black hair that was always messed up and in his eyes.

I thought he was going to throw the goddamn typewriter out the third-floor window of police headquarters. Instead, he just huffed again. He also didn't budge until I went over an pointed out the *p*. It was hiding where all good little *p's* hide, I told him as I pointed it out, "There, next to the *o*. Remember," I explained, "the *p* is always above the colon."

He made sure I was right, and checked out the *p* before quickly putting away the report he was working on, shoving it all in his desk drawer. "Tell me about it," he said as we went for our briefcases and headed for the elevator. I told him what I knew about the murder, which wasn't much.

As we passed the front desk of the Detective Bureau, the fat desk-sergeant laughed at us. Fat Phil Danton was sitting out his retirement behind the desk and usually laughed at any detective who had to work for a living. Especially anyone in Homicide, especially when it was a whodunit and he knew you'd probably be out all night.

"Want me to keep your girlfriend warm tonight?" He laughed as we walked past. He picked up the phone as if he were going to call a girlfriend and cackled as loud as he could.

"What a fuckin' asshole," Mark muttered as we waited for the extremely slow elevator to lumber up to the third floor.

"He reminds me of an armadillo," Mark added as he looked back at Fat Phil. "Got a little bitty head and a big ass."

He was right.

As we stepped into the elevator and waited for the door to make up its mind and finally shut, Mark continued, "He's a shit-eatin' armadillo and he couldn't keep a broad warm at night 'cause he's got a whisky dick!" and that was that.

Mark added, "What'd I tell you about tonight? Friday the fuckin' thirteenth!"

We turned on our police radios on the way to the scene. As usual, we would be the last to arrive. Every swinging dick above the rank of sergeant had already visited the scene, fucking up any possible evidence. And of course, the media was already there, along with a couple of K-9 units who had nothing better to do, not to mention a Community Relations car, two Urban Squad cars, a Tactical Unit from Algiers, two Louisiana State Police cars, a car from the Harbor police, and a very useful car from the Mississippi River Police, who could fuck up traffic anywhere, anytime. And of course there were district cars from each and every one of New Orleans's eight police districts. I'm fuckin' serious.

Cops are the noisiest people on earth. It's natural. Only they should know better about evidence and all. But they don't and no amount of written directives ever works. You can order them to stay away, warn them about not contaminating major crime scenes, such as murder scenes, and they still come. They all figure they know what they're doing and *they* won't contaminate anything, the other guy might, but they won't. That's just the way it is.

I had to park our car on Esplanade Avenue because of all the police cars blocking the streets. We stepped up on the sidewalk and I looked at the crowd down the street. It sure looked like a big scene. I had seen big scenes before, as a patrolman, back when I was going around contaminating scenes myself. But now, in Homicide, it was different. Now I had to write it, had to process that scene, looking at the crowd made my heart sink.

"Look at the fuckin' scene," I heard myself say aloud.

"It ain't so bad," Mark said. "It could be worse."

"Yeah?" I questioned.

"Yeah," Mark answered, "it could be Mardi Gras."

He was right. Nothing was worse than *that*.

I had been in Homicide exactly one month and I took out my notepad to write this scene myself. I started jotting right away a we walked.

"Arrived: 11:45 P.M. Temperature: mid 60's. Slight breeze. Area: houses and apartments. Scene: Corner Dauphine and Barracks Streets."

I followed Mark who began calling on the radio for our sergeant to meet us at the scene. We eased our way between the parked police units to the rear end of the crowd. We stopped a second for Mark to take out a sheet of paper from his side coat pocket. He called out to a lieutenant in the crowd and waved the lieutenant over.

It was a First District lieutenant, a big stupid-looking fella with red hair and bloodshot eyes. he casually strolled up to Mark with a bored look on his pasty face. Mark handed him the sheet of paper.

"Got something here for you," Mark said. It was a Xerox copy of the latest letter from the Chief of Police, which concerned the securing of major crime scenes, and which ended in instructing Homicide detectives to write down, for disciplinary action, the names of unauthorized personnel on the scene.

Mark gave the lieutenant enough time to read the letter, which took a while. Then he said, "Think you can clear away some of these morons?" Mark pointed to the crowd of assorted policemen's asses in front of us. That was all we could see of the murder scene, policemen's behinds.

"Especially that one." Mark pointed to one K-9 officer who was brilliant enough to have his dog out of the car on a leash. The dog was going through convulsions because of all the blood.

The lieutenant didn't take kindly to taking such orders, but we were right, as Homicide dicks usually were. So the looey did what looeys do best, which was annoy everyone so much they started to leave.

We kept the fist officer who had arrived on the scene, as well as a couple of other First District patrolmen for security. "No one above patrolman," Mark demanded. Patrolmen listen better.

Slowly, the crowed of blue began to melt away and, piece by piece, I was able to see the scene. It wasn't pretty. First one leg could be seen, naked and bloody, then the bottom half of the body became visible to me. Under the bright searchlights from the parked police cars, the blood was very red on the white flesh, on pavement and on the blue dress.

"Jesus fuckin' Christ!" I blurted out as the whole body became visible. "Jesus fuckin' Christ!"

"My thoughts exactly," Mark agreed as we took in the scene from the edge of the nearest parked police car.

I had seen many dead people before and lots of blood but no matter how many time, it was shocking. Right there on the sidewalk, in the middle of the French Quarter, there was a butchered body just lying there, naked and spread eagle for the whole goddamn world to see.

"Jesus fuckin' Christ!" I repeated.

Mark patted me on the back. "Never. Ever. Did this girl think she could possible end up this way." His dark eyebrows danced up and won, like a bear trying to impersonate Groucho Marx. He was trying for humor. It wasn't working.

"Think about it a minute," he continued. "That's it! That's all that's left of her. For the rest of her life she ain't moving outta that position. She's come to the end of the line and look what she looks like. She looks like *hell*. What the fuck's she doin' here all alone." Mark growled, leaned close and told the body, "This is *New Orleans*. You don't walk around alone at night.

Back to me now. "Think about it. In a minute the crime lab will be here and take pictures of her and all those cops gaping at her all spread-eagled like that." Mark shook his head. "I'll be deep down inside – she's embarrassed."

He had a point. I'd sure be embarrassed for her, for Mark, for me for trying to find something to chuckle at when there was nothing but horror here.

When the crime lab technician arrived I started drawing a sketch of the scene, placing the body in its position, placing the houses behind and the street in front. I noted the addresses on the houses and described the façade of each private home and apartment house in the entire are.

Mark glanced over my shoulder tor making sure I was doing okay, he stepped over and began to interview the first officer who had arrived on the scene. I overheard something about an anonymous call from a drunk sleeping on a sidewalk. That was real fucking cute.

I had processed two suicide scenes in my first month in Homicide, but this is my first murder. So Mark kept a close eye on me and I kept a close eye on the crime lab technician. The technician was a quiet fella with thick glasses and a very mater-of-fact way of thoroughly working through a scene. I followed along as he started by taking his first photographs. We stepped back and he took overall photos of the scene from different angles up and down Dauphine Street. Then we closed in, taking more photos, until we were up on the body, taking close-ups. He recorded it all on film.

I jotted notes: "White female. Early twenties, small build, long dark hair. Clothes – light blue wrap-dress, navy blue high-heel shoes, pantyhose torn, white panties torn, all clothes bloodstained. Jewelry – gold chain bracelet with gold pendant initialed *S*. Bulova wrist watch, gold in color and still running, gold ring on right ring finger with one red stone, all bloodstained."

I jotted a description of the body as the technician finished up his close-up photos of her face. "Nude," I wrote, "Lying on back, legs spread-eagled, right arm stretched out with right hand partially in gutter, left arm against side, mouth open, eyes open, body still warm to touch, lividity beginning, no visible wound on the front of body."

Her face was masked in that death look, that pale and lifeless color of the skin. Her mouth was open and there was blood on her front teeth. But it was her eyes that were the most telling. In death, eyes take on a glassy, unfocused look. Her eyes were hazel, cold and dead and faded hazel.

Next to her left hand I found a small can of mace. It was a purse-sized spray can of mace with the name *The Protector* on it. I did not touch the can but I did touch her and her hand was beginning to feel cool. Her fingers were still pliable and looked so small, almost like a child's hand.

"Mark," I called out, "come over here."

When Mark stepped over, I showed him the can of mace. He glanced at the can and then leaned over the face of the dead girl. He looked into her glassy eyes and asked, "Who did it? Who the fuck did this to you?" He said to the lifeless face, "You saw him coming, why didn't you "

"If only brains were made of video tape," I cut into Mark's conversation with the dead girl's face.

"You know it."

I continued to stare at the body as Mark stepped away. The technician was reloading his camera. I felt as if the dead girl and I

were alone for a moment, for a reason. I felt like telling her
something, telling her we'd get this rotten bastard. But I didn't say
anything. What do you say to a dead and embarrassed girl,
anyway?

I don't know. But I felt a closeness with her. She and I were
connected now. She was the victim and I was the hunter now. It
was as if those glassy eyes were asking me to get that bastard. It
was up to us, Mark and me, and it was a weight we would carry
around – those pleading eyes.

I found her purse against the way of the building about forty
feet from the body. It was in a heap, as if it had been thrown there.
There were even a couple of drops of blood on the purse, from the
blood splatter. In fact, there was a blood splatter on the sidewalk as
far as forty feet away, spots on the white masonry walls of the
building, and dots on the sidewalk.

The technician came over and carefully photographed the
blood splatter. Then he photographed the purse. And only after
Mark and I had gone over the scene once more, flashing lights
back and forth, for any other possible evidence, and found none,
did the technician put up his camera and take out his measuring
tape.

Mark held one end while the technician held the other and
called out measurements as I wrote them down. We triangulated
the measurements from fixed points. We took down the distance
from the corners of buildings to the street posts to the curbs. Then
we measured from the girl's right hand to the curb to a street post
to a corned of a building. We moved from hand to hand, from leg
to leg, until we had it all down, in case we had to put it back
together later – exactly to scale. We measured the width of the
street and the height of the curb and the length of the pool of blood
that had flowed in the gutter. We just let them have a little blood.

Then it was time to collect the evidence. The technician
collected the purse first, carefully picking it up and placing it in a
brown paper bag. Since the purse was made of cloth, there was no
use dusting for fingerprints, but there could be fiber evidence and
you never knew, the murderer may have left this name on a note in
her purse, you never fucking know until you look.

Wearing rubber gloves, the technician carefully lifted the wallet out of the purse and even more carefully sifted through for the girl's driver's license. And you guessed it, no note from the fucking killer.

The technician positioned the driver's license on the hood of his nearby police car and with a flashlight in hand, I looked into the smiling face of Marie R. Sumner, who used to live on Mirabeau Avenue in Gentilly, who used to stand 5 feet 2 inches tall and weight ninety-five pounds, whose eyes used to be bright hazel, back when she was alive, back before she decided to stroll down Dauphine Street in the lovely old French Quarter one fucking spring night. It's funny how many new Orleanians forgot that new Orleans is the city that care forgot. Fuck! Marie forgot but the city sure fucking didn't.

She was twenty-three years old and her parents were about to be visited by the angel of Death in the likeness of the police chaplain, who came quickly to the scene, took down the information from me and headed to Mirabeau Avenue. Sergeant Rob mason arrived about that time with the only two other Homicide men working our shift.

"Talk to me," Mason said as he walked up. I stepped forward and told him the story about Marie, carefully pointing out the can of mace and the purse and the blood splatter. Mason's face never changed expression from that lean chiseled look behind the ever present cloud of cigarette smoke.

Mason's small eyes darted from Marie to the purse to the blood, then around at the nearby buildings. He was a thin man, even thinner than the lean technician, and he looked like a P.E. teacher from the 1950's. He had short crew cut hair and still wore baggy pants, wide ties, and penny-loafers – that were all now back in style. Only Mason's clothes were the originals.

The other two Homicide detectives with Mason remained in the background, listening and saying nothing. I did not know them well, even though we were all part of the same squad. The taller of the two, Paul Snowood, was a good-ole-boy. He was from north Louisiana, spoke with a southern, county accent, always wore cowboy boots and looked just like Marshal McCloud from that old television show. And he sang songs, all of the time.

The fat detective was Cal Boudreaux. He was from New Orleans, always wore wrinkled clothes and looked like an unkempt hippo. He farted a lot, too.

"Hey" – Boudreaux took that moment to break his silence – "there's a roach doing the back stroke in this broad's blood."

Fuck still calls women 'broads'. Damn, this wasn't the Fifties.

Mason was not amused and gave Boudreaux a quick cold stare before asking aloud, "Now where the fuck's the Coroner's Office?"

I reached over and took Snowood's radio out of his hand and called Headquarters. I asked for the coroner's immediate presence. "Some time before dawn," I added.

"That was cute" – Mason shot me a narrow-eyed stare – "real cute, LaStanza."

Mason believed in the old adage, stay off the radio unless you have to and cut the cute remarks. We were Homicide. Pros.

So we waited for the Coroner's Office. Mason made good use of the time, sending Snowood and Boudreaux with Marie's driver's license back to Bourdon Street. Mason and Mark then started canvassing the area for any potential witnesses. Mason also sent two uniformed men around jotting down license numbers of every car parked within a mile of the body, in case we got lucky like the Son-of-Sam case. You never fucking knew, the murderer may have left his car behind. And later on, we could go back and interview everyone who was parked in the area, in case they saw someone murdering a girl and just didn't bother to call. It happens.

Some people won't say a damn thing until a policeman comes and pulls it out of them like a fuckin' dentist. "But, Officer, I thought you already knew that information." *Sure*, we know fuckin' everything. That's why they teach a class in clairvoyance at the Police Academy.

So the technician and I were left alone with Marie once again, waiting for the coroner's meat wagon to arrive. Actually we weren't really alone. Besides the roaches, the ever-present newsmen were still standing beyond the police cars, with their ogle-eye lenses pointing at us and the gory mess that once was a girl named Marie.

14

It was then, while I was looking at Marie again, that I noticed the bite mark on her left breast. "Look at that." I pointed it out to the technician. He had photographed her breasts before, but after we realized that the mark on her left breast was indeed a bite mark, he took out his camera again and took a real close-up of it. Then he swabbed each breast with a cotton swab, in case there was any saliva left by our killer.

"Fuckin' animal!"

Finally the Coroner's Office unit arrived, a white van manned by a acne-faced college student. Of course, no doctor bothered to come, doctors had better things to do than fuck with murder victims in gutters. So the acne-faced kid pronounced Marie dead about 1:45 a.m., March 14th. Acne gave me the name of some doctor to use in our official report as the man who *actually* pronounced death, pointing out that we should mention the doctor did so personally. We never did that. We always put down Acne's name. Fuck em! Mason had already told me to just put down the facts and fuck em all!

Acne then rolled Marie over. She was getting stiff by then and there was marked lividity, which meant that the back of her body – which had been lying against the concrete – was purple-colored from the blood left in her that had settled from gravity. Her whole back was bloodied with numerous stab wounds. There were at least twenty-five or thirty, but there would be time at the autopsy to get an exact number. What I had to make sure of now was that the weapon wasn't lying under her, or if was nothing else to note. All the wounds were in her torso, none in her neck or legs.

The technician added one last touch, he wrapped Marie's hands in paper bags, in case there was some evidence she might have touched the murderer, scratched him or tore at his clothes. We would scraped her fingernails at the autopsy.

When the technician finished, ole Acne zipped her in a black body-bag, while the television crews filmed away and the newspaper man shot pictures, and Marie bade farewell to the French Quarter. She never did make it to wherever she was headed. But she made the papers.

After the meat wagon rolled off, the media left and the technician, too – after he collected the remainder of the evidence, clothes, blood samples. And then I was alone with the big bloodstain. Down the street the patrolmen still blocked off the area to traffic. But it was just me left, me and the roaches.

Mark came lumbering back from up Dauphine Street a short time later.

"Find anything?" I asked

"Fuck no," he huffed

Mason was close behind.

"I came up empty too," Mason added. "As usual, nobody heard nothin', nobody saw nothin', nobody knows a goddamn thing."

I looked down at my watch and noticed it was getting close to three o'clock and I remembered I was supposed to call Jessica if I was gonna be late. That was supposed to have been around midnight. Fuck me!

"Just like this fuckin' city." Mark declared aloud, "nobody saw nothin'."

"Fuckin' ay," Mason noted.

"How the hell did someone just walk away from that?" I asked, nodding at the pool of blood.

"Maybe he didn't walk away. Maybe he lives right here." Mason nodded to a nearby building. "Maybe he's up there in a window right now watching us, beating his meat and laughing his ass off 'cause he knows we ain't going home tonight."

Facetious statement, but could be true. They'd knocked on every door in the area, woke up people. None with blood on their hands.

Mason tossed his half-smoked cigarette into the pool of blood in the gutter at our feet. "Let's get to work," he muttered. "Let's go find out what happened to the lost patrol." So we headed toward Bourbon Street.

"Guess this is my case," Mark said glumly to Mason, hoping for a miracle, hoping that Mason would assign it to the lost patrol. Fat chance. We worked the scene. And Boudreaux had caught a misdemeanor murder the night before.

For the first time that night Mason smiled that wily grin of his. "It's yours," he told Mark. "Cal caught that Thirty last night."

"That don't count," Mark argued. "It was a bar killin'. Black dude killed another black dude he knows. Just paperwork," Mark went on but it was no use. It was a Signal Thirty and it was Mark's turn.

Mason just shook his head and stopped to tell the patrolmen they could leave, after he secured the list of license plate numbers from them. He handed the list to me and led the way, on foot, to Bourbon Street, to find Boudreaux and Snowood.

There was no way they would assign that case to me, just one month in Homicide – not a whodunit like Dauphine Street, not yet. I'd handled two suicides already and assisted on three misdemeanor murders, but a whodunit was a whole different ball game. If it was a smoking-gun killing, a wife shoots-the-shit-outta-her-husband or a barroom killing in a low down bar, then all that was left was paperwork. But let a girl get stabbed to death, let it be a mystery and it gets serious.

We took a left on St. Ann Street and walked one block down to Bourbon. We left the quiet of Dauphine and Ursulines behind, along with the bloodstain and the roaches. We stepped into the neon bright lights of flashy strip joints and loud tacky bars.

Bourbon Street was a big whore of a street, all pimped up in plastic and neon make-up with rouge-red signs and mascara walls of blue and brown and tired yellow, where fake silicon-woman roam. There were plenty of strip joints where heavy, ugly women with sad, sunken eyes, would take their clothes off. Most of the women were middle-aged, women who anyone in his right mind would *never* want to see naked. And even if you *were* fucked up enough to want to see, you'd see nothing but blubber and pasties, no nipples and no pussy. That was against the law.

Bourbon Street was so dam gaudy, with its big-mouthed barkers who stood outside the joints, trying to coax the stupid passer-by into the sleazy bars. It's hard to say anything nice about bars that charge a minimum of ten dollars for one watered-down drink.

Bourbon had sidewalks lined in cellulite, which smelled of sweat and dirt and stale liquor all of the time. It was never clean. Buildings that would look old and quaint on nearby Royal Street, looked like tired whores on Bourbon. It was home for the plastic people, the fake women, transvestites, transsexuals, homosexuals and heterosexuals with grotesque fetishes, all sorts of fucking pimps, prostitutes, and other various scum.

All of which made Bourbon Street a very interesting place to visit – like the Audubon Zoo. It was enough to bring Marie Sumner visiting on a Friday night she should have stayed home. Then maybe I would have been with my girlfriend, Jessica, instead of walking down Bourbon Street with two other tired cops.

•

We found Paul Snowood standing outside a strip joint, talking to a girl with bright blue hair. The girl had on a leopard skin jumpsuit and was skinny, thinner even than lanky Snowood and skinny Mason.

"So, you go out much?" Snowood asked the girl as I stepped up behind him.

"Yeah man," the girl answered, cocking her head to one side like a parrot, "I hang out." She shifted her weight to her right foot and cocked her head the other way. "Say man, you really a cop?"

"Just like you're really a fuckin' whore," I interjected as I stepped up, regretting it as soon as I said it. Maybe she wasn't a whore at all but my Sicilian was up and I was in no mood.

The girl sneered at me and put her hands on her hips. "Is this short one with you?" she asked Paul.

"Yep," Paul answered in his southern twang. He put his arm around me and added, "He's ma lover."

I looked up at his silly face and asked if old blue-hair had seen our victim that night. "Don't rightly know," Paul answered. "I was just getting' warmed up when you come."

He let go of me and handed blue-hair the driver's license of Marie Sumner and asked her if she'd ever seen the girl.

"No," was the answer. "What'd she do?"

"Got herself murdered," I answered and grabbed the license from the girl and headed into the sleazy joint where Boudreaux was watching a fat woman take her clothes off.

Needless to say, the other team had surfaced no useful information. Mason lit another cigarette and called us together for a minute. He decided to split us up. Mason would take Boudreaux and go to Marie's house and find out what they could about her, for all we knew she could have been *with* someone, or gone to meet someone, or maybe her father butchered her, you never knew.

Mark and Paul and I remained on Bourdon Street to prowl the bars. And that was just what we did for the next three hours, in and out of scum-bag joint after scum-bag joint until it was after six o'clock and Mason Called on the portable radio.

We all met down at the Café DuMonde on Decatur Street. We took a table in the outside area of the café, ordered hot, strong café au lait and exchanged notes. Mason had come up with some things which he told us about as he wrote them down in his notebook.

Marie left home alone with no definite plans. Parents did not know where she hung out but we had a list of girlfriends to interview later. No known current boyfriends. Las known boyfriend was in the U.S. Navy in the Mediterranean.

Her car had been located on Esplanade Avenue by Mason. It was locked and looked clean.

Mason handed Mark the victim's address book. It went without saying that we would check the names in the book against the names of the cars parked in the area and then go down the list and dig and dig.

First thing I learned in Homicide was that eighty percent of all homicides are committed by friends or relatives, so you never knew.

Mason leaned back in his chair and took a deep gulp of coffee, then asked me what we got so far. I took out my own notebook and listed the following facts:

Multiple stab wounds in her back.

Clothes removed after, and body positioned that way on purpose.

"He wanted her found that way," Mark injected.

She saw him coming because she had the can of mace in her hand.

"Maybe she always carried the mace," Paul said.

"Could be," I agreed. So I put a question mark by number three.

The bite mark.

"What bite mark?" Snowood and Boudreaux both sat up.

So I explained. There was no doubt in any of the faces around me that the bite was a *very* interesting fact. "I had it swabbed," I added.

"Good." Mason nodded.

We placed Marie in two bars. In both instances, she was alone and only the bartenders remembered her, and both vaguely. I took oral statements from each bartender. The only reaction came from bartender number two, who said, "You don't say," when I told him what had happened.

Bourbon Street reeked with compassion.

A quick check of each bartender proved neither had left the bar after coming to work. And of course, no one saw anyone following Marie out.

"You sure about those bartenders?" Mason asked. His eyes were closed as he leaned back in his chair.

"Yeah," Marked answered, "I went to school with the bouncer in one joint and the tender never left, and the second joint has a cop on duty at the front door and their tender never left either."

"So" – Snowood frowned – "we don't know so much." At least he was listening. Boudreaux was too busy with his second order of *beignets*, those hot powdered-sugar donuts that I used to love as a kid.

"We know it's a man," Mark stated matter-of-factly. "And he's a real sicko, especially the undressing and the spread-eagle bullshit."

"We don't know much more," Mason added from his leaning position.

I finished my coffee and ordered another cup. Boudreaux started in with his bad jokes about sex and how a pussy can get more people in more trouble. Snowood told a joke too, and Mark added a recent dago joke. Joke, and it breaks the tension. Keep serious and the tension builds. So we joked about the body and about Bourbon Street and even about each other. I cut in with a remark about Snowood. He was the only man I ever knew who could dip Skoal and drink coffee at the same time. I have no idea how he knew when to spit and when to swallow.

"So what's next?" I asked finally.

"Paul and Cal go home," Mason said. "Get some rest."

Mark and I were going to the autopsy at 8:00 a.m. Mason stood up, stretched and went back to work himself. He went to Headquarters to prepare a formal press release. He would do it the usual way, which meant he would put in certain errors, on purpose. It was an old trick, not to report the whole truth to the media, because the murderer will read it. You'd be surprised just how many murderers go around correcting police statements about murders, to their relatives and friends and even casual acquaintances, and then eventually we find out that there was someone who knew what he should not know. It was a proven fact that certain elements of all murders should remain known only to the police and the murderer. It was a link that might one day bring us together.

So Mason would say there was only one stab wound and *never* mention anything about the bite mark. He would also say there was an important clue left behind by the murderer, who would *shit* when he read that, unless he was sick enough not to give a shit. Mason would keep the whole mess as vague as possible and it would work.

Until some pain-in-the-ass reporter, who had some sense, would go to the Coroner's Office and secure an official copy of the autopsy report and tell it all in the morning paper. Autopsy reports were *public record,* so any swinging dick could waltz in and get a copy. And some suck-ass reporter will always do it, "Because the public has a right to know."

Fuck the public! The public doesn't count. Only the victim counts. And for the time being, only we knew the facts, us, and the rotten mother fucker of a killer.

•

There was no dignity in death, especially at the New Orleans Coroner's Office. The morgue had a more appropriate nickname, to anyone who ever visited the place, it was called THE CHAMBER OF HORRORS.

Built in the Thirties, the *chamber* occupied the basement area of the old Criminal Courts building at the corner of Tulane Avenue and Broad Avenue. Its morgue looked as if it had not been cleaned since World War II. It reeked of death and formaldehyde, or whatever that fucking chemical was that stunk up the palace. Its walls were dotted with bloodstains from autopsies conducted long ago. Those same walls, with their moldy, peeling paint, were about fifteen feet high, for ventilation. But the only ventilation was one lone half-opened window on the right side. It was not a nice place to even visit.

Mark and I arrived early and found our body easily. She was in the top body-bag. She was lying atop two old black men who had no body bags, all they had were tags on the toes of their stark naked bodies.

The *chamber* had nine coolers for bodies, but the coolers were *always* full, so the most recent cadavers were stacked in the hall. You always had to watch where you stepped because you were always stepping on hands or stumbling over someone's dead feet.

Mark quickly grabbed one of the workers and asked if he's put Marie's body up first, since we had to witness the autopsy. No use sitting through other autopsies. The worker was large, black and obliging, and, with the help of another silent helper, he lifted Marie's body bag and tossed it on the stainless-steel table on the right side. At least we were closer to that lone window.

I watched the workers quickly unzip the bag and roll Marie out. They never said much. They were quiet and quick workers, a little ghoulish-looking, with tired eyes, but very efficient. Since they got paid by the body, instead of by the hour, they worked fast.

They had Marie's head propped up on a small black headrest before the doctor came strolling in behind his big black cigar. Now, the doctor was a real ghoul. If you looked up *ghoul* in the dictionary, his picture would be there next to the word. He looked a little like Peter Lorre, like a toad with a cigar.

He was a walking cliché, munching an egg salad sandwich as he glanced at the bodies. There was the body of a young Oriental boy on the left autopsy table and Marie on the right. It was then he noticed us an shook his head.

"Another one, huh?" he chuckled and took a bite of egg. He gave Marie a quick look-over for a second and added, "She wasn't a bad lookin' girl, damn shame." He nodded to his helper, who knew exactly what to do. The helper took out a swab from a nearby cabinet and spread Marie's legs wide and swabbed her vagina. He put the swab in a vial and then swabbed her anus with another swab, which was put in a separate vial. Mark took the vials and held them for the crime lab technician. They would be analyzed later, for semen.

Marie was then rolled over on her stomach and we started counting wounds. About that time, our crime lab technician arrived and took pictures of the wounds and then removed the paper bags from her hands. He scraped Marie's fingernails for any evidence and put each scraping in separate vials.

Then the helper turned Marie on her back and washed down her pallid white body with a small hose at the end of the table. The dried blood liquefied and drained off her skin into the trough on the side of the table. The technician then took close-up photos of Marie's cold face.

We counted thirty-four stab wounds. Only five of them were deep, the others curiously very shallow stab wounds. They had punctured the skin and gone past the yellow-orange fatty tissue, but they did not go past the ribs.

After the wounds were counted and measured and logged and noted, the tall assistant, a light skinned black man, rolled Marie over on her back and quickly opened her up. With quick slices, starting separately from each shoulder and cutting under each breast , the razor scalpel laid Marie open.

I stepped back when the cutting started. I didn't like to see that razor cut the flesh. It was too quick, too sharp, and too rough on flesh. And I also did not like that initial smell when a body's laid open, even a fresh body had a stale smell inside when first opened. I stepped back while the helper cut Marie under her breasts and then down in one deep slice all the way to the top of her pubic hair.

I looked away as the helper sliced the flesh away from the rib cage, then I heard the snippers clip through each rib until the ribs and sternum were lifted away.

I guess I just wasn't used to autopsies yet, like Mark. He was right on top of the assistant. I was getting better, though. On my first day in Homicide I had to witness three autopsies of a double murder-suicide case. But Marie was the first female autopsy I'd witnessed.

At least my stomach didn't turn this time. Maybe I was too tired or maybe, as Mark assured me, I was getting used to it. After a few minutes, after that initial stale smell had scattered or been diluted by the other stink, I found myself standing next to Mark as the helper carefully cut out the organs.

The doctor strolled over and examined each organ to determine just how many of the wounds punctured which organ. There was a great deal of blood around the heart and lungs and it did not take the pathologist long to determine which wounds were fatal.

As each organ was removed, examined, and weighed, a piece of the organ was secured and placed in a vial for analysis. Urine was collected for analysis, as well as blood, bile, the contents of her stomach, and liquid from the eyeball. The eyeball was pierced with a long needle and liquid was withdrawn. Eyeball liquid was the best place to determine if Marie had taken any drugs or alcohol. At least that's what the doctor said.

The doctor returned to the Oriental cadaver as his helper started on Marie's head. I watched as the large black hands took the razor scalpel and sliced along the back of Marie's skull. Then he pulled her scalp forward and cut the small membrane that held it to the skull, until her face folded down and her entire skull was visible.

The doc returned for a quick look at the skull before the helper started the silver bone-saw and cut away Marie's skull. The sound of a hundred finger-nails on a hundred blackboards echoed through the cold room. Even Mark stepped back with me, but there was no escaping the sound. You just had to wait it out.

The helper lifted Marie's skull-cap from her head and handed it to the doc for another quick examination. Then the brain was carefully removed and brought to the other end of the autopsy table where it was placed on a stainless steel scale and weighed, the moved to piece of wood next to Marie's feet. It was a cutting board. And there, the doc sliced the brain like a meatloaf, in neat thin slices, one after the other. He examined each slice for clots or whatever.

Human brains look just like soft cheese, a little red on the outside from the blood vessels, but chalky white inside. On my first autopsy the doctor put gloves on me and gave me a piece of brain to feel. It felt just like rubbery mozzarella cheese.

A Homicide detective can learn a lot from an autopsy by watching, more than he can get from reading a report. He can see the wounds, the angle and depth and force used to kill. Only five of Marie's wounds were possibly fatal – three of them punctured her lungs and two severed the aorta. The other twenty-nine wounds were not deep enough. The barely reached the back ribs, more punctured than stab wounds.

"Could be someone small," I told Mark as we walked out of THE CHAMBER OF HORRORS.

"Could be." Mark wasn't in any hurry to come to conclusions.

"Could be someone weak, maybe a woman?" I asked, not believing a work, just fishing.

"No way," Mark came right back. "It was a man all right. It's a sex crime. Probably a frustrated freako, but definitely male, that's why the exhibitionism and the piquerism."

"The what?"

"Piquerism," Mark repeated. "It means when a man sticks a knife in a woman in order to receive sexual satisfaction from the plunging. He might think he's doing it hard, but he's just sticking it in her, feeling the knife plunge in and out, a substitute penis." Mark stopped outside the building and yawned at the morning sun. "I learned all that shit at a class about sex crimes last year. It's from the French word 'piquer' – to prick."

"So," I said as I yawned myself. "What'll we do now?"

"Now we sleep," Mark answered. "Take me back to Headquarters, then go home and get some sleep. I'll call you tonight." So we left THE CHAMBER OF HORRORS and Marie's leftovers behind.

They had unfolded her face, tossed her organs back into her hollow torso and sewed her up with a large liver sewing needle. Then they tossed her on top of the finished pile of yesterdays' cadavers, to lie among the other naked bodies. I last saw Marie lying face down atop the body of an old black man.

No, there was no dignity in death, just leftovers.

•

It was nine o'clock, Saturday morning, when I got home and tossed my suit in a corner of my bedroom. After a visit to THE

CHAMBER OF HORRORS, everything went to the cleaners, even the tie.

I brushed my teeth for at least ten minutes, put fresh toothpaste on my brush and continued. I looked at myself in the mirror. There were dark circles under my eyes. And those newly acquired age lines on my face showed more clearly, along with the new gray hairs at my temples.

I looked at the Italian face in my mirror and for some reason thought of my father. I was actually beginning to look like him, more and more. At this time in the morning my father would be reading his morning paper.

I almost fell asleep in the tub, but managed to get out and into bed. I reached over and lifted the receiver from the phone and called Jessica. She would still be asleep but I wanted to talk to her, about it.

The phone rang about fifteen times before her familiar voice answered.

"It's me," I said. "You awake yet?"

"Of course not" – she sounded groggy – "what time is it anyway?"

"About ten."

"Yeah?" Her voice took on that annoyed quality it had when I did something wrong. Again. "What happened this time?" she asked.

"We had a murder," I answered. "At eleven-thirty. An all-nighter. Just got back from the autopsy."

"Please," she said quickly, "you're not going to tell me about brains and mozzarella cheese again, are you?"

"No, I just wanted to tell you why I didn't call."

"Yeah?" She sounded more awake. I could picture her sitting up in bed, her head in her hand, that hurt, annoyed look in her dark green eyes. "Guess there weren't any phones near you last night. Where were you, China?"

Oh yes, I could see those sharp green eyes as plain as if she were next to me. Funny how you get to know someone well enough to tell those things over the phone.

"I was in the Quarter," I attempted to explain. "A girl got herself butchered last night right in the street."

"Please," she shot in, "no details. I just wish you'd call, Dino. I still have supper waiting, " her voice trailed off and sounded more tired.

"I'm sorry," I said again for the hundredth time. I had been sorry a lot lately.

"I guess you couldn't help it," she added, but she didn't mean it. "I just miss you."

I felt the hair on my neck prickle at that. "I miss you too."

It was the same conversation we'd had the last few weeks. Time just seemed to be slipping away from me. She had been the first to notice. Jessica was always the first to notice everything. I don't know, but we both had expected for me to have more time to myself after leaving the Sixth District for Homicide. In Homicide, you had regular days off, unless there were some bad murders. But I could count the times on one hand that I had seen Jessica in the last few weeks. And there was little hope of it getting better.

After a brief pause in the conversation, Jessica started telling me about how I'd become more and more like *her* father. Jessica's father was a retired police sergeant and she told me I was like him.

"I just don't understand it," she said. Then she told me again about how her father had grown so insensitive that it had driven her mother away. It was an old story, a typical cop story about another defunct marriage blamed on the job. I thought Jessica would understand more. But she was so scared.

I almost fell asleep on the phone.

She realized it and told me to go to sleep. "Call me when you get up," she add.

"Okay," I agreed and hung up. We'd talk later. I could have bet she was holding her head again. I wished she were holding mine. No, I didn't wish that at all. I just wanted to be alone and go to sleep.

I was so damn tired.

And I could not understand how the hell that Fuck-head could have walked out of the Quarter, covered in blood, and no one noticed.

Fuck! Fuck! Fuck the whole goddamn world!

*Chapter 2*
Prytania Street


Dino LaStanza had that dream again. The bad dream about the Harmony Street Wharf came to him again. It was a vivid dream and very real. And it was the same as before, in slow motion, and he could not get away fast enough.

The scene was familiar, that black wharf on the Mississippi River in a dark corner of the Sixth Police District. And in the dream he could see himself moving closer and closer to the wharf, like a movie camera closing in, closing in.

And then he saw that face again, that evil face of the man kneeling next to him. Dino placed a pistol in the mouth of the evil face and watched the eyes of that face plead with him as he slowly squeezed the trigger. Dino felt the gun kick and saw the body roll over, .

But then it was no longer night, no longer dark. It was daylight in his dream and he could not get away and there were people everywhere. They could see him, could put him at the scene, they knew what he had done. And then there was another familiar face there, staring at him. It was Sergeant Mason, and he knew. And he smiled.

Dreams have little meaning sometimes. and sometimes they express one's deepest fantasies or one's deepest fears. The Harmony Street Wharf was Dino's deepest fear. It haunted him, visited him late at night when he was most vulnerable. And he could tell no one about it, could reach for no help because it was his secret. it was his tragic flaw, his personal nightmare. And he was safe only because no one else knew. It was his secret, and it would not leave him alone.

•

The phone woke me a few hours after I'd fallen asleep on the morning after the Dauphine Street murder. I was dreaming again, that same damn dream about the wharf. I woke up afraid, like a little kid. I woke to a pair of eyes staring at me, pleading with me. I woke to a vision of Marie's eyes and they were pleading with me to catch her killer.

The phone kept on ringing until I picked up the receiver.

"Well, Mr. Big Shot Detective," said the voice on the phone, "you did it again. Front page news!"

I knew the voice well. It was Stan, Stan-The-Man, my old partner from the Bloody Sixth District. He was always one for perfect timing.

"What the fuck are you calling me for?" I grumbled, trying to sit up in bed.

"You asleep?" he asked in a voice that told me he knew very well I was asleep.

"I *was.*"

"You lazy wops are all alike, sleep, sleep, sleep. I just called to congratulate you. You're on the front page of the *Picayune* again. You little publicity-seeking wop."

"What are you talking about?" I asked, still groggy.

"Go get your morning paper," Stan told me. "I'll wait."

I looked at the receiver. I just knew the crazy son of a bitch was smiling at me. He was a stone-fucking nut. "Why are you fuckin' with me, Stanley?" I asked. "I got two hours sleep."

"Candy-Ass," he cut in, "go get your paper. You're famous. I'll wait."

There was no use arguing with him. Ever since he broke me in as a rookie, Stan felt like I was his little duckling. He looked after me, taught me everything he knew, and called me any time he damn well pleased. Years together in the Bloody Sixth taught me there was no use arguing with a crazy man. If I hung up, he'd just call back. If I unplugged the phone, he's just come over. So I got up, stumbled to my front door and retrieved my paper.

I opened it on the way back to the phone. And there I was, right on the front page of *The Times-Picayune*. There was a picture of the murder scene on Dauphine Street. I was in the center of the photo, standing at the edge of the street, writing notes on my pad, my side to the camera. Behind me, in the lower portion of the picture, you could see the bottom part of Marie's spread-eagled legs. That's the last New Orleans saw of Marie Sumner, a pair of spread-eagled legs. There was a caption beneath the picture. It read:

"New Orleans Homicide Detective Dino
LaStanza stands over the nude and bloodied
body of a twenty-three-year-old woman who
was murdered in the 1300 block of
Dauphine Street Friday night."
There was a story on page two. I didn't bother to look, I just
picked up the phone again.

"Ya' see," Stan told me, "so how's the big shot getting along?
You don't talk to none of us peasants no more, huh?"

It was one of the oldest stories in police work. When you're in
the same district, you and your padnas are *so damn* close, and the
minute you get transferred, it all slips away. I knew it. Stan knew it
too. No matter how hard you try to keep in touch, you can't. You
get on different shifts and work at different stations, and time slips
by.

So I sat up in my bed, with my *Picayune* spread out in front of
me, and we talked about the case for a while, then we talked about
other things, like the usual blood and violence of the bloodiest
police district in the entire south, the Blood Sixth of Old New
Orleans.

•

Some background information should be provided at this
point. I am Italian-American. And there is an old saying that
Italians make the best criminals or the best cops. Well, I grew up in
a house full of blue uniforms, so that made the choice easy.
Besides my father would have broken both my legs if I would have
grown up to be anything else. There were times when I thought he
*had* broken something, when I was a kid and getting into trouble. I
had a strict upbringing, living under the roof of Captain LaStanza.
But I guess I needed it.

I grew up next to City Park, between the park and the Canal
Cemeteries. I grew up playing football in the park, and hide-and-
seek between the crypts and sepulchers of the old cemeteries. In
New Orleans, tombs are built above ground because of the high
water table. Most of the city is below sea level, built where no city
should have been built, on miles of mush and swamp. So our
cemeteries look like small villages of the dead, with walled tombs

and crypts and brick paths with sharp turns where you could hid and get lost forever.

As a kid, I grew up in the shadow of my big brother, Joe. He showed me the ropes, how to play football and baseball, and how to hide in the cemeteries so nobody, and I mean *nobody*, could find me. He also told me about the werewolves of City Park and the vampires that prowled Odd Fellows Rest Cemetery at the corner of City Park Avenue and Canal Street. When I was real little, you could not pry me from the house at night. Joe was pretty smart about that. He was getting into his teen-age years ad there were lots of young girls to hang out with at tight – when little brothers should not be around. and I wasn't. I was inside.

When I got a little older, Joe gave me a break and let me tag along sometimes. I used to sit up in the bleachers I in the old canteen near the park and watch Joe and the other teen-angels put moves on the girls at the sock hops. I remember how I used to think all those teen-age girls were movie stars. I told them that, and they loved me for it. "He's so cute." I learned early about flattering girls. It paid off later.

Looking back now, I could have died at eight and been eternally happy. I guess all childhood days seem better after you grow up. My father was a shining blue knight to me then. Infallible. Invincible. He would have never grown old and gray and gotten to drinking too much. My mother would have never grown so quiet, have never lost that light that used to shine in her eyes when she was a young mother. And my bother would have outlived me, as he should have.

There would have been no Vietnam for me, no dismal housing projects cropping up around the city for me to work in and arrest desperate people. There would have been no Sixth District madness and no funeral for my brother. I would have been spared that agony, spared burying my brother in that blue uniform.

Joe was killed in the line of duty. He was murdered because he wore that blue uniform. But that's a whole different story. And I took care of all that. I took care of my brother's murder long before I started taking care of the murders of strangers in Homicide.

I have done a lot in my first twenty-nine years – plenty to be proud of and plenty I'm not proud of. I guess that's why I have nightmares. I used to have nightmares about Vietnam, now I have them about the wharf. Scenes of death stay with you, in the jungle or on an old streetcar – or mass death when an airliner fell from the sky on a cold New Orleans night when I was a rookie.

New Orleans is dirtier than it was when I was a kid. It's so much sadder. I can remember when streetcars seemed magical to me, like trolleys to faraway places and how the French Quarter seemed like a trip into a time machine. New Orleans has grown much darker and bleaker. The streets have grown worn with traffic snarls and potholes. There is *so much more* crime and violence and so many more people.

And then there were love affairs that died, too.

I once knew what it was like to truly love someone. I once loved a girl with blue-on-blue eyes and bright yellow hair. Her name was Guinevere and she was a young Orleanian beauty, and she loved me so. But, as new Orleans beauty goes, she faded.

A poet would say she's with the angels, or that God took her into his arms. But I'm no poet and I've seen what God has allowed to happen in this world and I know better. I know she is gone, forever. One evening she died, and I tell you, New Orleans lost so much for me. New Orleans and I have both lost a great deal.

But there is no place else for me. New Orleans and I are too much alike. Our roots are here, our families, our heritage. I guess we're just a couple of losers still hanging in there in case there's a bit of romance left.

·

I managed to get a few more hours sleep after Stan hung up, but Mark called me later and said he'd be by that afternoon to pick me up. It may have been Saturday and my day off, but he was coming to get me.

I took a long shower and got ready, managed to get two strong cups of coffee-and-chicory in me before Mark arrived. I had time to read the newspaper story about the murder and laughed at how many mistakes they managed to put into one story. Mason couldn't have misled them *that* much. What a buncha fucking clowns.

When Mark arrived, he was smiling.

"What the fuck you smiling about?" I asked as I let him in.

"I love my work," he answered. "Don't you?"

I had another fucking nut for a partner. First there was Stan and now this grizzly-bear idiot. I shook my head and went back in my bedroom to finish getting ready.

"Want some coffee?" I asked.

"No thanks." He followed me into my bedroom, still smiling. I ignored him and kept looking for the ankle holster for my new snub-nosed, stainless-steel, Smith and Wesson .357 Magnum. Rubber grips that grew tacky when wet so the weapon did not slip in sweaty hands.

"What are you looking for?" Mark finally asked me. "Lost a blonde or something?"

Married men seem to think unmarried men have blondes hiding in various places around their pads. Mark walked to my closet, opened the door and peeked inside. "No blondes here." He chuckled.

Before he searched anymore, I told him what I was looking for.

"What do you need that for?" he asked, still smiling.

"To carry my gun." I don't know whey I bothered to answer, but I did, as I looked under my bed.

"How many times I gotta tell ya," Mark started in with his senior-partner-instructor voice, "you're in Homicide now. You don't need a gun. All you need is an extra ball-point pen."

I grabbed my shoulder holster and my unneeded Magnum, *and* an extra pen, and we left. The shoulder holster wasn't as comfortable as the ankle holster but it was better than listening to Mark while I looked. On our way out the door, Mark asked me if I had a good sleep. He was smiling again.

He was strange, sometimes. But no more strange than the rest of us, I guess. Police work does that to people. It makes bad comedians of us all. You need humor for a release.

"You gotta admit," Mark said as he drove, "this is a helluva case, a once-in-a-lifetime caper, and it's all ours." He winked at me. "That is," he went on, "until the administration decides to get involved. Hopefully, we'll have this wrapped up by then."

He didn't have to remind me about how a case can be fucked up once politicians get involved. When I was on the road I saw many a big case go to the dogs after the mayor ordered the police chief to assign a *task force* to a case.

"You gotta realize," Mark concluded as we pulled up at Headquarters. "there will never be another time like this again. When we're old men we'll be able to tell our grandkids about the way we solved this famous case."

He sure was an optimist.

The mood in the Homicide squad room was anything but optimistic. Mason was waiting for us with his cigarette, skinny brown tie tonight and maroon sport jacket. Mason owned three sports coats, all with narrow lapels from long ago. One was navy blue, one was bright green and one was maroon. This was his day to wear his favorite maroon coat. Boudreaux was there, looking through his collection of police patches he kept in his lower desk drawer. Snowood was present, in a loud yellow cowboy shirt and blue jeans. He was humming his favorite tune, which was the theme from M*A*S*H, the movie, not the limp-dick TV show, a real upbeat tune entitled – *Suicide Is Painless.*

There were some Robbery detectives there also. They were a little upset because they had been pulled and told to work with us that day. If you ever want to piss off a Robbery detective, put him in Homicide for a while. He will suddenly have to be in on time, and will have to time to take care of 'personal business', such as meeting trampy women and other informants. But worst of all, they have to wear *ties.*

As the last ones arrived, Mason waited for everyone to settle down before he started in. He spoke in careful sentences and had a way of getting people to do whatever he wanted – by asking them, instead of telling them. And he only asked you to do what he did, which was work hard. He would be there every inch of the way, so how could you argue?

Mason was very tired as he gave out instructions. He would take most of the Robbery men back into the Quarter and give the place a more thorough canvass. He gave Mark a lead and asked if he'd take Boudreaux with him while he gave Snowood and I another lead.

34

Mark waited until he could get Mason on the side and quickly asked, "Why separate me and Dino?" It was a good question. I had the same one in mind.

Mason rubbed his tired eyes as he cigarette dangled precariously from his lower lip. "You get the best lead," he told Mark, "and since Boudreaux came up with it, he goes too. I want Dino to handle the other lead because it's in the Sixth District." He looked over at me. "Figured Dino knows the Sixth fairly well."

He made sense, as usual.

The lead Mark had sounded pretty good. It seems a recent parolee from Angola State Penitentiary, who had been sent up for three rapes in which he used a knife to carve his initials on the victims, had been seen in the Quarter the night before by a couple of First District patrolmen, prior to the murder. At least it was something to work on, and you never knew.

Snowood and I got lead number two, which involved a certain black citizen named Latman Whitley. It seems Latman was arrested on Bourbon Street the previous night – after the murder – on a warrant for failing to appear in court on a molesting charge. He was flagged in the police computer as a career criminal, known to be dangerous and *always* carried a knife. He had previous convictions for carrying concealed knives, rape, and armed robbery. He had just spent seven years in Angola for manslaughter, he had cut up his common-law wife.

And he was already back on the street that morning because some benevolent judge let Latman out on bail again with a quickie bond. Now, Latman had been arrested for failing to show up in court previously, so it makes a lotta fucking sense. One fucking judge puts a warrant out and another lets the asshole back out on bail, again.

"How'd we find out about this?" I asked Snowood as we walked out of the office to the elevator.

"Boudreaux," he explained. "Seems Mason had him check the arrest register at Central Lockup this morning."

On our way downstairs, I dropped by the Records Section and got a mug shot of Latman.

"I know this mook," I told Snowood. "I've seen him around Prytania Street before, Euterpe Street, too." Paul shrugged his shoulders as we climbed into his car. He had spent his uniformed years in Sleepy Hollow, the Seventh District, which was up against Lake Pontchartrain in New Orleans East, with miles and miles of undeveloped swamp and some new subdivisions and apartment complexes, as well as the biggest swamp within the city limits of any American City – Bayou Sauvage.

The Seventh had none of the charm of the Sixth District, with its four huge housing projects and enough poor blacks to cast a few hundred Tarzan movies. The Bloody Sixth got its name from those blacks who bloody each other with great regularity on such lovely streets as Felicity (pronounced fell-a-city by the local mooks) and Melpomene (pronounced mell-pom-many) and Terpsichore (tap-si-core) and Euterpe (U-tap) and of course the ever popular C-L-ten. They call it C-L-ten because the street sign reads – CLIO, and so if you're a snotty-nosed mook growing up in the Melpomene Project and saw a street sign like that, you'd call it C-L-ten.

I took another long look at Latman's mug shot as Snowood drove off in the wrong direction. "What's the matter with you?" I asked. "Don't you know where it's at?"

"Sure I do," Paul claimed as he took the long way, the white people's way to St. Charles Avenue. "This is the Sixth, ain't it?"

"Take a left here," I told him. After a few more turns, we pulled up at Freddie's Blue Note Bar, corner Baronne and Euterpe.

Freddie's was a social climbing bar, where the young men of society hang out. It occupied the bottom of a two-story wooden building that was painted bright blue. Freddie's had no front door, ever. It was always open and always dark as hell inside, even in the middle of a bright Saturday. That was because old Freddie painted all the walls black a long time ago. The bar was also know as the 'No Door Bar' by some of the street thugs. There was no sign.

I led the way into Freddie's, with a cautious-stepping, country-assed Snowood following close behind. As I stepped in, I saw three black men playing pool on the only table in the place. There was a large, fat black whore sitting at the bar but I didn't see Freddie.

"Freddie," I called out as I kept moving in. I glanced at the pool players who were checking us real hard. I ignored them as I stepped up to the bar. "Oh, Freddie!" I called out again. "It's the police."

An old, bald-headed man with a face that was actually black, instead of dark brown, stepped out of the back room behind the bar. He came and said, "Say what?"

I smiled at Freddie and he took a couple of seconds to recognize me.

"Well, I'll be," Freddie said a moment later. "You sure look different."

"I know," I agreed as I leaned my hands on the bar. That was the first time Freddie had seen me out of uniform. I glanced over my shoulder at Paul, who was busy keeping an eye on the pool players. I turned back to Freddie and took out the mug shot of Latman and handed it to him. "I'm in Homicide now," I told Freddie as he looked at the picture. "Know what Homicide means?" My voice was loud enough for the pool players to hear we weren't narcs – not that narcs *ever* wore a coat and tie get-up.

"Means killin'," Freddie answered correctly. He handed the picture back to me and said he never saw the man before. So I thanked Freddie and walked out, with Snowood right behind. On my way out, I waved good-bye to the pool players and winked at the fat whore at the bar. She smiled broadly at me. God, I missed the Sixth District already. Where else were there such nice funkball bars?

"Well, where to next?" Snowood asked as he jumped into his car.

I let him pull away from the curb and down the street before I pointed to the nearest pay phone. "Pull up over there," I said to him. I stepped out of the car, dialed Freddie's number and waited for the old man to answer.

"It's me," I said.

"Yeah," Freddie answered. "Dat was Latman. He stays on Tap-si-core by Coliseum. Big green house. He downstairs in front."

"He come see you much?" I asked.

"Sometimes. But mostly he go to Fade-Out."

"Thanks, Freddie," I added, "*Means killin'?* You got that act down pat."

"They thinks I'm a chump." He snickered and hung up.

As I stepped back to the car, I remembered how working with Stan-The-Man paid off. Stan and Freddie went back a long way. Most Sixth District street people wouldn't piss on a cop if he was on fire, much less talk to one, or *ever* give information to one of us. But Stan saved Freddie's ass one time by putting a certain pie-faced dick head in Charity Hospital after the dick head went after Freddie with a pool stick.

And when that same dick head returned to Freddie's after he was released, Stan put the zap on him again, just for setting foot in Freddie's. Sometimes one ass-kicking wasn't enough. But a second one from Psycho Stan usually got people's attention.

So we get along fine with Freddie. We stayed away and let him gamble, run his whores, deal a little pot from his back room and we got information. It was a bargain.

"Who'd you call?" Snowood asked when I jumped back in the car. He took a fresh dip and put it between his teeth and lip, then let it sit a second before spiting a gob of brown shit out the window.

I told him what Freddie had said about Latman.

"That's fuckin' good." Paul was impressed as he wheeled toward Terpsichore Street. He let out another big gob of shitty-looking spit as we pulled off Baronne Street.

He was easily impressed. But if there was one thing I knew, it was the Sixth. It was the best place to grow up as a cop. Smack in the middle of the city, the Sixth was sandwiched between the rich uptown section and the downtown business district. The Sixth had everything, from the plush, well-manicured lawns of the Garden District to the four big housing projects, known to Orleanians as places to avoid, like the *plague*. The Melpomene was the biggest housing project in the Sixth, then there was the Magnolia, the St. Thomas, and the unique and world-famous Calliope Housing Project, where the only grass that grew, grew in pots that were hidden from the view of the 'ma-fuckin' police."

Whoever invented housing projects should be fucking hanged. Putting all those poor and uneducated people together had produced one result, more poor and uneducated people. There is nothing more depressing in the whole world than Christmas in the housing project, where runny-nosed little kids play in the streets with no hope in their eyes.

There are no fences around the projects to keep anything in or, and when they're old enough, the kids can walk out. Only by that time they are already lost in the fleeting pleasures of drugs and sex and the easier way of just stealing.

Some parts of the Sixth were dark even in the brightest hours of daylight, like alleys in the projects, like dark wharves along the river, and like Freddie's Bar.

The Sixth had everything you'd want to see as a cop fresh out of the Police Academy, so you grew up fast. And you grew up hard. You went from calling them blacks, to calling them scumbags, to calling them their fit and proper Sixth District name of mook.

A mook was different than a black man. You could tell a mook by the vacant look in his eyes. A mook was hopelessly uneducated and usually poor because it was easier to steal than work steady. Stealing wasn't steady but it was the fastest way. A mook was usually of the Negro persuasion, but there were many white mooks, too.

A black man may one day go to school and become a doctor. But a mook was nothing more than an animated cadaver, just hanging around until it was his turn to visit THE CHAMBER OF HORRORS at Tulane and Broad.

•

Latman wasn't at his house. And since he didn't work, he was either in a bar or leaving a bar or heading for another bar. Paul and I stepped off the front porch of the house in which Latman stayed. Paul spit on the white steps and left his calling card.

He spit again just outside the Fade-Out Bar at the corner of Melpomene and Prytania Street, right next to a famous New Orleans street sign. The street sign, with the words 'Melpomene' and 'Prytania' printed on it was where a mook named Jeffery Vick died one night long ago.

Jeffery Vick was shot in the Fade-Out Bar on a certain Saturday night. He had stumbled out of the bar and fallen against the street sign. Some college kid happened by and took a quick picture before getting the hell out of there. The picture wound up on the front page of the morning paper, instant fame. When Stan and I arrived in our neat blue uniforms, the cameraman was gone. *Everybody* was gone. There wasn't a soul in or around the Fade-Out, not even a bartender. Ole Jeffery was there by himself, looking stupid as hell, with his tongue hanging out and rigor mortis waiting around the corner for him.

All by himself, Jeffery had been a busy man in the Fade-Out that night. He had six highballs, drank three cans of cold beer, played the juke box, smoked five cigarettes simultaneously and had enough time to shoot himself. He fired his gun and ran around in front of it far enough to leave no powder burns, and dispose of the gun before the police arrived. That was all done before he staggered outside and expired against that street sign that Paul Snowood so rudely spit upon.

Yes, the Fade-out was a very familiar place to anyone who wore little silver sixes on the collars of their blue uniforms. It was familiar – and unlike Freddie's – dangerous. It was a place where you kept a wary eye out before you even got out of your car. I warned Paul before we stepped in, and he kept both eyes sharp as I tried to get the attention of the bartender.

There were two pool tables in the place and seven black men who stopped playing when we entered. They stared at us, pool cues in hand. A couple other blacks were sitting at a table. They got up slowly and moved to the far end of the bar. Paul and I remained close to the door, just in case.

"Say you," I called out to the bartender, who was pretending he did not see us. I had my badge and credentials in my left hand and waved them at him. He knew who the fuck we were all right, ID unnecessary. What other white boys in suits, carrying portable radios, would ever walk into the Fade-Out?

"Come here," I instructed the bartender when he eventually glanced our way. I knew him. His name was Tyrone and I was sure he remembered me. Stan and I had arrested him once for shooting a customer. The customer didn't die and did not show up in court to press charges, also Tyrone went free. Of course, the court gave Tyrone back his gun and sure enough, not a week later, Tyrone shot another customer.

It so happened that at that exact moment, a certain patrol car was passing outside and heard the shot. Two wild-ass policemen rushed into the Fade-Out and found the customer with a fresh wound in his arm and Tyrone hiding behind the bar. and nobody knew nothin'.

So Stan and I took it upon ourselves and closed down the place, locked the front door and ripped the place apart until we found Tyrone's gun hidden behind the bar. Stan took the gun outside and destroyed it by beating it to death against Jeffery Vick's street sign. And of course, Tyrone went free.

So Tyrone knew me when he approached, although he tried to hide behind those large dull eyes of his.

"Keep your hands where I can see them," I ordered him.

Tyrone smiled and put his hands on the bar across from where I stood. He had no front teeth and looked somewhat like night crawler, with those reddish-yellow eyes.

I knew it would be no use, but I asked anyway. "Where's Latman?" I asked the toothless one.

"Don't know no Latman," Tyrone answered, looking down a the bar when he spoke. Lying mook couldn't look me in the eye.

I showed him the mug shot and asked him again. He shook his head. At that moment, I heard the squeal of brakes outside. I glanced at my watch and smiled at Tyrone as four rather large uniformed officers, with silver sixes on their collars, walked in.

They put everyone against the wall and shook down all of Tyrone's nice customers, while I shook down Tyrone. The somewhat illegal search surfaced three knives, all sorts of pills, enough tees and blues to knock out the senior class of Nicholls High School, and one .25 automatic. The uniformed men made two arrests and ran everyone else outside.

We stayed inside with Tyrone. "Now come on," I chided him as he still stood in the position against the wall. "We're all alone now," I reminded him, "so just tell me the truth. I know damn well you know Latman and you know where he's at. So just tell me and save us all a lot of trouble."

Tyrone said nothing and scaring him wasn't about to work, so I tried something else.

"Say, Tyrone, don't your momma stay over on Dryades Street?"

He said nothing. He'd see his share of Cagney movies and he knew he was a tough guy.

I turned to one of the Sixth district men and told him where Tyrone's mama lived, "above the cleaners, on Dryades, next door to Snookums Grocery."

"Know the place," the uniformed man replied.

"Go get her," I came right back.

"Say, you leave my mama alone," Tyrone snapped as the uniformed man started to leave.

"You're in no position to give orders," I reminded Tyrone as I pulled out my handcuffs. "We're all going to your favorite police station," I told him, "the one on Felicity Street. And if you won't tell us where Latman is, maybe your mama will."

"She don't know nothin'," Tyrone told me.

"I don't give a fuck what she knows," I said calmly. "We're just gonna fuck with her like we fuck with everybody until you remember where Latman is." I put the cuffs on Tyrone and started him toward the door. On our way out, Paul spit on the bar and left a large glob of shit behind.

"Say, man," Tyrone said to me as we started out the door. "Why you *doin'* this?"

"Because I'm a prick," I answered him, 'and because you're a lying bastard and we *both* know it." I spoke in that very calm voice I reserved for when I wanted to make myself very clear. I stared back into Tyrone's glaring yellow eyes. "Why don't you just tell the truth one day, why can't you just tell the truth, whey do you gotta lie when the police ask you something? The truth just *once*."

Tyrone continued to stare at me real hard.

I smiled at him and leaned closer. "What you got going with Latman?" I asked. "Could be Latman's a punk? You like to fuck each other?"

Tyrone laughed at me. "Latman not a punk. He just stupid."

"So you *do* know Latman." I laughed back at him. "Now you know why we're bringing you in. That's a felony. Lying to the police during a criminal investigation."

Tyrone stopped laughing and stopped walking. He huffed and looked down at the ground and said, "He at eat."

I looked back at him and asked, "You mean Latman?"

"Yeah, he at eat."

I took the cuffs off Tyrone and signaled to Paul that it was time for us to be leaving.

"Say," Tyrone added, "You stop dat an goin' to my mama's."

"He never went," I told Tyrone over my shoulder. "It's my turn to lie to you." I pointed my finger at him, "Now we're even." I smiled. "But if you're lying about Latman, I'll be right back."

I thanked the uniformed men before Paul and I drove off. Paul seemed relieved when we left, but he was a little puzzled. "Where to now?"

"We go get Latman."

"You know where he is?" Paul asked.

"He at eat," I repeated Tyrone's statement.

Paul looked at me for a second. "And what the fuck does that mean?"

"It means, he at eat," I said, unblinking.

"I think you been around these ass-holes too long," Paul concluded as I told him which way to go. We finally pulled up at the corner of Euterpe and Dryades. I got out and Paul followed. As I stepped around the corner, I turned to Paul and pointed to a sign across Dryades Street. It was a big yellow sign with the word *EAT* hand-printed in bold black letters.

"He at eat," I said to Paul.

Paul coughed up some more brown shit and started laughing.

"I told you," I went on, "he at *eat!*" I pointed to the sign again. "Don't you just love the fuckin' Sixth?"

•

*EAT* wasn't a restaurant. It was a soup kitchen of sorts. It had a cafeteria walkway in front and long rows of tables for customers to munch their two-dollar meals and cold drinks. It had a regular clientele of bums and other degenerates. It was a nice place to visit, but I would *never* eat there.

Latman Whitley was sitting alone at the end of one of the tables. He was finished eating but was still sipping his cold drink when I sat next to him, placing my portable radio on the table next to his plate. Latman looked at me as I showed him my badge and credentials. I asked him a couple quick questions and received some slow, slurred answers. Latman had what was commonly called a 'slow brain' in the projects. Which meant that not only was he stupid, he was slow.

Snowood added little to the conversation. He began to hum his suicide song again. And while he hummed and Latman slurred his answers, I fished for a couple simple facts.

"Just tell me where you were last night?" I asked. "About eleven o'clock?" It was the third time I had to ask the question.

And for the third time I got the same answer, "Jail." The Fuck-head kept insisting he was in jail at eleven.

I turned to Paul and said, "Guess we should bring him in."

"What if he pukes in my unit?" was Paul's reply.

I asked Latman again, and again he insisted he was in jail before eleven. He told me he just got out that morning and couldn't understand why we didn't know that.

A long time ago I learned that when a mook *insists*, he just may be right. And it was easy enough to check out. I left Latman with Paul and moved over to the pay phone at the rear of *EAT* and dialed Central Lockup. After I checked twice, I had all I needed.

"Come on," I told Paul when I stepped back. "Let's get the fuck outta here.

"What about Stupid here?" Paul asked as I started away.

"Leave him, just fuckin' leave him."

Paul waited until we were in the care before he asked the obvious.

I answered him with a question, "Boudreaux was the one who came up with this, huh?"

"Yeah, he went to Central Lockup and checked it out," Snowood answered and started to laugh. "What's the matter, old Boudreaux fuck up again?"

"Well, somebody did," I said in disgust. "We just spent three hours tracking down a man who was arrested at nine fifty-five last night. At nine fifty-five, our victim was still in Pierre's Bar."

Paul continued laughing, spit out the window. "That fuckin' Boudreaux will fuck up anything." He started laughing louder.

"Did you hear about the time Boudreaux put out a warrant on a dead man?"

"No." I shut my eyes and leaned back in the seat while Paul told me the delightful story of how a warrant was issued on a dead man.

"Seems ole Boudreaux was so bent on solving a particular murder case," Paul began. he told me how Boudreaux always believed the first thing he was told about anything.

"He never checked up on anything either," Paul went on, "so it was easy for him to put out a warrant on a dead man. Boudreaux was told that a certain man named Tom Quick was the killer. So Boudreaux secured an arrest warrant for a man who had been dead two years.

"Then the ass-hole contacted the *Picayune* reporter in the press room, on his own, and gave the reporter an old mug shot and the story on Tom Quick. And sure enough, it hit the papers the next day that we were looking for Tom Quick and had an arrest warrant for committing a recent murder.

"Well, the Quick family was quick enough to call the paper right away to tell them that Tom could be found in St. Vincent De Paul Cemetery. And when the reporter gave the information to Boudreaux, he refused to believe it until Mason took him to the cemetery and introduced him to Tom Quick's headstone."

That was the story.

"And how does he last?" I asked.

"Civil Service." Paul Laughed so hard he almost swallowed his Skoal.

"What a fuckin' waste," I added.

Paul composed himself a moment and chuckled. "I don't think it was a waste of time, we got to meet a few interesting people, didn't we?"

I opened my left eye. "The big whore in Freddie's right?"

He laughed even harder.

•

Paul Snowood and Mark Land seemed to *enjoy* their work. That was something I had to learn from them. They each had another quality I had to pick up on quickly. They could *talk* to people. Not like the way I talked to people – like a street cop – but with patience.

Snowood was very laid back and that helped him. On our first suicide case I watched as Paul talked to the family in a patient and comfortable way. I had to learn that. In Homicide, you talked a lot differently to people than you did in the Sixth.

You had to almost pamper them in Homicide. Anything to get the right information, you eased it out of them. Paul was good at that. Mart was even better. Surprising as hell watching that grizzly bear morph into a teddy bear.

I sat with Mark one evening after a typical mook-barroom killing and watched as he coaxed and pampered and convince the killer to give a statement in full detail. Mark also got the killer to give us the murder weapon and the names of two witnesses. Sometimes you have to build a case against someone with their own help.

"There's nothing better than a confession," Mark said to me that evening. "Especially a confession on tape. Because our D.A.'s office ain't the brightest in the world and you gotta tell them a story before they'll listen. All the circumstantial evidence in the world don't make the D.A. listen like a confession.

"You gotta get down to the criminal's level," Mark added. "To get a good confession, you gotta get close to them, almost become friends with them, and maybe they'll tell you enough for you to send them to Angola forever. Or the electric chair."

I had a lot to learn.

•

When Paul and I got back to the office, I found Mark sipping coffee with a disgusted look on his face. Boudreaux was already gone. Mark told me how Cal had sent him on a wild goose chase also. Mark had found the parolee who was in the Quarter, but the man was on crutches with a cast from his ankle to his crotch.

"Fuckin' Boudreaux," Mark muttered between sips.

"You're fuckin' right," Paul agreed.

"So," I said, "where to from here?"

Mark took a deep breath and noted we had to handle the registrations of the cars parked in the area, to check the list of known deviants, and of course we could run down the residents in the area of the murder who had criminal records. We'd start in the morning.

The fuckin' killer was out there. All we had to do was find him.

It was Saturday night and I was tired as hell but there was no way I was not going to keep my date with Jessica. I had been spending less and less time with her lately and being tired wasn't good enough. I wasn't about to let another Saturday night slip away from us.

I took a long shower but even that didn't revive me. I was that tired. All I felt like doing was curling up and sleeping. But instead, I splashed cologne on my face, put on the light gray shirt and black pleated pants she had given me for my birthday. Then I gave myself a good look in the mirror. I looked tired. I also needed a haircut. In that mirror, my very Italian face stared back at me, looking older by the day. My Mediterranean shade of skin kept me from looking as pale as I felt. but there were gray hairs peeking out from between my dark hair.

It was fortunate that my VW knew the way to Jessica's house by itself, because I must have yawned twenty times on the way. It was a route my car and I had taken hundreds of times in the last two years, to that one-story brick house in the Lakeshore subdivision. it wasn't a fancy neighborhood, regular middle-class houses built new in the fifties and sixties, about a mile from Lake Pontchartrain. It was a nice quiet house that Jessica lived in with her father.

My car parked itself in its usual parking spot in front and I slowly moved to the door. I was only a half hour late which wasn't bad, considering.

She opened the door before I even knocked and greeted me with those very green eyes of hers. She had a way of looking at me that made me feel like I had just returned from doing something I should not have. She took a long look at me, shook her head and sighed before turning around to get her purse from the couch. She was telling me I was late, again.

I watched her move to the couch, watched her hips move beneath her tight red skirt. There was a long slit up the front of the skirt that reached halfway up her thigh. And I could see that smooth thigh plainly when she turned back to me. She wore a silky white top that was cut low around her nice round breasts. She looked great beneath all that long dark hair.

I looked into her eyes as she moved back to me. I looked for something in her eyes, and it was still there. It had been there for a while, even before I transferred to Homicide, but I didn't pay much attention to it. But it was there all right, a look of fear, a foreboding, a sadness in her eyes because she felt it was slipping away. We didn't talk about it. Maybe we should have.

We had a quiet dinner at a Chinese Restaurant and then went to a movie at the Robert E. Lee Theater, which had the most comfortable seats of any theater in the city, which was all I needed. she woke me with a nudge after the movie was over.

"Come on," she said, "it's over."

"Thanks," I answered as I stretched and yawned.

"You just want to take me home?" she asked with those disappointed eyes.

"No," I answered as we stepped from the theater into the warm night air. There was a nice breeze coming off the lake. The breeze was warm and wet and it felt fresh on my face, so I left the windows down as I drove back downtown to my apartment next to City Park.

I made some coffee for myself and some hot chocolate for Jessica while she kicked of her high heels and turned on the television. When I stepped back into my living room she was curled up on the couch.

I curled up next to her and it did not take long before I was running my fingers through her hair and kissing her softly on her neck. Then I kissed her mouth not so softly as we both slowly reclined on the couch. I ran my and over the tightness of her skirt and the smooth silkiness of her stockinged legs. My hands traced the familiar curves of her body until I reached her breasts. I rolled my fingers gently over them and began to unbutton her blouse.

She rolled beneath me as I removed her bra and began to kiss, then gently suck, the small nipples of her full breasts. I cupped my hands around each and squeezed gently as my mouth moved from one nipple to the other. I kissed her up and down from breast to mouth to breast again.

I worked her skirt up until it was above her waist and looked down at the length of her legs and her thin white panties beneath the pantyhose. She spread her legs as I climbed on top of her and began to slowly move against her.

I could feel the tightness growing between us as we rubbed, as she moved against me – at first gently and then harder and harder until there was no use in clothes. Her breath was deep and hard in my ears and I kissed her hard before sitting up. I pulled her up to me and unbuttoned her skirt and tossed it across the room, then I tossed her blouse and bra after it. I ran my mouth down to her navel as I pulled her pantyhose and panties down all in one. And as she stepped from them and we moved to my bedroom, I threw my clothes off on the way.

Jessica lay down on my bed, on her back, the light from the living room falling on her body, illuminating her from the waist down while the rest of her remained in semi-darkness. I moved to her and kissed her lips as my hand began to run over her body – from her neck to each breast, to her thighs. Slowly, I kissed my way down to those breasts and then traced my hand down past her thighs to her knees, and then up again, deliberately skirting her soft pubic hair.

I took her thighs and spread them as I kissed each leg again and again, moved my fingers up between her legs and began to rub them into her gently, in and out very slowly as I kissed my way up then down the length of her body. I looked at the dark hair between her legs and then up at her face. Her eyes were closed and her mouth half open. I quickly moved up to her mouth and plunged my tongue inside as I climbed onto her.

I took my time, moving within her, moving slowly and firmly. I took the time to hold myself back, to hold it all in until her movements grew into quick rhythms and she gasped in my ear, "Come on, babe, come on."

It had been a while and it felt so good.

I thought I would fall asleep right away. But I did not. I think Jessica did because I could feel her soft easy breath on my neck as she lay snuggled in my arms. But I could not sleep. Not right away.

•

Jessica and I were very much alike, maybe too much alike. We were of the same clay, the same mold, the same city, same police families, same Italian upbringing – Catholic schools, po-boys, and Barq's root beer-with-seafood summers.

We even looked a little alike with the dark Italian looks and small bodies. We liked the same things and seemed to dislike the same things. And yet it was slipping. I could feel it and could not understand it. Not really. There were strains at the edges.

I remember when we first started out together, she told me she didn't want to lead her mother's life of loving and then leaving a man who was forever a cop. And maybe that was it. She was leading her mother's life. And I was leading my father's life. so where did that leave us?

## Chapter 3
## Bayou St. John

He lived in an attic apartment on the third floor of an old wooden house on Urquhart Street, not more than nine blocks from the lower French Quarter. The house was once a single-family dwelling that had long ago been converted into seven separate apartments. It had a large front porch and a small backyard and a landlord known to its occupants only as a post office box number. It was a worn-out house, occupied by plain people in a drab neighborhood of lower class whites, blacks, and Hispanics.

The man who lived in the attic apartment lived alone and never spoke to anyone else in the house. But that was hardly noticed by occupants who rarely spoke to anyone anyway. He was a pudgy man, in his mid-twenties, who liked to wear plaid shirts and read the newspapers. He read *all* the newspapers, from the front page through every classified ad, except for one section. He never ready the Sports section. Ever.

He was born and raised in New Orleans, a product of Louisiana's public education system, who dropped out of school in the tenth grade to become a janitor. He was still a janitor and still felt like he was on the outside looking in on the rest of the world. He always felt that way, especially after his only parent died. His mother passed away of old age before his twentieth birthday. She was a seamstress, who worked all her life to wind up with gnarled hands and the one troubled son.

There were times, very late at night, when he felt so alone, as if he was the only being alive. He felt as if he were a stranger, a wanderer from a faraway land who was lost on a strange planet. *Alienated* was the word, but he never knew it.

But he had *finally* done something. He had done something he dreamed of doing for a long, long time. And after he had done it, he had returned to his attic apartment, changed his clothes, sat up in his bed and waited for the morning paper. He waited until dawn that Saturday morning after his journey to Dauphine Street, and then quietly slipped downstairs and walked to the self-service newspaper stand on Elysian Fields Avenue.

His triumph was on the front page. He slipped fifteen cents into the slot with a shaking hand. He made sure no one was looking and then quickly removed three papers. His eyes watered when he looked at the picture on the front page. He wiped his eyes, tucked the papers under his arm and walked briskly back to his apartment house.

He made sure he was not followed before taking the three steps up to the front porch. He waited just inside the downstairs doorway and checked again before ascending the stairs, three at a time. And only after he carefully locked the four locks of his apartment door and made sure the lone curtain of his lone window was secure, did he jump on his bed with his papers. He took a deep breath and read about himself on page one.

*He had don't it.* He had *really* done it. And it was there for the world to see and read, and best of all, there was a *picture.* He could see her legs in plain view behind the policeman who stood over her. It was *perfect.*

He read the article twice, and with each reading he became more excited. As he read, he rubbed his crotch. he looked again at the picture of the policeman standing over the body and knew the policeman could see all of her, all of her body, between her nasty legs. The policeman was writing something on a pad, probably something about him. The policeman looked dark and mysterious and he knew the policeman was at a loss.

He liked the picture so very much, especially the policeman. He decided the detective would be his great enemy. He looked at the name under the picture, LaStanza. A strange, foreign name. A great name for an enemy. Not an American name at all.

When he felt himself close to erupting, he put the paper down and picked up the object he had earlier placed so carefully on his night stand. He lay back on his bed with her bra in his mouth and masturbated. He fucked her right there, in the picture with the camera looking and the jealous detective watching. He fucked her nasty pussy. And it was the highest climax of his life. It was *fantastic.* It was an explosion from inside him, from deep within.

And after, he slept.

•

When he woke he was hungry, so he got into his 1966 ford Falcon and went to the Speedy Burger on St. Claude Avenue. He liked the burgers there and liked the drive-up window, so he could stay in his car and not go inside where people could stare at him. He ordered three burgers and a vanilla shake. He ate one burger on the way home and then wolfed down the other two after he was safe inside his locked room. He wished he'd bought more.

But he had work to do now. He had to wash the clothes he'd worn because of all the blood. he had already washed down the front seat of his car. He would use his sink, next to the old refrigerator with the rusty bottom, to wash the clothes.

Then he had to clip the newspaper and put the articles in his new scrapbook. Then he had to hide the bra somewhere, maybe in his closet, or maybe behind the loose boards in the wall behind his bed. Yes, behind the bed would be better, because he would sleep next to it.

Then he would masturbate again. He wanted to do it until he was drained, until he was ready again, to go out.

He hurried. He washed the clothes and hid the bra in a paper bag behind the loose board. then he curled up on his bed again with the newspaper article and began to rub himself. His eyes stopped at one word: 'Baffle'. He wasn't sure what the word meant but figured it meant 'scared'. That was what the police were. they were *scared*. The whole fucking city was scared now. He felt a power within him that crawled up from his stomach and lodged itself in his throat and made his eyes water. He was so *powerful*.

He had dreamed of the day he would be famous. He dreamed of the day when his name would be spoken in fear, just like Jack the Ripper.

A long time ago, he was baptized by a Catholic priest and given the name Jerome Hemmel. Now, he decided to change his name. On the day after he killed the girl in the blue dress, he changed him name to Jack Hemmel. No longer was he the simple janitor named Jerome, who the students at Loyola University ignored as if he were a urinal in the latrine. He was *Jack*.

•

During the following week, Sergeant Rob Mason, Detective Mark Land, Detective Dino LaStanza – as well as their supporting cast of Paul Snowood, Cal Boudreaux, and several angry, tie-wearing Robbery detectives worked every lead they had. They worked long and hard. And in the end, had nothing.

Another Friday came. A man came home on that particular Friday night at about eight o'clock. His name was Cesar Rodrigues Corona and he lived on Zinnia Street in a red brick house with his wife, Teresa, and their two children. Cesar owned a pet shop on Magazine Street and was a jazz musician on weekend nights. He had a ten o'clock gig that Friday night, so he was in a hurry when he got home.

"Teresa," he snapped as he opened his front door.

His wife put their two-year-old baby back in his bed and went into the living room. Cesar was already in the kitchen.

"What's for supper?" he huffed as he sat heavily at the kitchen table.

"I'll make you a sandwich," Teresa said as she moved slowly over to the refrigerator. She was getting ready to tell him about the helluva day she'd had, about how their daughter had fallen while playing in a tree and cut her forehead, about the washer that was leaking, about –

But Cesar spoke first. Being large and powerful, and being the hot-blooded *Man-of-the-house,* Cesar jumped up, knocking his chair over. He bellowed at Teresa and cursed her.

"I want a hot supper when I get home!" He proceeded to throw whatever was within reach across the kitchen. He kicked the chairs around and slammed kitchen cabinet doors until he realized that Teresa was not in the kitchen. She was in the living room. He went in and continued yelling until Teresa rose heavily from the sofa and took another one of her walks.

Teresa walked out the front door and headed down Zinnia toward Bayou St. John. She would walk until Cesar was gone. She crossed Beauregard Avenue and walked up the levee next to the dark waters of the bayou. On the other side of the high levee, next to the deep bayou, Teresa felt as if she were separated from the rest of the city, separated from troubles, at least for a while.

The water looked silvery under the moon, smooth and glassy. Teresa had taken walks before along the bayou. Her walks were becoming more frequent as Cesar's tantrums increased. She would walk until he calmed down or went off to his gig. Then she would go home to her kids.

She did not see the man sitting next to the bayou until she was almost upon him. "Oh!" She jumped. "You scared me."

He stood up nervously from his place next to the water and backed off a step.

"Sorry," he said as he looked down at his feet. He looked up at her for a second, then looked away again. Teresa examined him a moment, then turned and walked away toward the old bridge by the ruins of the Spanish Fort. The man was young and pudgy and looked, like a wimp. He was a wimp, she decided, and if he followed her, she would bat the living shit outta him.

She was mad enough at Cesar to do it, too. She clenched her hands into fists and thought about how she would like to bat the shit out of Cesar. She had tried once. He gave her a black eye and a bloody lip.

Teresa stopped by the old Spanish Fort and looked around for the pudgy fellow in the plaid shirt, but he was gone. She sat down on the worn brick steps and looked at the silvery water.

It was a very old fort, which had long since crumbled into faded brick ruins, overgrown with grass and mounds of earthen levee that protected the city from flood waters from nearby Lake Pontchartrain. It was small and quiet, next to the tranquil bayou, where violence was a stranger.

She did not see the pudgy man in the plaid shirt, carrying a thin, long-bladed knife now as moved over the grassy ruins in a mating dance of death. His heart pounded in his chest as he slowly moved closer to the woman sitting on the steps next to the bayou. He crept closer, stalking her. In a moment he would be upon her and there would be such a climax in blood –

•

Murder cases were usually named for the victim or for the murderer. Victim names, such as Marcus-Nelson and the Lindberg Murder cases are common titles. Cases like Leopold-Loeb and the Son-of-Sam Murders were named for the culprit, just like the Jack the Ripper Murders.

In New Orleans, where thing are done differently, naturally, murders are usually referred to by their location. Therefore, the murder of Marie Sumner was know as the Dauphine Street Murder. The only exception occurred when there was a murder in a housing project. Project murders weren't given any name because they weren't murders. They were killings. There was difference, at least from the point of view of over-worked homicide detectives because in those cases, the victim and killer usually knew one another.

The Bayou St. John Murder occurred on a Friday night while I was trying to sleep off the exhausting week of dead-end leads. Mark called me and said he was on his way to pick me up. Our killer had struck again, and there went my weekend, again. It was the same killer all right. Only at Bayou St. John it was worse.

This time it wasn't a girl who came out of a French Quarter bar. This time it was a housewife, in a residential neighborhood, and there was no chance for Jessica and I for that weekend. I was thinking of how I was going to tell Jessica as Mark and I pulled up near the Spanish Fort on Beauregard Avenue.

The murder scene was on the other side of the levee, next to the bayou. Of course, there was the usual entourage of dignitaries assembled at the scene. This time, there were a couple captains mixed in with the usual number of patrolmen, Levee Board Police, ambulance drivers, reporters, and that same K-9 officer with his same hungry dog.

Mark handed another copy of the chief's letter to one of the captains. I asked another captain, "who's got the olives?"

"Huh?" was his reply.

Mark then stepped over to that particular K-9 officer.

"Why don't you just get the fuck outta here with that thing?" Marked said.

"This *thing* is a K-9 officer," the man holding the leash snapped back at Mark. "And I wouldn't get too close because the leash might slip outta my hand," he added with an evil grin.

"I was talking to the dog," Mark snapped back.

Mark's eyes became tiny slits. "Let go of the leash and I'll put three slugs in that K-9's head before you can bat an eye." Mark leaned closer and his voice rose, "Then I'll beat the fuck outta you, toss your fat ass into the bayou right in front of the TV cameras." Mark pointed at the mini-cams going up the levee.

"Now get the fuck outta here," Mark snarled, "and I better *never* catch you on another homicide scene again!" Mark walked off without a second look.

The K-9 officer had to have the last word, so he said that he hoped we'd need him someday so he could be sure and not be around. Then he left. That was a typical cop reaction. If you don't like another cop, just threaten to not be there when you're needed.

*"Fuck you!"* Mark yelled. "And the fuckin' dog you rode in on too!"

•

We met the case officer on top of the levee. He was from the day shift, from the other Homicide platoon. At least Bayou St. John would not be our headache. Mark and I didn't say it, but we both were thinking the same thing, at least the rank had something else to think about besides Dauphine Street. But this was a helluva way to get their minds off our case.

The case officer was a nearsighted fellow named Albert Ruston who wore thick spectacles that made him look like a half-blind owl. Albert had short stringy hair that barely covered his huge ears. He was friendly but *lazy*. There was no way Albert was gonna solve this thing that suited Mark fine. Because Mark and I were gonna solve it, period, just ask Mark.

At the top of the levee Mark stopped and spoke to Albert while I moved to the body and started taking notes. What was most obvious was what I noticed first. She looked a lot like Marie, at least by her description. She was a white female, early twenties, 5'1" to 5'2", ninety pounds, long dark hair, slight build.

I watched the crime lab technician finish his routine and waited until he went up to meet with Albert and our lieutenant. This time the commander of Homicide was out with his boys. Lieutenant Bill Gironde was an old Homicide man who was smart enough to let his boys work as free as he could let them. He never pressured anyone and that was a blessing. Only he was the nervous type who drove his sergeant batty with administrative bullshit. He loved his boys but was hell on his sergeants.

While the lieutenant met with Albert, Mark and the technician, I moved closer to the victim next to Bayou St. John. She was naked, her legs open wide, and there were stab wounds visible around her vagina. She lay in a great pool of blood, deep red, sticky liquid that was slowly changing into dark globs of jelly like goo. her clothes had been thrown aside on the grass at the base of the levee.

I needed no flashlight. The bright white light of the moon cast a silver glow on the face of the lady next to the bayou. Her open eyes gazed skyward in that dull, unfocused stare. In movies and in cheap detective novels, it is said a victim's face is 'masked in terror'. In real life the face is masked in a dull look, with no expression, only a pair of lifeless eyes that seem to stare far away, into another world. I found a bite mark on her nipple. Only this time it was on the right nipple. When Mark and Albert came down, I pointed out the bite mark.

"So," Mark snapped, "we learn something else about our man."

"What's that?" Albert was quick to ask.

"He's ambidextrous."

It went right over Albert's head, right over the lieutenant's head also. But Albert wasn't about to be outdone. He had a question of his own. "Are we standing on a batture?" he asked. "I mean, is this the bayou batture?"

"I'm not sure." I answered. Mark wouldn't even answer him. I never heard of a bayou batture, but I knew the land between the levee and the Mississippi River was called the river batture and the land between the levee and Lake Pontchartrain was the lake batture. So I guess you could call the land between a levee and a bayou, a bayou batture.

Then again, who gives a fuck? It's a colloquial term. There's no way you could look it up in a dictionary. New Orleans was full of terms like that. In New Orleans we call a sidewalk a *banquette*. A median was a *neutral ground*. A dime was called a *silver dime*. A covered porch was a *gallery*. And of course, everyone knew *lagniappe* meant something extra. So what did *batture* have to do with a murder? Then it hit me, Albert's writing his final report already. Another unsolved murder to file away.

Albert stood scratching his head as the coroner's driver arrived and zippered up the body in a black bag.

When a patrolman arrived to say the victim's husband was by the police cars, Albert suddenly had something to do. He and Lieutenant Gironde crossed the levee to start in on the first, natural suspect in the murder of a housewife – her husband.

Mark and I walked over the levee to the street side. "We got ourselves one helluva fuckin' problem," mark said as he rubbed the stubble on his chin.

"We got a fuckin' maniac," I agreed.

"It's our turn," Mark added. He meant the city. It was New Orleans's turn.

"Well," Mark said, "we may as well help on the canvass." So we moved across Beauregard Avenue. When we stepped to the other side, I stopped and looked back at the dark levee. I could see the bright TV Lights illuminating the large oaks on the other side, long Spanish moss dangling like gray ghosts.

"What's the matter?" Mark asked me.

"Don't know," I answered. "There's something about this scene, like Dauphine Street, only I can't put my finger on it."

"Well," Mark huffed as he turned away, "Whenever you put your finger on it, let me in on it."

Mark took the houses on Beauregard from Phlox to Jay Street. I took the houses from Phlox down to Robert E. Lee Boulevard up to Phlox. Whatever was bothering me, it kept rattling around in my brain. Something about the scenes.

"It'll come to me," I told myself, "probably in the middle of the night."

Eventually, as I neared Robert E. Lee Boulevard, I saw a black man sitting at the bus stop. He wasn't there when Mark and I drove up earlier, but he was there now. He was listening to his BFR as I approached, so he didn't hear me. BFR is project talk for a Big Fuckin' Radio, which was usually kept next to the ear of a mook and turned up very loudly.

I could see there was no blood on the man as I walked up to him. He didn't see me until I was almost on him, but he knew who I was right away, a white man, in coat and tie, carrying an LFR – Little Fuckin' Radio.

"Let's see some I.D.," I told him.

"Sure." He smiled at me and looked around to see if I was alone. God only knows how he missed that caravan of police cars and ambulances up the street, but he seemed surprised to see me.

"Say, what's going on, man?"

"Murder," I told him.

"A what?" His eyes grew wider as he handed me the rest of the papers in his wallet. He stood back and quickly emptied his pockets on the concrete bench. "I'm clean man," he assured me.

"Can you turn the BFR down a second?" I asked him. He was quick to oblige. I stepped back and called Headquarters on my LFR and ran his name through the computer. it was obvious by the man's attitude that he'd been handled by the police before. It took only a minute for the computer to tell me the man had the usual number of city arrests and misdemeanor arrests, but no felony busts.

"What you doing' here?" I asked him.

"Visiting," he answered.

"Who?"

"Family." He looked down at his feet.

"You got family around here?" I asked in a louder voice, knowing that no blacks lived anywhere near there. I stared hard at him and when he looked back at me I could see he was scared. I twirled my finger around and pointed to the bench. He assumed the correct position so I carefully patted him down.

"Now, take me to your family's house," I told him.

"Well – " he shuffled, "she ain't ma family, zackly" He started putting the papers from the bench into his pockets.

"Then what is she, zackly?"

"She is more like my woman," he told me.

It got more interesting by the minute.

He led me a few houses up Beauregard to a one-story brick house with a Japanese garden in front. He knocked on the door. After a couple knocks, a woman's voice asked, "Who's there?"

"Tyrone," the mook said. Another *Tyrone*. I always wondered if Tyrone Power was that popular with black women.

The door opened and a white woman in a bra and panties stood in the open doorway.

"The bus will be along," she said.

I stepped from behind Tyrone and put my credentials in front of her nose.

"Police," I said as I walked into the house. I signaled for Tyrone to follow me and we all gathered in the living room. It was a dirty house, cluttered to the ceiling with books and stacks of papers. It took only a couple of strategic questions to get the whole story. The woman admitted that Tyrone had just fucked her. He was on his way back home, in the St. Bernard Housing Projects, by bus because there was no way she was driving anywhere near there at night. According to her, they had been together most of the night. She was nonchalant about the entire matter. It was a friendly conversation. I appreciated the candor and told them.

"Didn't you see all the police cars out front?" I asked the logical question.

The woman pointed out that the bedroom was in the back of the house and Tyrone had slipped out the back door when they were finished.

After I took a quick look in the back of the house I called Albert on my LFR. I figured he might want to know about this. It took about two minutes for Albert and the lieutenant to arrive. I introduced them to the fat lady and Tyrone and then I stepped back. Mark came a minute later and watched as Albert went into action.

He was actually excited. Maybe because the woman was still in bra and panties. Ole Albert had something to work with, an urbanite in a strange neighborhood. But I felt sorry for Tyrone as the questions started. I guess I should have just let it all go, but I was still new and who knew. I didn't want to be wrong.

As the questioning continued, I looked at the woman again. Not bad looking, pushing forty and a little hippy but she had a pretty face and large brown eyes and completely comfortable in just her bra and panties. Then it came to me – the something that was rattling around in my head. *Brassiere.*

I grabbed Mark by the arm and led him outside the front door.

"No bra," I told him.

"What?"

"That's what was rattling around in my head," I explained. "I was going over my notes on Dauphine Street and I felt something was missing, there was no bra with Marie. And there's no bra tonight." I pointed to the nearby levee.

Mark rubbed his chin again and started grinding his teeth.

"We gotta talk to the husband," I told him as I started walking away.

"Hold on a second" – Mark didn't move – "a lotta women go braless," he argued, but it was a faint argument.

"And lots more wear bras," I came right back.

He looked at me real hard and a smile began to work its way under that bear moustache. "Are you thinking what I'm thinking?"

"Yep," I assured him. And I thought of it *first*.

Mark's face broke into a broad grin. "This could be fuckin' good." We left the woman with Tyrone and Albert and the good lieutenant. We headed straight for Zinnia Street

Cesar Rodrigues Corona had finished crying by the time we arrived. He was sitting at this kitchen table with various members of the family, mostly Latin women, who were still crying. Mark and I took Cesar aside and asked him one simple question. As far as he knew, his wife *always* wore a bra.

It may have been the middle of the night but there was no way Mark and I were *not* going to Gentilly. We parked in front of the Sumner house on Mirabeau. Mark called the Detective Bureau on his LFR and had Sergeant Ass-Hole Danton call the Sumners and tell them we were outside and had to talk to them right away. When the light on the front gallery flicked on, we stepped out of our unit and approached the house.

Mr. Sumner was a skinny old man with droopy eyelids visible behind horn-rimmed glasses. He looked frail and tired and Mark apologized for the late hour before we all sat in the living room.

"Mr. Sumner," Mark started, "something important has come up and we gotta know if Marie wore a bra last Friday."

The old man's droopy eyes grew somewhat wider and a little more awake. He stared at Mark as if he were looking at a crazy man. He cleared his throat and whispered, "I have not idea." Mark asked him of he could ask Mrs. Sumner.

The old man hesitated a moment, then got up slowly and walked toward the back of the house. It took him a few minutes. I sat in the dark living room and looked around at the mementos of a lifetime, a scarf of the Blessed Mother above the couch, an oil painting of a couple from the twenties. And in the center of the room, on the coffee table, was framed photograph of Marie. She was in cap and gown, and she was smiling.

Mr. Sumner re-entered the room and told us that Mrs. Sumner had not idea either.

Mark thanked him and we started for the front door, Mr. Sumner cleared his throat again and added, "The missus says Marie wore a bra most of the time. But she don't know about that night."

I thanked Mr. Sumner again and walked out.

"If only she had a boyfriend," I said to Mark after we were outside. A boyfriend would know, or even a close girlfriend would know, but Marie was such a loner, such a quiet girl.

I started thinking about Jessica as we pulled off. She went braless occasionally, but only with certain clothes. I was thinking about her boobs under that blue velvet dress she wore without a bra. It was past midnight already and she was probably asleep. I close my eyes and dreamed of Jessica in bed, her long dark hair spread out on her pillow, her face clear of make-up, so soft and pretty, and peaceful. Only I knew she was not peaceful. I should have called her from the Tyrone's lover's house.

Mark drove me home and came in for a minute for some coffee. He sat at my kitchen table and we talked a while about the case.

"We may have something," Mark said, "in that bra thing." He started rubbing his eyes and added, "But let's keep this between you and me for the moment."

I agreed.

"If someone else figures it, then that's good for 'em," he went on, "but right now only three people know it, you and me and the killer."

"And," I thought to myself, "that's a bond that might bring us all together one day."

I poured two cups of hot coffee and sat back in a chair across the table from Mark. He stopped rubbing his eyes and glanced at his coffee before looking around the kitchen. "It's awfully bright in here," he grumbled.

I knew what he meant. Lots of kitchens in old New Orleans houses were painted bright white with bright tile floors and all-white appliance. Those 150-watt bulbs I had put in didn't help.

"The bulbs are too bright." I pointed up at the lights.

Mark nodded, then took a gulp of coffee before sitting back and rubbing his eyes again. He started chuckling and then let me in on the joke. "I'm sure glad you found that mook."

"He sure looked silly," I added and started laughing too, "but not as silly Albert once he got started."

When he finished chuckling, he drank the rest of his coffee in tow more large gulps and jumped up to leave. "See you tomorrow night," he told me on the way out.

"No," I argued, "Really?"

"Yeah." He wasn't kidding. "We got some people to talk to in the Quarter, got some snitches to check on. Saturday night brings out all the freaks and fruits."

I closed my eyes and had one thought, "Fuck me!"

•

Jessica had a way of staring at me that made me feel like a little boy who had to apologize right away. I would say, "I'm sorry," automatically. But sometime it was no use.

That was the look that greeting me early Saturday evening when I picked her up for dinner. But I did not say I was sorry this time. I just kissed her softly on the cheek. She said nothing. And she remained quiet until we were blocks away from her house.

"Are you sure you can spare the time to have dinner with me?" she asked.

I already told her I was meeting Mark at the office later, that we had to make it an early supper, that I had to work. What else could I say? So I said nothing. I just gritted my teeth and waited for her to continue.

"So," she went on, "why don't you tell me why you have to work again?'

I looked at her face in profile. She would not look back at me. She stared straight ahead and told me to watch the road. So I did just that. I felt like hell, tired as hell and tired of what was happening between us.

Jessica was changing right in front of my eyes and it was my fault. And worse, I could do nothing about it. She was becoming a bitch. No – I was turning her into a bitch. She had never bitched at me before. Even when I was working midnight shifts and twelve-hour power watches at the Sixth, she didn't bitch. But Homicide was a different matter. On the road you had regular time off. Homicide was a ghost that followed you home and came between you, even when the two of you were alone.

•

We had dinner at a restaurant on the lakefront. Seafood was always her favorite, so we had shrimp and watched the sailboats drift on the lake. The restaurant was built on pilings over the water and our table, next to the window, provided a open view of the dark waters of Lake Pontchartrain.

Jessica waited to speak until after the main course was served. Then she took her time and spoke quietly and carefully. She told me she was not happy. She told me she was worried about what was happening to me and to us. I listened as she said I was no longer dependable, no longer there when she needed me. She talked, and I could see how unhappy she really was.

As she spoke, I looked out at the water, at the sun that setting in the western sky. It looked as if the sun were sinking in to the lake itself, a bright red disc sinking and sizzling in to the salty lake waters. It was a bloody red sunset. And as Jessica spoke in the background, I felt as if something were staring back at me from beyond that sunset, as if something wicked, something evil and ugly was staring back at me.

As the bloody sun sank, I felt murder's cold and lifeless eyes staring at me from the edge of the sunset. And I felt a chill.

*Chapter 4*
Algiers

Life in a pressure cooker. That's the best way to describe police work. You get out of the Academy, get the badge and get right into the cooker and the pressure starts building, and building, and building.

I remember one night, when I was a patrolman, there was a call from a man who said he was going to shoot the first policeman who showed up at the corner of Euterpe and Constance Streets. The man claimed to have a shotgun and was waiting.

Stan was driving that night. He wheeled our car around, floored the accelerator and we *still* were not the first ones there. Two other cars had beaten us. I was disappointed because we weren't the first to arrive, because the man was already in custody. And I was disappointed because the man turned out to be a drunk with no shotgun, just a lone shotgun shell in his pocket. What a letdown.

But for a moment, when we were wheeling toward the man, not knowing if there would be a shooting or not, heading headlong toward the unknown, I was so excited. Even then, in my first year, I learned that I was not afraid. I thought then that I was born to be a cop.

But I know better know. It was the pressure cooker. The cooker had started in on me then. It begins with the first death you witness, a car wreck, then maybe a suicide or two and a rape or two, and then more death and death and death. You become conditioned. You become indifferent to human pain, saturated with being a constant witness to violence.

You begin to feel it doesn't affect you. You begin to handle each scene easier and easier and believe you can handle almost any situation. Because *you are the police*, you figure you can handle it. You begin to be less and less affected and les and less fearful until there is *absolutely no fear left*.

And so, when you hear there is a man with a gun waiting for you, you fly there, not from bravery not because you're crazy, but because you've seen it all before and you *know* you are the one

who lives on. You are a perpetual witness to the misery of man.
And if that stupid mother fucker *does* have a gun, then you're just
gonna blow his brains and eyes and teeth and hair all over the
fucking place, period.

I'm no philosopher or great writer who can illustrate in subtle
scenes just how the pressure affects you. Just take my word for it,
it does. And there is little relief. Some cops turn to drinking, some
to sex, and some to other pleasures that can be addictive and eat
away your mind. Some just resign themselves because they can't
handle it. Some can neither handle it nor escape it and it will
eventually destroy them.

What little relief I have found usually comes in the form of
humor. You learn to be a cheap comedian. You have to be. You
have to joke about it, to let the pressure out. After a particularly
bloody scene, you have to joke when you eat pizza later. The red
sauce looks too much like blood, and the mozzarella cheese bears a
striking resemblance to the brain matter you just watched ooze
from the skull of a man who blew his brains all over the ceiling of
his bedroom.

You try not to joke about things that that but you have to.

It's living in a pressure cooker. And Homicide is the pressure
cooker you take home with you, so you can simmer overnight and
wake up with the case staring you right in the face. You brush your
teeth wondering if you're canvassed everywhere that should have
been canvassed. You shave and wonder if there was one person
you missed. You dress and remember all the Homicide clichés.

"You don't solver murders by sitting on your ass," was the
oldest cliché. "You gotta hit the streets, gotta dig the information
and keep digging until you solve it, because the information is out
there, you just gotta find it."

You drink strong coffee-and-chicory in the morning and the
murder is sitting right there across the table. Cold dead eyes stare
at you asking when you're gonna catch the bastard. You find
yourself jotting down little notes to yourself, so you don't forget,
because you can't keep everything in your brain.

I jotted the word *car* down during my second cup on a right
Monday morning. I wanted to remember it because that was
something we knew about our killer. He had to have a car. To get

to and from the Quarter and to and from Bayou St. John with bloody clothes, he *had* to have a car. He couldn't get on a public service bus with blood all over him and not be noticed. To be sure, I had spent the previous weekend checking with all the bus drivers who worked the nights of the murders on Dauphine and Bayou St. John. I did it on my own. *Car* wasn't much, but it was something.

As I drove to pick up mark, another cliché came to mind. "Eighty per cent of all homicides involve people who are acquainted with one another." It is know as 'murder among friends, relatives and associates'. It was common knowledge, and it turned out that way, eighty per cent of the time. People kill people they know, husbands kill wives, and neighbors get pissed off on a hot summer night and kill each other, or drug dealers kill their partners. That meant twenty per cent of homicides involved total strangers. And it looked like we were in the lucky twenty, with random, serial killings. *Fuck me.*

I made another note to myself, wondering if maybe there was a connection between Marie Sumner and Teresa Corona. It could be anything, maybe they used to work at the same place once or went to the same school. Maybe they went to the same bank or same hairdresser or any fucking thing. Maybe they had the same fucking gynecologist or took their driver's license test the same day. It could be anything.

I rooted through my briefcase as I drove, steering with my left hand and jotting down my newest note to myself. When I finished I felt a little better. I had two ideas. Yet deep down, I knew it wasn't much. The chance of Sumner and Corona being connected was miniscule. The only thing they had in common was being in the wrong place at the wrong time. The killings had *random* stamped all over the. And that was scary.

As I turned on to Bienville Avenue, near Marks's house, I heard something on my police radio that made me sick to my stomach. It was Mason's voice. He was talking to Headquarters, and from the staccato messages, I knew we were in trouble. Headquarters was calling for a Homicide team, on another murder.

Mark was waiting for me outside his house, Leaning on the bottom post of his front-porch steps as he sipped a cup of coffee. He lived in a bright blue shotgun double house with a long front gallery and concrete steps that led down to the sidewalk. Mark lived on one side of the double. He parents lived on the other side. His mama did all the cooking. She was bigger and louder than Mark and was amazed that I was so little and skinny, for an Italian. Mark had his radio with him, but as usual, it was turned off. So I told him about the murder. "It's in Algiers," I said as we started downtown toward the Greater new Orleans Mississippi River Bridge.

"Fuck! Fuck! Fuck!" was Mark's only reply.

"But it's not our boy this time," I added.

"Fuck."

"There's a dude with a hole in his head next to the river," I advised.

"Double fuck!"

Mark was right. Double fuck us because we were headed across the goddamn river to another murder and we had enough to do as it was. You get elbow deep in murders and then someone else comes along and leaves another body lying around. So we crossed the Mississippi, took a left on General DeGaulle Drive and eventually found the murder scene on the river batture just south of the Algiers Dry Dock. There weren't as many people at this scene, only a few extra Harbor Police and only one mini-cam.

"Where's that fuckin K-9?" Mark asked loudly as he glared around.

"Looks like he skipped this one." I noted.

Mason was standing on the sandy part of the batture, about thirty feet from the river's edge. He was standing next to a blue pickup truck. Mark and I climbed down the levee and took a roundabout way to Mason, walking far away from the other policemen, who were adding their footprints to the sand.

"What's up?" Mark asked as we stepped up.

Mason, who lit another cigarette with the end of the cigarette he was about to throw away. He looked at me and nodded his head toward the body behind him. "This one's yours," he said to me.

I already had my notepad out and started right in on the scene. The body was lying in the sand three feet from the driver's door of the pickup. It was a young man in his late twenties, white male, red hair, blue eyes, six feet tall, thing build, wearing a gray tee shirt and blue jeans and white tennis shoes.

The body was lying on its back with its arms spread out and its left leg twisted beneath it. Its right leg was extended straight out. There was one visible wound to the left temple, a large bullet hole, which appeared to be an entry wound. It was surrounded by a flash mark with black gunpowder plainly visible. And when I looked closer, I could see the imprint of a large muzzle in the debris of he lesion. It was a contact wound. The skin was jagged with sharp cutting edges along the side of the wound where the muzzle had been placed against the skull, against the bone, causing the gasses from the gun to get between the skin and skull, rupturing the skin outward. I made note of all this and pointed it out to Mark when he came up behind me.

"You're learning fast." Mark patted my shoulder. "See his eyes." Mark pointed to the swollen purple-black eyes on the cadaver. "Head wounds always blacken the eyes."

I continued my note taking, sketching the scene until the crime lab technician came. Then I followed him through his meticulous steps as he processed the scene. There were three empty beer bottles in the sand a few feet from the body. One was broken, and closer examination revealed the broken bottle had been shot. We dug a large caliber projectile from the soft sand beneath the bottle.

Mark found three semi-cool beers from the remainder of the six-pack on the floor of the pickup. It was then that Mason called Mark and I over to the front of the truck.

"Know what this looks like?" Mason asked from behind a cloud of smoke.

Mark hesitated a second, in case I was going to answer, but when I didn't, he nodded at Mason and said, "Fuckin' suicide."

Mason nodded also and added, "This looks just like a suicide, except the gun's missing. See the way the leg is twisted under the body."

Mark added, "Like he was just standing there when" – Mark pointed his index finger at his temple, then pulled his thumb back and fired – "and he just fell down."

"It's a shame the gun's missing," I said.

"This is a mook neighborhood," Mark declared as he glanced around the batture. "If you were a mook and came upon a nice gun lying there, wouldn't you pick it up?"

Mark looked at Mason and asked, "Who called this in?"

"Anonymous call."

I was still looking at the body and asked, "What about the shot at the beer bottle?"

"Hesitation shot," Mason answered. "Common."

"He wanted to make sure the gun worked," Mark added.

Mason and Mark became more convinced by the minute about their suicide theory. Mason gathered his notes and announced, "You two finish the scene and I'll go over to the guy's house and see what's up there." He took the victim's driver's license after I copied down what I needed.

I went back to work, making certain the technician swabbed our victim's hand for a neutron activation test, then the FBI lab could tell us if the victim fired a gun recently. I was beginning to hope this was a suicide. All it would involve would be paperwork.

But as usual, the scene was not easy to process. As I looked around the sand I could see too many damned footprints, footprints of the asshole cops who were traipsing through the scene long before Mason arrived. I dream of one day having a truly clean murder scene. I guess I'll have to be the one who finds the body. I wouldn't tell anyone, except for the technician. He and I would have the scene all to ourselves, except for the body.

But that only happens in daydreams. Back at the Algiers scene, I watched the technician carefully dust the pickup and the beer bottle for fingerprints. You gotta process suicide scenes just like murder scenes, because you never knew.

•

It was high noon when Mark and I pulled up in front of the small frame house on Homer Street, about a mile from the levee and the death scene. It was a mixed neighborhood, lower middle-class black and white. Mason's car was parked in the driveway and the front door was open. We called out and he told us to come in.

It was dark in the living room. Mason was sitting on the tattered couch next to a woman in her twenties, her hair in a yellow bandanna, a Kleenex in her hand. She was wiping the tears that streaked her red face. Mason stood up and moved over to us. He explained quickly that it was looking more and more like suicide. Seems our victim attempted suicide twice before with pills and had just purchased a new .44 Magnum the day before.

"I gave Snowood and Boudreaux the receipt from the gun store. They're heading over there now," Mason added. "The only thing missing is a suicide note." Mason concluded. "I haven't had a chance, you two look around for it." He led the wife into the messy kitchen, cleared a space on the kitchen table and took a statement from the woman while Mark and I searched the two bedrooms and bath for a note.

We found none and eventually joined Mason back in the kitchen while he finished the statement. I gathered my notes, still hoping this was a suicide so I would only have to write a report after I attended the autopsy the following morning. I leaned against the refrigerator and finished my notes as Mason put the finishing touches on documenting the short and sad marriage of our victim and his wife with the red face.

The victim's name was Peter Green. His wife was named Meryl and they were married two years, no children, no job. Peter had been laid off from the oil rigs recently. Neither one had finished high school. Peter's favorite move was *Dirty Harry,* Meryl explained, so he bought a .44 Magnum to end it all. When the statement was finished, Mason explained to Meryl how to claim the body from the coroner.

I started to step away from the refrigerator, when something caught my eye. I took a second look at the side of the fridge and almost laughed out loud. I bit my lip, shook my head and signaled to Mark to come over and take a look. Mark almost laughed too. "Boy," I thought to myself, "we sure are some fuckin' detectives!" On the side of there refrigerator, in bold crayon printing, was our suicide note:

"Meryl. I killed myself. Send police to levee. Peter A. Green"

I waited for the crime lab to come and take a picture of our note on the side of the refrigerator. And later, back at the Bureau, I told Snowood and Boudreaux about how we stumbled on the note.

"Think that's funny?" Cal Boudreaux roared loud enough to rattle the light fixtures. "You ain't gonna believe what happened at the gun store."

Boudreaux was laughing so hard he couldn't talk, so Snowood told us, "When we got to the gun shop, the owner showed us the sales record. Green bought a .44 Magnum yesterday. The owner still had the check and showed it to us." Snowood's voice choked off in a roaring laugh. "And when we told him what happened, he picked up the check and ran right out of the store, and I mean *ran!*" Paul Snowood had to sit down he was laughing so hard, and Boudreaux almost fell on the floor, holding his fat sides.

I looked at Mark and sighed. "The guy must have looked funny when he ran." My statement brought tears to Boudreaux's eyes. Mark and Mason walked away from the two idiots but I hung around for the punch line. It took a full minute for Cal to get it out. "He didn't run funny. What was funny was where he was running to."

"Where?" I had to ask.

"To the bank!" Boudreaux roared again, "to cash the fuckin' check!"

•

It wasn't until the net morning, after the Green autopsy, that I had a chance to tell Mason and Mark my ideas about the murders. We gathered in Mason's small office, kicked our legs up on Mason's desk and leaned back with some coffee. I told them about what was obvious, the car.

"Well the, it's about time we worked on those registrations," Mason declared, "but I still think it's a long shot, then again, we got nothing else."

"I have an even longer shot," I went on. "I'd like to dig into the pasts of Sumner and Corona." I told them about trying to find a connection between the two, maybe a common link would surface, because you never knew until you looked.

They listened and Mason smiled from behind his smoke. "You're fishing," he stated. "But don't get me wrong, you're eager. I just don't think there's anything there. I also don't want you killing yourself working up blind alleys. Suppose we go after the car registrations first?"

Rob Mason leaned far back in his chair. He closed his eyes and I thought he was gonna doze off. I watched his lean face become very still. In the long moments that followed, Mark started telling me in a low voice how Mason could fell asleep anywhere. Once Mark told me, Mason fell asleep in the middle of a statement Mark was taking from a prominent lawyer. It wasn't too bad until Mason started snoring.

"I heard that," Mason told Mark.

"It's fuckin' true," Mark declared.

"I never snore."

"Next time I'm gonna bring a tape recorder."

Mason's eyes never opened. He just leaned back and spoke to us. "I've been going over my notes from the Homicide School I went to at he Southern Police Institute a couple years back. I had a couple classes on the psychology of sex killers. They are classified into three groups – the Psychopath, the Sexual Inadequate, and the Abnormal. I think our boy is an Abnormal style sex killer."

"You're right he's fuckin' abnormal," Mark shouted. "He's stone-fuckin' nuts!"

Mason waited for Mark to calm down before continuing. I was eager to listen to this. "Abnormal killers are a very small percentage. But their trademark is that they leave a bizarre scene."

"Bingo!" Mark said. "Our boy sure is fuckin' bizarre."

Mason went on, "He kills because of some inner conflict in his personality. His mind's distorted."

"He's fuckin' nuts!" Mark blurted.

Mason continued, "The only motive is it's a sex crime, he loses control. He has a distorted sex drive and can explode with incredible power." Mason's voice became lower as he instinctively used the old police trick of getting one's full attention by lowering your voice so the listener has to concentrate to hear. "Abnormal killers leave a bizarre and extraordinary crime scene. They are guiltless and kill on an impulse. They have frequent delusions and fantasies and sometimes experience hallucinations."

"Is this some sort of theory?" Mark asked.

"No, it's statistical fact. Jack the Ripper was classified as an Abnormal Killer."

"Fuck," Mark complained, "that's all we need, Jack the fuckin' Ripper."

"That's just what we might have here," Mason acknowledge. "According to past cases, he lives alone, grew up in a family dominated by an older female with no male father figure, has a very limited social life, if any at all, and he will strike again, usually at random." Mason's eyes opened suddenly as he started coughing that hacking smoker's cough of his.

"Fuckin' cigarettes gonna kill ya." Mark reached over and put out the cigarette smoldering in the ashtray on the desk.

Mason chuckled and leaned forward and lit up another cigarette. "I'm afraid our boy's a serial murderer, and we've just been handed chapters one and two."

"Jack the fuckin' Ripper," Mark repeated in disgust.

"And they never caught him," I added to the conversation.

"Yeah," Mason agreed, "that's what I have written on the bottom of my notes."

"Well, that's encouraging," Mark huffed. He stood up and stretched his massive arms. He yawned and shook his head from side to side like a snarling grizzly. "Well, that abnormal Fuck-head better look out because *I'm coming after him!*" Mark bellowed.

When I think back on it now, Mason sure was subtle in his motivation.

•

We caught two more homicides in the following two days. One was a barroom killing in the Fifth District, not too far from the lovely Desire Housing Project. Snowood caught that case and occupied himself with some paperwork.

The second wasn't a homicide at all. A fat old lady went out for a walk and stumbled into a canal along the Almonaster Industrial Corridor. A truck driver found her about a week later. She was really ripe and about to pop from a week in the strong spring sunshine. Boudreaux was the first Homicide man on his scene, and, after a quick look at the body, he went and stood by his car and waited for the meat wagon.

We found Boudreaux leaning on the hood of his car. He was surprised to see Mark and I. "What are ya'll doing here?" he asked.

"What you got?" Mark answered with a question.

"Old board, floater. Just hope she's got no knife in her back or bullet holes." That was the extent of Boudreaux's investigation, some brief notes and a wing and a prayer. He just *hoped* there was no physical evidence on the cadaver that would tend to lean to foul play.

Boudreaux didn't even go to the autopsy. We found him sitting at his desk early the next morning. Mark laughed right away, because he had predicted Boudreaux would not go to the autopsy of a body in such a state of, stink. I was too tired to laugh at Cal. Tired and thankful that it was our last day on the day shift. The next day we were due back on evenings and thankfully away from all the heat and headaches of working days at Headquarters. It was a pain working around the brass all the time and with no place to park your police car and the stifling New Orleans springtime heat. I hated the day shift, even if it was the only time I could see Jessica regularly. But what the fuck, I hadn't seen much of her, anyway, the whole month since Dauphine Street.

"Skipped the autopsy?" Mark asked as we walked past ole Cal, who was busy munching on a moon-pie. Cal ignored Mark's question. I stopped by the message desk and glanced at the daily reports on the sergeant's clipboard. Something caught my eye. It was Boudreaux's daily on the body of the woman. He had classified her death as a possible boating accident, a *fucking boating accident*. I chuckled as I brought the daily over to Mark. He jumped up and ran over to Cal. "What the fuck's this?" Mark bellowed.

"My daily," Cal answered between bites of his moon-pie.

"Boating accident? What the fuck are you doing?" Mark cried. "Boating accident?"

"Fuckin' Ay!" Boudreaux roared back. "I found a fuckin' rope next to the body, man. How do you fuckin' know she wasn't water skiing?"

There was no use even trying to reason with Boudreaux. Mark should have known better.

A little later that morning, Paul Snowood came in from the front office. He was leading a middle-aged couple, a mousy-looking woman and a scarecrow-looking man, into the back office. He led them to Boudreaux, introducing him as the man responsible for the investigation of the old lady's death. After grunting a brief hello, Cal explained to them that they were in the wrong place. He told them to go to the Coroner's Office for the body.

"But we want to know about the investigation," the scarecrow complained.

"There ain't no investigation," Boudreaux calmly replied.

"What about the autopsy?" the scarecrow asked

"I don't know nothin' about it," Boudreaux explained as he leaned back in his chair. "I told you the Coroner's Office has all that information. You don't think I'm gonna go to an autopsy of a stinker, do you?"

He actually called the woman a *stinker*. The scarecrow's face snapped back as if he's been slapped. He told Boudreaux he didn't appreciate his mother being referred to as a stinker.

"She was under water for a week. You didn't smell her at the scene," Cal explained. "I did."

And I though the Sixth District was madhouse.

On my last evening off for a month, I called Jessica as soon as I got home. She was drying her hair and told me to call back. I lay down on my couch and promptly fell asleep. The next thing I knew, Jessica called me. There was something in her voice I didn't like.

"I'm free tonight," I said. "Let's have dinner." There was a time when we had dinner together every night, but lately –

"I can't," she answered in that same low voice.

"What?"

"I can't," she repeated. "I'm going out, and I'm late."

"Out? Where?"

"I'm going with Julie, to a movie."

"Oh, yeah?"

"Yeah."

I waited a second before asking, "Why?"

Her voice picked up an octave and I could see I was annoying her. "What do you mean 'why'?"

"I mean *why?*"

"Because I want to," she snapped.

"You want to go to a movie, instead of, uh?"

"Yes. Exactly."

"What the fuck are you saying, *exactly?*" I heard myself asking.

She exhaled loudly and then spoke carefully, "Look, I haven't heard from you in almost a week. So I'm going out with a girl friend."

"But why?"

"Because she asked me and I can't depend on you," she cried, "and I'm tired of it."

"Well, I'm tired too," I snapped back. "I'm so fuckin' tired I don't even know what fuckin' day this is!"

There was silence on the other end of the line. I guess I was yelling, again.

"Listen – " Jessica sighed. "Julie will be here in a minute. Let's continue this later." Her voice was low and calm. "Why don't you just rest?"

"I don't want to rest," I said.

"Well, I've got to go," she said hurriedly.

"Then go," I advised. I could hear her breathing at the other end of the line. She sighed again and repeated, "I've got to go. We'll talk tomorrow."

"Yeah." I hung up. I guess I expected her to call right back, but I wasn't surprised when she didn't. I remained on the couch as the sun set outside and darkness invaded my living room, and soon I was asleep.

When I woke up, I woke up with a start. I didn't know where I was and in the blackness I tried to get up, stumbled over the coffee table and fell face first on the carpet. It took me a couple seconds to realize where I was and to remember. It was then I realized I had my Magnum in my hand. I was holding my revolver in a hand that felt anything but steady. I reached over and flicked on the lamp at the end of the sofa and sat there with my head aching, trying to figure how I came up with my gun when I went down.

I put my gun on the table and went into the kitchen. After letting my tired eyes adjust to the bright glare of the kitchen, I made my way to the refrigerator to get something to eat. I hadn't eaten and the clock above the fridge said it was almost two o'clock in the morning. I didn't eat. My stomach was all knotted. So I put on some coffee and after one hot cup, went back into the living room with my second cup and called Jessica. There was no answer.

I leaned back on the sofa and tried not to think about it, tried not to think about Jessica, and wound up thinking about Marie – and that was worse. It was too late to call my parents. I hadn't talked to my mother in awhile and I should have.

More coffee and still not Jessica and I couldn't sleep. So I called another number – just in case someone was home – and after a word or two it was decided. "Should I bring a couple of six-packs or what?" the voice at the other end of the line asked.

"Why not?" I answered.

About a half hour later there was a knock at my door and in stepped Stanley Smith of the lovely Sixth District, with a case of cold beer. "You look like shit," he greeted me as he entered. "This'll cure ya." He took the beer straight into the kitchen.

•

By five o'clock in the morning I was zonked. Stan was pretty zonked too, sitting on the living room floor and singing, "Nothin' would be finer, than to be in her vagina in the morning, Nothin' would be sweeter than her suckin' on my peter in the morning, .." He looked over at me and shouted, "Come on, sing the chorus!"

There was no chorus. And even if there was, I couldn't have sung it. I could barely talk. My tongue was so swollen I couldn't keep it in my mouth. I was sticking out of my mouth. My tongue always did that when I drank too much beer, fuckin' useless tongue.

Stan continued singing as I tried to call Jessica. I don't know why I bothered, because even if I got her on the phone, I couldn't talk. My fuckin' tongue was sticking out of my head.

•

It was daylight the next time I woke. There was the worst taste in my mouth. I tried brushing my teeth, but that didn't help – all it did was hurt my tongue, which was still swollen enough to be in the way. And the first cup of coffee didn't help either. All it did was confuse the taste buds and leave my stomach howling for relief. I hadn't eaten since the previous morning and hadn't had a square meal in days. There was an unending ache in my stomach that was either from lack of food, or from the beer and coffee, or from the relentless pressure of the Homicide pressure cooker.

Stan made his way into the kitchen a while later. He looked like a werewolf on drugs, his pretty blond hair sticking straight out like it was starched. He passed on coffee and, instead, opened another beer, splashed part of it on his face before joining me at the kitchen table.

"It's so fuckin' bright in here." he muttered between loud beer belches.

"Too white" – I waved at the walls – "and too much light." I pointed to the 150-watt bulbs overhead.

Stan staggered over to the light switch, managed to flick off the 150's and fell back in his chair.

"You wanna call your wife?" I asked.

"Fuck her."

"It doesn't bother her when you stay away," I asked him, "on your night off?"

"She don't care" – he belched again – "that's what keep us from splitting up. We never see each other."

I poured myself another cup as Stan started telling me about the dream he'd just had. He started getting real excited.

"Remember that tree we arrested?" he asked.

"How could I forget?" It was the only tree we ever arrested.

"I dreamed about that fuckin' tree," Stan explained in a voice growing more and more excited. "The mother fucker was chasing me down Felicity Street."

"So."

"So, I was shooting at it and hitting it and it kept on coming!"

"That's the trouble with those things. They won't go down," I added.

"The little mother fucker kept coming and its branches were reaching for me." Stan stood up and started wrestling with the branches. "They were trying to *strangle* me!"

I picked up my coffee and his beer just in time as Stan twirled around and crashed on the table, still wrestling the branches. He rolled around and then fell on the floor. When he was safely away from the table, I put the beer and coffee down and waited for him to finish off the tree. It took him a few minutes, but when he finally broke free he jumped up and stomped it a couple times for good measure. Then he stepped back to his beer. "That was a real mother of a tree," he concluded, "but I fucked it up *real bad* this time."

He went back to his beer and nothing more was said about the tree. I sat there and thought back to the night we came upon the real tree. It was a small tree that stood in the Magnolia Housing Project, one of the new trees planted by the city, between two of the old brick buildings. Stan and I were searching for some fuckin' street thug that night when Stan ran headlong into the tree. After a few moments of frenzied fighting, Stan managed to uproot the tree, which was only about six feet tall. He kicked the tree silly, handcuffed it and tossed in the back of our unit.

Then we drove the tree to the Sixth District Station where Stan booked it for Simple Battery on a Police Officer and Resisting Arrest. He put it in the holding cell and then later, when no brass was around, Stan sneaked into the cell with a Greater New Orleans telephone book and beat the living shit out of the tree. He used the phone book because it didn't leave marks -- in case the tree went to Internal Affairs and swore out a police brutality complaint against him. You gotta hand it to Stan, he thought of everything.

When Stan finished his beer, he belched again and then started talking about his marriage. His wife was too opinionated, he explained. She didn't agree with Stan's opinions about marriage and women. Stan was a simple guy who simply wanted his wife to be good in bed, good in the kitchen, and good in the laundry room. 'Fuck me, feed me, and wash my dirty clothes' was Stan's philosophy of marriage. And he couldn't understand why it wasn't working.

The clock above my refrigerator said it was nearly one o'clock in the afternoon. I wondered about Jessica. Stan continued talking, this time telling me about his newest girlfriend, an eighteen-year-old rich-uptown-bitch he had been fucking regularly for the past few weeks.

"Every time I fuck her," Stan bragged, "I leave her babbling like a fuckin' idiot." She just sits there babbling, 'Dick, dick, dick." I think I'm fuckin' her brains out.

•

It all came to a head late one evening. Jessica called me at work and asked me to stop by after I got off. It came to a head on her turf, at her house, after midnight on a hot and humid New Orleans night. The air was thick and sticky outside. She was waiting for me inside her air-conditioned dining room. She was sitting at the table with a fresh pot of coffee.

"You look tired," She told me as she stood and poured me a cup. She put in two sugars, stirred, and placed the cup on the table in front of me. Then she sat down across from me.

"I'm exhausted," I admitted as I sat down heavily next to the coffee.

"Then I'll make this short," she said in a voice that was almost a whisper.

Jessica Anne Blanc had bright green eyes that could see right through me. And even when some of that brightness dulled, when that spark between us began to fade, she could still peer deep inside me with those eyes. There was no place to hide, nowhere safe from those searching, sad eyes.

It was not easy for her, but she took her time, remained calm, and, in a whisper-voice, she told me that since I had not time for her anymore, she had no time for me. That was how she put it.

"That's it?"

She nodded at me with those piercing eyes that could see things in me I thought were hidden from everyone. She knew exactly what I was going to say. I felt it. I swallowed hard as the knot in my stomach twisted again. I took a sip of coffee and heard myself asking, "Is there someone else?"

"Of course not."

"Then what the hell does all this mean?" my voice rasped.

"It means we're not going to see each other anymore." She kept her eyes riveted to mine. Her lips tightened as she added, "Not that we see each other anymore, anyway."

I looked away.

"I can't take it anymore." she went on. "I need more and, and, Her voice trailed off. The room became so damn quiet. I could feel a drop of sweat work its way down the small of my back. I looked at her as she sat staring down into her coffee. After a while, a tear fell into the cup. I reached over to touch her hand and she yanked it away.

She glared at me and through gritted teeth declared "I'm not going to cry." Her lips were trembling. "I am *not* going to cry."

I could see the pain in her eyes. The hurt and the fear and the anger slowly rose in Jessica as she looked at me. She wiped the tears from her face with a defiant hand and snapped, "You are not the man I fell in love with anymore."

"Then who the fuck am I?"

She shook her head and looked away from me. "You see? You know how I hate it when you curse like that." I watched her face, watched as the hurt slowly melted away and anger emerge. She looked at me with eyes that were thin slivers. "I thought you were different, Dino. I thought you were better, but you're not. You're just like every other cop. All you love is your work."

"Just like your father," I had to add.

"Yes! Just like him."

"So why did you ever go out with me?" I asked in a voice that was growing louder by the second. "You knew what I was like form the start."

The anger was still there in her eyes. But I knew the hurt was also there, lurking, waiting to come out. I didn't want the hurt to come out again in her eyes. So I quickly rose and then became lost between the door and Jessica. I hesitated, turned around and faced her until she looked me in the eye and said, "Get out."

I turned away and stepped out quickly and that was it. I didn't look back after I turned away, for fear of seeing the hurt in those eyes. I didn't look back because I could feel the hurt creeping within me from my chest up into my tight throat. The hurt time came to me and there was no way to get away from it.

•

I have a picture of Jessica taken when she was sixteen, long before I knew her. She showed me that picture once and I kept it. She had long hair, then, that fell to the small of her back. And she was so pretty. She had a shy smile and bright eyes filled with all the wonder and mystery of a young girl. The wonders of a woman lay before her.

I wish I'd met her then. I wish I would have know her then, back when I was a teen-ager, when the world was so much brighter and I had all my hopes in front of me. It would have all been different. I would have never hurt her. Never. Long before I joined the long blue line.

But I was older now and everything was so much more complicated, so much colder. And I knew in the core of my soul that no matter what happened between Jessica and I from that night on, it would never be the same.

"So fuck it!" I said to myself. "Fuck it all!" Sometimes I just wanna shout out all the obscenities we cops use. Sometimes I wonder why they just don't have a class at the Police Academy that teaches us to curse: Fuck you, Fuck the public, Go fuck yourself, Get fucked, You've got to be fucking me, It won't fucking work, Beasts the fuck outta me, Beautiful, just fucking beautiful, Lovely, simply fucking lovely, Big fucking deal, Merry fucking Christmas, Jesus fucking Christ, Fuck it, just fuck it, Tell it to someone who gives a fuck, Don't get fucking wise, I just got fucked, I don't give a fuck, Fuck the whole fucking world!

•

I had believed in love. With Jessica, I really became close to a woman for the first time. It was as if we were married. We never actually made wedding plans, but when we talked about the future, we always said, "When we get married, "

I remember the night we met. Jessica was standing on the veranda at Longue Vue Gardens under the bright white moonlight. The moonlight had picked her out like a movie spotlight. Her face was soft white, snowy white under the moon. I'll never forget the sparkle in those bright eyes when she smiled at me for the first time, and the softness of that first kiss in the garden.

I would miss her. I would miss her late at night, in the darkest part of the night when all is quiet and I was alone and she was nowhere for me. I would miss her skin next to mine. I would miss having her there to talk to, to be with, to depend on. But most of all I would miss the fire lamps of those bright eyes when they were in love with me.

•

Jerome Hemmel took out the dog-eared paperback book and sat on his bed under the bare light bulb. The book was the only book he ever read from beginning to end. It was about Jack the Ripper. Actually, he had not read it all. He had skimmed over some of it until he had gotten to the good parts, the juicy parts. Those parts he read over and over again.

"Yes," he thought to himself as he searched for another favorite part of the book, "I'll call myself Jack from now on." He would not be Jerome anymore. He was Jack. And like the first Jack, he would have "the luck of the devil' – as the book said. He would come out "like a shadow and strike and disappear."

Jerome especially liked the letters Jack had written to the police. He wanted to write one. He planned to get some paper, maybe from the bookstore at Loyola where he worked. Then he would write a letter to the police, like Jack did. Maybe he would send it to the detective in the picture of Dauphine Street. The one with the odd name.

He would tell the police how he had the luck of the devil and how he would strike 'any woman, anywhere, at any time'.

## Chapter 5
## Exposition Boulevard

The third body was found by a young couple taking a romantic stroll along Exposition Boulevard at the edge of Audubon Park. The boy spotted something shiny between two rows of dwarf palm trees in the park. It was a pool of blood.

I heard the call on the radio and knew right away it was our killer again. I listened to the shaky voice of the first office on the scene. "Uh, we're gonna need a, uh, Homicide team," the officer stuttered.

"Ten-four," Headquarters replied.

"And the coroner," the first officer added, "and uh, the crime lab, and get some rank over here."

I listened to the inevitable chatter on the radio as I wheeled my unit around and headed back to Mark's house. I had just dropped Mark off early for the first time in weeks. It was a quiet Thursday night, just before nine o'clock. It was over two weeks since the Bayou St. John murder and we were gearing up for another Friday night. But he came back early, on a Thursday, the rotten mother fucker came back early.

There ware times when you want to take that little fucking radio and throw it as far away as you can and scream that you've had *enough*. You want to quit, absolutely fuckin' quit. You want to take the next flight to Australia and live in the outback with the kangaroos and the fuckin' wallabies. And fuck America.

Fuck New Orleans and all the dark-skinned mooks and lily white-faced mooks and even the fucking police. Let them kill each other until there is no one left to kill. *Fuck it all.*

But, you find yourself rushing through traffic to get your partner and then rushing to the scene. You hurry to get there. No matter how much your insides ached for the soothing comfort of another world, no matter how disgusted you are, you hurry. You park your car on St. Charles Avenue across the streetcar tracks from the sacred spires of Loyola University and the large white statue of Jesus Christ who stands with His arms open wide to Audubon Park. You walk slowly toward the patrolmen standing in their baby-blue shirts with their big flashlights. You follow the flashlight beams through the large oaks and they gray Spanish moss that hangs ghostlike in the black Orleanian night. When you arrive at the scene you say nothing, until you are ready.

And then, as even more cops assemble. along with ambulance attendants, reporters, television crews, passers-by, as all the various parties assemble, you stand there and realize you are the only one who knows. You are the only one who knows *exactly* what to do. All the others wait for you to act. In the end it is just you and your partners. Our Division – Homicide. The best of the lot. Nothing else mattered.

•

Exposition Boulevard was not a boulevard at all. It wasn't even a street. It could be found on any map of New Orleans, nestled against the downtown side of Audubon Park, but it wasn't a roadway. It was a sidewalk, a walkway given a fancy name so that the large houses and mansions that line the edge of the park had a fancy address.

The body of the young woman rested not fifty feet from the double-wide sidewalk called Exposition Boulevard. She lay between a line of dwarf palm trees, a little over a block from St. Charles Avenue. She had long brown hair and faded brown eyes. She was about 5 feet 2 inches tall and weight all of many ninety five pounds. We found her small, gold silk purse, dug out her driver's license. Few, if anyone, looked good in their driver's license photo. Our latest victim was gorgeous, smiling at us.

She had worn a yellow sundress, white sandals, white panties and a gold chain with a gold crucifix. When we found her, she was only wearing the chain and crucifix. Her clothes had been ripped from her and lay in pieces between the palms, in the large bloody pool. There was no bra.

"I'll bet there's no blood left in her," Mark mumbled as we stood over the body. She was on her back, between two dwarf palms trees, her arms and legs spread wide, her lifeless face masked in blood. There was so much blood.

Mark found more blood in the direction of St. Charles Avenue. "Looks like our boy walked off toward St. Charles," Mark called out to me as he searched around. I walked over and he showed me gobs of blood on the grass. The killer had dripped his way to the brightly lit avenue with its big street lights and spotlights that illuminated the lofty spires of Loyola.

Between the palms and the avenue stood a large concrete shelter. Mark found more blood in the wash basin on the side of the shelter. "Jesus fuckin' Christ, look at this!" Mark cried. No doubt. Our boy washed up at the shelter before he left.

When Mark and I started back toward the body, I pulled him aside and whispered, "No bra."

"I know," he nodded and put his finger over his lips.

The crime lab technician had arrived and I helped him. I held a ruler next to the bite mark on the left breast of our victim as the technician took a photograph. Then I withdrew the ruler so he could take another close-up picture without the ruler in place. Mark found a pool of vomit several yards from the victim in the direction away from St. Charles Avenue. One of the patrolmen advised us it was from the boy who found the body.

And so we went through the meticulous, repetitive steps, measuring and photographing and securing evidence until the body was removed in another black bag. Then the technician went to photograph and dust the shelter for fingerprints near the basin and faucets, take samples of the bloody water.

When Mason arrived we all gathered at the shelter and gave instructions. Several patrolmen were sent to St. Charles Avenue and to all the side streets around Loyola University, as well as the streets behind Exposition Boulevard. They went to copy all the license plate numbers of all the cars, and to sop any passers-by who might have seen or heard *anything*. Mark took a couple of eager Second District follow-up officers to each of the mansions on Exposition Boulevard, starting at the corner of St. Charles, to ask if, by chance, anyone was gazing out their upstairs window and happened to see a fella dripping blood all over the fucking place.

Our victim lived in the 1400 block of Exposition Boulevard, a block from the murder scene. She lived in a three-story mansion, an old-fashioned southern veranda home with a six-foot black wrought-iron fence surrounding the property. There was a wide gallery around the entire first floor of the immaculately white wooden house. On the gallery, just to the left of the cut-glass front door, hung a double-wide swing where you could sit with your sweetheart on a moonlit night and look out at the open expanse of Audubon Park, at the brooding oaks and lazy lagoons, or listen for the lions and tigers to roar at feeding time at the Audubon Zoo by the river.

Above the gallery stood two sets of balconies one each floor, wrought-iron balconies of black lacework, which matched the fence surrounding the property. They were familiar balconies, in the timeless tradition of the French Quarter. Our victim's name was Lynette Anne Louvier. She was twenty yours old.

Mason and I waited for the police chaplain to arrive before we knocked on the cut-glass door. A black woman in a white maid's dress answered the door. She was polite and surprised to see us. It was obvious that no one in the mansion had seen the commotion down the way. Those mansions that lined Exposition Boulevard were special places where the ugliness of the city was kept beyond six-foot fences. But even a six-foot fence did not prevent this mansion from a visit by three Angels of Death.

The chaplain asked for Mr. Louvier. He was not in. So the chaplain asked for Mrs. Louvier and the maid went up the long spiral staircase. She hurried when she reached the top. The maid was from the part of town that knew exactly who we were and what our visit meant. We waited in the foyer. Mason reminded the chaplain that it was important we find out where the victim had been going and if she had been with anyone that night.

I stretched as I stood under the bright chandelier of the foyer, and my stomach pinched in a deep, sharp pain. I had not eaten supper again. I was still living off coffee and that was no good.

A dark-haired boy of about eight came downstairs first.

"Hi," he called out as he stopped up with big smile on his face. I tried to smile back. A middle-aged woman then came down the stairs. She also had dark hair, cut short. She was an attractive woman for her age, in fact, she was damned good-looking and the closer the came, the harder it was to tell her age at all. She wore a powder-blue designer jogging suit with matching powder-blue jogging shoes that appeared to have never jogged anywhere. She tried to force a smile as she greeted us, but the maid probably told her. When the chaplain confirmed his identity, when he told her he was the police chaplain, it was as if he's punched the woman in her stomach. She almost buckled. I thought she might fall, but she stood her ground as her eyes darted from the priest to Mason and then to me, quickly searching our faces for something, anything. I looked away.

The chaplain asked if we could speak with her privately. The woman led us into a formal living room at the front of the house. He waited until she was seated and then asked if she was Catholic. She was. So the priest knelt next to her and began speaking to her in almost a whisper. I heard him ask if she had a daughter named Lynette, and the tears came immediately. He leaned closer to her and whispered in her ear as her head sank and she began to sob.

Mason led me back into the foyer. He asked the maid for the phone number where we could reach Mr. Louvier. Then he stepped over to the phone.

"What's wrong?" the boy asked excitedly.

"Your mother's going to all right," I tried to assure him. What a fuckin' liar.

Then I signaled for the maid to take him way. Take those pleading young eyes away from me because there was nothing I could do, nothing anyone could do. It amazed me that a moment ago this house was a happy one. Even though Lynette was dead, they were still happy in their ignorance, until we had to come and tell them.

"The father's on his way," Mason told me as we stepped outside. Mason found a patrolman standing outside the gate, called him in and sent him into the foyer. Then we went back to work. We left the sobbing behind. It was a sound that cut right through me. Another night lay before us, a night of knocking on doors and asking the same questions, jotting the same notes and looking into the same fearful eyes of people behind half-open doors. We worked through the hours.

When we finished, we met at the concrete shelter where the mother fucker had washed up from his night's work. I gathered the notes from the patrolmen and follow-up officers and tucked them safely away in my metal clipboard, notes of license plate numbers and names and addresses of people who knew nothing.

"Did the priest find out where our girl was going?" Mark asked Mason as the good sergeant lit up another butt.

"No," Mason growled in a weary voice, "family's too upset. We'll get it in the morning." He took the cigarette he'd just lit out of his mouth, took a good look at it and then threw it on the concrete floor of the shelter. Then he stepped on it. Without looking up, Mason pointed his finger at Mark and said, "You go to the autopsy, it'll start in about an hour."

"Autopsy?" Mark asked, "at three in the morning?"

"Yeah," Mason advised, "they're gonna post her early." He looked up at Mark and shrugged, "Rich people got their privileges."

"Yeah?"

"And that ain't all," Mason added. "Me and the case officer here" – he point to my chest as he went on – "we gotta be back at the Louvier house at seven, we gotta meet the family, and the Chief."

"The Chief?" Mark groaned, covering his eyes with his hands. "Now we're in for it! Here comes all the political shit."

Mason nodded in agreement.

"Why did the mother fucker have to kill a rich girl?" Mark complained aloud.

"Not just a rich girl. The Louviers own banks. More than one and it's worse than that," Mason said, "Mr. Louvier is a old friend of the Chief."

"That's all we fuckin' need." Mark added as he reached over and patted me on the back. "We're gonna get fucked on this one, believe me."

"I'll bring the Vaseline," Mason said as he walked off.

Mark drove me home and had a cup of coffee with me before leaving for the autopsy. I couldn't find anything to eat except for some Grape Nuts, so I ate a bowl before crashing headlong onto the bed. But it was no se.

At three o'clock in the morning, I cranked up my old Volkswagen and drove to THE CHAMBER OF HORRORS. The crime lab technician was just arriving and we walked in together. Mark was trying, without success, to strike up a conversation with the ever silent black assistant when I stepped into the room.

"What the fuck you doing here?" Mark laughed at me when I strolled in.

"I can't let you fuck up my first case," I told him.

Mark chuckled. "It's getting to you. You'll be a stone-fuckin' nut just like me before you know it. You're a born Homicide man, my boy."

I let Mark take the notes. I just watched for a while, watched it all start again, the cold naked body lying on the stainless steel table, the photos, the swabbing of the vagina and the scraping of fingernails, the hose rinsing off dried blood and grass stains to reveal cold white skin. Then came the counting of wounds.

"She put up a helluva fight," the doctor concluded.

There were wounds in her chest and stomach and in her arms and legs, there were wounds in her throat and in the cheeks of her face. There was a stab wound through her lower lip and one in her chin, and defensive wounds in both hands and both feet. She'd put up her hands and feet to fend off blows. There were slices of toes missing and deep punctures in the soles. The were gaping wounds in and around her vagina and, of course, there was a bite mark – on her left breast. The bite mark appeared deeper than the previous marks and Mark pointed out that it looked as if one of the killer's teeth was chipped. "When we find him, we'll nail him with his chipped fuckin' tooth," Mark declared.

Lynette Anne Louvier had one hundred and twenty-one stab wounds in her petite body. And as we counted those punctures and logged them and noted their locations, I kept thinking the monster was still free. He was still out there, the rotten mother fucker. He was free, but I was not. I was the case officer. I was responsible, from the moment she gasped her last breath, I was responsible for her.

In the cold light of the autopsy room, as I stood watching from the corner, I remember thinking that I was responsible long before that last breath was taken. I had not caught the rotten mother fucker. If I were a better man, I would have caught him before this, he would be mine and Lynette Anne Louvier would be warm and asleep in her mansion overlooking the park.

And so I watched as the assistant took his razor scalpel, placed it on the body and laid Lynette open. I watched her disemboweled before my eyes and there was nothing I could do. In the background I heard the doctor tell Mark that at least twenty-five of the wounds were potentially fatal. I left before they started up the skull saw.

At five in the morning I went home and took a long, long shower. I washed away the dirt and grime from my body. I turned up the water as hot as I could stand it and tried to wash away the sick empty feeling within me. But it was no use. All I felt was exhaustion. I was sleepwalking, shaving in my sleep, blow-drying my hair, and dressing in my sleep. I put on the new navy blue suit that Jessica had bought me on my last birthday.

In my bedroom mirror an image stared back at me. It was a young man in a navy blue suit, with dark hair and a moustache. It was a sharp image, a lean figure of a man, who looked like he was heading out for a big date. In the mirror, I looked surprisingly good. Maybe it was the way my hair turned out after the quick blow-dry. I looked far better than I felt. Only my eyes gave me away. They seemed hollow and dark. My eyes looked like the eyes of an old man.

It was still dark when I pulled up on St. Charles Avenue, parked and walked into the blackness of the park. I crossed the open grass, past the shelter, past the rows of dwarf palm trees and even past the roadway next to the brackish water of the lagoon. I stopped at the gazebo between the road and the lagoon and sat on the wooden bench.

I looked over at the Louvier Mansion standing on Exposition Boulevard, lit up like a house on fire. All the other houses along the boulevard were dark, except for the sad mansion where death had stopped by earlier. I watched as a car backed out from the mansion and drove away. There were several cars parked at the house now. I leaned back on the bench, placed my little fucking radio next to me on the bench and turned up the volume on the detective channel and waited for Mason to call me.

It wasn't long before faint streaks of light began to creep up behind the mansions along the boulevard, slowly illuminating the images of Audubon Park. The looming oaks, with their moss beards, took shape in tones of shadowy gray. Ever so slowly, the grayness gave way to a black and white scene as the park became visible. In the early morning twilight, I looked over at the black lagoon as the eerie morning mist rose from the still water. In the dimness I thought I saw a figure standing next to the water, a girl, in a long white dress. She was staring at me with tear-filled eyes. It was Lynette.

I closed my eyes tightly, but she was still there when I looked back. Her arms were outstretched, reaching for me. She pleaded with me and I knew exactly what she wanted. I cleared my throat and told her I would get him, no matter what, no matter how long it took, I would get him. I promised her. She did nothing but stand and stare at me with those eyes that glistened. The muted colors of the park became clearer in faded brown and dull greens as the sun crept higher. I could feel is warmth on my face. I closed my eyes to the sunlight and listened to the cars passing up and down St. Charles Avenue.

Mason woke me a little after six thirty. I rubbed my eyes and looked over at the lagoon. She wasn't there. Mason tapped my shoulder and pointed toward Exposition Boulevard to a man standing in front of the Louvier mansion. There was a uniformed officer pacing in front of the mansion, a tall man without hat. I could see his full head of gray hair. Mason did not have to say anything. I knew it was the man with the upside down badge.

Only one man wore his star-and-crescent police badge upside down and that was the Chief. It was an old tradition, started long ago when all the star-and-crescent badges were alike, before numbers were put on them. The Chief was the man who stood apart from the others. He wore his badge upside down.

Our Chief was a native son who had worked his way up through the ranks. He name was Sal Rosata and there was a long scar on the right side of his dark olive-skinned face, which looked even darker under the full mat of gray hair. He was a tall man who stood a full head taller than Mason, a burly man with muscular arms that protruded from his short-sleeved police shirt. His dark face wore an ugly expression that morning. I could see it from fifty feet away and it didn't look any prettier as I got closer.

"Were you sleeping over there?" the Chief scowled at me as I stepped up.

"No sir," I answered, "I was thinking."

"About what?"

"About sleeping."

The Chief almost smiled but caught himself. He narrowed his eyes and stared real hard at me. "Just like your old man" – the Chief sighed – "smart ass wop!" He should talk. Rosata was a big a dago name as LaStanza. And he was, literally, a far bigger wop, and he knew it. The Chief looked at Mason and ordered, "Show me where it happened."

I followed them to the dwarf palms and the big bloodstain and the clumps of grass chewed up in the struggle. Mason then led the Chief to where the assailant had dragged her from the boulevard. "See how he dragged her over the palms." Mason pointed out the marks in the grass.

"She put up a helluva fight," the Chief muttered, half under his breath. He looked around at the houses and asked, "Any witnesses?"

"Nope," Mason answered as he lit another cigarette.

The Chief turned away quickly and started back toward the mansion. "Come on, let's get this over with." He shook his head as he walked. "Don't the Louviers have other children?"

Mason answered, "They've got a son who goes to Holy Name of Jesus School, and another daughter, who's in college up north."

The Chief nodded and said, "I know Mr. Louvier. Nice fella. Never met the family. This is bad, real fuckin' bad." He opened the iron gate of the mansion and then looked back at me. "So you're the case officer, huh?"

I nodded.

"First whodunit?"

I nodded again.

The Chief glanced at Mason's chiseled expressionless face and then looked at me. "How's your Pop?" the Chief asked me.

"Fine," I answered, "drinking and fishing."

"And your momma?"

"She's fine, too."

"Good," the Chief said, "Tell 'em I said hello. I been meaning to see them, but I been busy and, you know. Just tell 'em I asked about 'em, okay?"

"Yes, sir," I answered as he turned and started up the stairs of the Louvier mansion.

There are things in my childhood I remember vividly, as if a tape recorder existed in my mind. Sometimes I can hit the rewind button and play it all back, like the night we thought my father was killed. A rookie patrolman named Rosata was driving my father that night, when their patrol car skidded out of control during a high-speed chase. The car flipped over into the Palmetto Canal. Rosata came out with a deep cut on his face, but my father didn't come up. Rosata went back down but couldn't find him.

I remember the men at my front door and my mother crying. I wasn't until day light that they found my father. He had come up all right and started swimming. But just like a dumb wop, he swam lengthwise in the long canal that was only about fifty feet wide. He finally crawled out of the water near the Jefferson Parish line. Then he passed out on the concrete wall. That was how our Chief got the scar on his face and my father received his first *Dumb Wop Of The Month* award. There was also a *Dump Mick of the Month* award, both dating back to the turn of the century.

A man with deep-set eyes greeted us at the front door of the Louvier's. He was a distinguished-looking man in a black pinstripe suit. His face was composed and his voice firm as he spoke, but his eyes gave him away. Those deep-set eyes were filled with a sadness that I've seen before. It was a sadness that cannot be hidden, cannot be relieved, even with time. It was a sadness that just hides with time, but never goes away.

I've seen that sadness before, in my father's eyes some years back when we buried my brother in St. Patrick's Cemetery one autumn day. I can see that sadness in my mirror sometimes. You can hide it, but it never goes away.

When we stepped into the house, Mr. Louvier pulled the Chief aside and asked Mason and I to step into a room across the foyer from the living room. Mason followed me into a dark, cool room. It took a couple of seconds for my eyes to adjust to the darkness and to see that we were in a library. The Chief leaned inside the room a moment later and asked Mason to join him in the foyer. They closed the door and I was left alone in the dark library.

I stood looking around the room. I could see the rear wall was covered with books, floor to ceiling, and so was the wall across from the door. The only light that peeked into the room slipped through a crack in the long silken drapes along the French doors of the front wall, which faced the gallery and the sunny park outside. My eyes followed the sliver of sunlight as it streamed across the room illuminating tiny particles in the air that made the light look like a thick sliver of sterling silver.

The air was cool in the library and that made me feel my exhaustion that much more. So I stepped over to a large easy chair in the middle of the room and sank heavily into it. The chair faced a fireplace along the wall next to the door to the foyer.

As I sat, my eyes followed the sliver of sunlight to its destination above the mantel of the fireplace. The light fell across a large portrait, a portrait of Lynette. I leaned back in the soft easy chair and studied the painting. The girl in the portrait wore a white gown that was low-cut and draped over her shoulders. She looked like a drawing I'd once seen of a Greek goddess, her hair long, dark brown with a hint of red highlights.

She looked so young in the painting and so alive. Her neck was smooth and white, like alabaster against the dark background of the painting. Her lips were full and unsmiling, but not pouting either. Her face had an expression of confidence and beauty and full of emotion. Her red lips looked, moist. "It must be the sunlight on the shiny oil," I told myself.

He eyes were large and sad. They stared at me. And I knew, that if I rose, those eyes would follow me. It was on of those paintings where the eyes follow you. No matter where you move in a room, the eyes follow you. She was very pretty indeed in the portrait. And it made me feel that worse as I continued to stare back at her, tracing the outline of her face with my eyes as the long dagger of light fell across the vivid colors of the painting.

It pained my heart to look at her. This was a great New Orleans beauty, a dark haired brunette daughter of the city, a face sweet and gorgeous, wide eyes and full, sensuous lips. And she was gone.

For a moment, my mind flashed back with cruel realism to the scene from the autopsy. So I closed my eyes to shut it all out. I could feel my arms slowly sliding down the sided of the easy chair. I remember thinking I would rest a minute, but soon the easy breathing came and I dreamed.

I dreamt I heard a noise in the room but my eyes would not open. They were too heavy to open. I struggled, and finally my eyes opened to an unfocused vision, of someone moving in the room, in slow motion. I felt myself lean forward as a girl moved in the room. She moved to the painting and then turned slowly to me. Those same sad eyes from the portrait met my eyes. It was the girl from the portrait, it was Lynette, standing beneath the portrait and looking at me as I rose sleepily from the easy chair.

As she faced me, the dagger of sunlight fell on her face and her eyes looked like dark gold gemstones staring at me. A moment later those topaz eyes became misty with tears that began to roll down her small round cheeks.

"You're alive," I heard myself saying to the girl who was crying in front of me.

She quickly brushed away the tears from her face and in a quivering voice asked, "Who are you?"

"I'm a detective."

"What are you doing here?" she asked as more tears began to roll down her cheeks. I could not answer. She tried to compose herself and in a voice somewhat deeper she announced, "I'm Lizette, Lizette Louvier. Who are you?'

I fell back into the chair and tried to clear my thoughts. I remember shaking my head quickly, as if that could straighten out the mess in my mind, as if that could clear it all. *Twins.* I thought to myself.

She looked back at the painting and something snapped in my mind as I realized this was all real. This was no dream or hallucination. This was *real.* Suddenly I was very awake. I rose again from the chair and told her my name and fumbled in my coat pocket for my credentials. I handed my badge and I.D. to her. She took them and stared at my I.D. for a long time. Her lower lip began to tremble as she tried to hold on to whatever composure she had left, but there was no stopping the tears that streamed down her face.

"I didn't know Lynette had a twin," I told her.

She handed my credentials back to me and turned again to the painting. Through trembling lips she told me how she had just gotten off a plane and, as an afterthought, she whispered something about Brown University.

I looked back at the painting, traced again the fine delicate lines of the beautiful face. "Is it Lynette or you?" I knew it was a dumb question as soon as I asked it. So I just shut up.

"I didn't know anyone was in here," she said suddenly.

The room seemed to become stuffy, growing hotter by the moment. I watched her staring at the painting and I felt a shiver race up my back to the base of my neck and back down again. I could feel sweat on my forehead and in my palms. Part of me wanted to fade away and leave this girl alone, but another part of me wanted to stay with her. I could not stop staring at her, at those lines of that pretty face. She was a small girl, about 5 foot 2, with straight dark brown hair that ended at her shoulders in a curl. She wore a dark brown jacket and skirt, with a neat high-collared white shirt. She looked exactly the way a rich uptown daughter of old French Creole blood should look, beautiful and aristocratic.

After a while I could see her composing herself as she stood more erect. She spoke to me in a stronger voice, "My mother told me that you have been working on this killer," she almost choked on the work, but continued, ",for over a month." She turned to me with narrowed eyes. I nodded in response to her statement and felt the room becoming insufferably not.

"Why haven't you stopped him?" She asked in a voice barely audible over the deep sob that followed. She choked back the sob and asked, "What have you done?" Her eyes were filled with pain. I looked back at her and felt the knot in my stomach stab me.

"You're useless," she cried in a voice that cut right through me. "Useless!" she repeated as she turned and hurried from the room. I started to follow, but stopped myself. She wrenched the door open and slammed it shut as she ran into the foyer. A second later the Chief stuck his head into the room and snapped at me "Taking a break LaStanza?"

"No, sir."

"Then get out here," he ordered. He led me into a large dining room and made quick introductions around the table where Mr.

and Mrs. Louvier sat. There was a priest present and a doctor and several attorneys. I sat next to Mason as the Chief started telling them about how we would leave no stone unturned, spare no expense.

Then Mason spoke. He told them everything we'd done so far, and managed to get in a question about where Lynette had been that night. Mr. Louvier explained that Lynette was coming home from an evening class at Loyola University. I wrote it down. Then Mr. Louvier gave the Chief a list of Lynette's girlfriends and boyfriends. She was a popular girl.

I tried to catch anything that was said that was important, but I could not stop thinking about Lizette and about what she'd called me, "Useless!" The word worked on my mind and my stomach.

Mason had to ask me twice before I heard his question about the autopsy. "He's pretty exhausted," Mason explained as he finally got my attention. The Chief was glaring at me with the same look my father used to give me.

"Yes – " I hesitated as I gathered my thoughts. Then I gave them a brief account of the autopsy. Mr. Louvier was not satisfied. He was a tough fella and asked me outright about the wounds. I hesitated in case Mason or the Chief wanted to step in, but when they didn't I told him everything, about the one hundred and twenty-one wounds, about the twenty-five potentially fatal wounds, and about the defensive wounds on the bottom of her feet. I could see the color drain from Mr. Louvier's face as he slumped back in his chair. A doctor escorted Mrs. Louvier out of the room. And shortly after, the interview was thankfully ended.

On the way out, the Chief gruffly told me to go home and get some rest. "Then I expect you to work your ass off."

I was the case officer. We would work the case as a team and put in the long hours as a team, but it was my case. I was responsible for solving it. I wasn't supposed to let it become a personal thing, but how could I not? It was a very personal thing, because her death belonged to me now. Her life was hers, her body was now the mortician's, and her casket would soon belong to the cemetery, but her death was mine.

I was the case officer and I knew I would never do anything as important as this for the rest of my life. And I knew I was never going to give up, not ever. I wanted this murderer so fucking badly.

I was so tired when I got home, all I did was fall into bed. I closed my eyes but my mind wouldn't let go. I kept hearing those words echoing in my mind.

"You're useless," she said. Those agonizing eyes had asked me why I had not caught him, and what could I say to those eyes?

It didn't matter how hard we worked, didn't matter how many meals I'd skipped, didn't matter that my stomach was knotted up like a twisted towel, didn't matter how much sleep I missed, didn't matter how many things we'd done right in the investigation, because we didn't do the most important thing right, we hadn't caught him. It didn't matter if I'd lost Jessica. All that mattered was that he was still out there and Lynette Louvier was lying among the cold cadavers at THE CHAMBER OF HORRORS. All that mattered was that *he was still out there.*

Lizette Louvier had known me for only a couple minutes, but she knew me very well. I was useless, totally fucking useless.

•

The rain threatened all day on the day they buried Lynette Anne Louvier, but it did not rain until that night. During the day, the sky remained ugly and dark with gray-black clouds gliding overhead like lost galleons on a stormy sea, with humidity so high that the air felt wet on my lips as I stood behind the crowd at St. Vincent's Cemetery.

St. Vincent's on Soniat Street was a small graveyard, one square block of white masonry sepulchers and gray cement tombs surrounded by a red brick wall. Along the Duffossat Street side of the cemetery stood a long wall of tiered tombs, oven tombs. Atop the wall stood a life-sized stone statue of Jesus on the Cross. At His feet there were three statues of women in bronze, praying for Jesus, or praying for the other poor souls entombed in the wall.

I stood at the rear of the crowd, behind a raised plot where forty-seven headstones marked the burial site of forty-seven nuns, *Sisters of Charity of St. Vincent DePaul,* read the marker. Each headstone bore a Sister's name, 'Sister Mary Annette, Forty Years Vocation." Above the raised plot of earth stood a white stone statue of Jesus' mother. The Virgin Mary stood with her head bent so she could look down upon the dead nuns at her feet.

From my position behind the dead nuns, I watched the robed priest spray holy water over the steel-gray casket that bore Lynette's body. I watched the coffin as it was slipped into one of the walled toms just below the statue of Jesus. I looked around the crowd and tried to spot anyone who was out of place, But the only person out of place was me. I thought that maybe, just maybe, he would show up, lurking behind a sepulcher, with a maniacal leer on his hideous face. I would see him and know him, and he would be mine.

But there were no maniacs present. There were only quiet people in dark clothes who crowded next to the walled tombs with their head bent. I watched them until it was time to leave. I looked for Lizette and found her as the Louviers moved away. I stood back, away from everyone, but Lizette's eyes found me. She gave me a cold hard stare as she passed.

I was the last to leave that afternoon. I waited until the workers came forward to seal up the hole in the wall in which Lynette's coffin rested. Then I walked down the wide center walkway of St. Vincent's, leaving behind the dead nuns and the Virgin Mary and Jesus on the Cross and the three bronze women, and Lynette.

The rain fell heavily that Saturday night, turning the street outside my house into a small canal. I sat on my couch and watched the rain slam against my living room windows, watched the world blur away in front of my eyes. I thought about Jessica as I sat there, wondering what she was doing that dark, rainy night.

I leaned back on the couch and listened to the steady beating of the rain. I thought about my brother and his tomb in St. Patrick's Cemetery and how we used to play in the rain when we were kids, and how cemeteries were made to play in. Sometime later, the rain lulled me into a deep sleep.

•

Lizette answered the phone after the first ring. I did not expect her to answer. "This is Detective Useless," I said in a voice still scratchy from the sore throat I'd been unable to shake.

"Yes," she acknowledge in a voice as cold as the stare she gave me the day before. "What do you want?"

"I would like to come by, if it's convenient?"

"Why?"

"I need to have a look at some of your sister's things," I told her. "Your father said it was all right to come by," I added. "Is this afternoon all right?"

"My father didn't tell me anything about this," she snapped, "and he isn't in now." She paused and waited for me to come back. I didn't want to put it off. I wanted to do it right away. It was my case, but it was her sister.

"I'll call another time," I said reluctantly, with a sigh.

"Do you have to?"

"Yes, I *have* to," I came right back. "And I have some questions for you, too," I told her. "That is if you *want* to help solve your sister's murder." She said nothing as I went on. "But since you don't want to talk to me, I'll have my sergeant contact you, maybe you'll feel like talking to him."

I heard nothing at the other end – not even breathing – for a long time. I found myself holding my breath until she finally asked in a voice that sounded distant ands ad, "What were you doing at the funeral?"

"My job. I was doing my job," I answered. "I was there to provide security. What if the killer showed up?"

She didn't answer me, So I waited. Then she said I could come by that afternoon at three o'clock.

"Fine," I agreed and hung up.

•

It was still wet in the park from the heavy rain the night before. I managed to keep my shoes clean so I wouldn't track up the fine hardwood gallery as I walked up the front steps. The maid let me in and asked me to wait in the library for Miss Lizette. I went into the library and immediately noticed how different it looked with the curtains open and the bright daylight filling the room.

I examined the portrait again, this time in the bright, golden sunlight. I gazed at the alabaster skin and the full lips that still looked moist. The large, sad eyes indeed followed me as I moved around the room. I took a good look at the room for the first time and felt uncomfortable, felt out of place.

I'd been in Garden District mansions before, been in the houses of the richest people in New Orleans before, but this day I felt jittery. It wasn't the wealth, although the Louvier mansion reeked of wealth. The finest Oriental rugs covered the shiny hardwood floors. Crystal chandeliers hung from the high ceilings, and the stately furniture looked as if it were plucked from a museum exhibit – like unused pieces in a timeless collection. Each piece had been perfectly positioned, polished, neat and clean, by someone with impeccable taste. The mantel above which the portrait hung was made of ivory-white marble. And around the room there were other oil paintings – magnolias in gold-leaf frames and plantation homes on sunny days in long ago Louisiana.

No, it wasn't the wealth that made me jittery. It was that face, the face in the portrait and the same face in the other photographs around the room. There were pictures on the desk and tables, large framed photos of that face on the other walls, photos taken in the park among the trees, dark hair flowing in a breeze that made the strands of hair each out and glitter in the sunlight. I looked at the face and saw how truly beautiful it was. It was a perfect face.

I felt intimidated by that face. My heart sank as I looked at the pictures because I knew she was beyond reach. She was too pretty to touch, to pretty for anyone like me to ever touch or ever know. And something in me wanted to know her. I felt a powerful attraction to her, but I would never feel those lips, never touch that skin, except maybe in passing, if we bumped.

As I stood uncomfortably in the study of the rich people, I felt like a poor Italian immigrant, as my grandfather must have felt all his life, a black dago in the land of English-speaking white people. I was a peasant all over again with as much chance of knowing the girl in the pictures as a serf had of knowing a princess. It didn't matter if I was a big shot Homicide Detective, because she knew me as I really was.

•

Lizette came into the room wearing a typical uptown preppy outfit, a crocodile shirt, khaki safari shorts and sandals. She looked fresh and clean and young, younger than she had looked before. She was a small girl, a petite body and breasts too large for her size. Her big eyes looked at me, golden eyes the color of crisp autumn leaves. Except for a touch of sadness in those eyes, she looked every bit the part of a rich uptown hussy. That look was inbred.

I followed her small rounded hips up the long spiral staircase to her sister's room, a room with stuffed animals, Tulane and Loyola pennants, and a large bed with a ruffled lace canopy.

"What exactly are you looking for?" she asked.

"I'm not sure. Did Lynette keep a diary?"

"No," Lizette answered as she sat stiffly on the edge of the bed.

"What about an address book?" I asked.

"Yes." She pointed to the roll-top desk across the room and then asked, "What do you need that for?"

I answered without looking at her, "Because eighty per cent of all homicides are committed by friends and associates, people who know each other." I thumbed through the address book before slipping it into my coat pocket. In the confinement of the bedroom, Lizette's perfume seemed stronger, although it wasn't a strong scent, a sweet feminine scent that filled my nostrils. I looked at her as she sat on the bed. Her face was masked in puzzlement as she looked back at me.

"Do you think she knew him?" she asked.

"I don't know. But I've got to check it out."

"I don't think you know what you are doing," she stated calmly. "I think you're going about this all wrong."

I was about to cut her down, to ask her how she became an expert on homicides, but when I looked back at her I felt a sadness. Those eyes looked at me with such pain. I turned away from Lizette and continued searching.

"What have you done so far?" she asked, "in the investigation, have you come up with anything? Anything at all?" Her voice had a cutting edge to it.

So I told her how we had traced Lynette's activities on the night she died, traced her from when she'd left her class at Loyola. Lynette had crossed St. Charles Avenue and left two female classmates at the streetcar stop on the avenue. But no one followed her as she walked down Exposition Boulevard. We had also checked out every male in her class.

"Next, we'll check out every Loyola student and then start in on Tulane," I concluded.

"You think someone at Loyola or Tulane?"

"You mean a nice college boy? You never know." I remembered Marks' reaction to that same question as we checked out Lynette's classmates that Friday evening. "No way." Mark scowled. "No fuckin' way!"

I could tell by the way she looked at me that it didn't matter if I hadn't slept because I was checking out classmates, didn't matter if my voice was scratchy and my throat sore from lack of rest. None of it mattered because we were no closer than we were the night Marie Sumner had bought it. Zero results meant zero.

"We know that he was waiting for her," I declared. "We don't know if he was waiting for her because she was Lynette or if he was just waiting for any girl."

Lizette said nothing. So I took out my useless notepad and asked about her sister's boyfriends. She had none at the moment. Her old boyfriend was an intern at a hospital in Los Angeles. I wrote his name down anyway. I also listed the names of Lynette's girl friends as Lizette gave them to me reluctantly.

"How about new friends?" I inquired. "Coworkers? Any creeps who bothered her? Any weird neighbors? Anybody from the French Quarter?"

"Lynette didn't work. She's a student, like me."

I swallowed hard and asked her my next question. "Do you know, by any chance, if Lynette usually wore a bra?"

"What?" Lizette's eyes lit up as she looked at me with increasing suspicion.

"You know the outfit she wore that night?" I asked. "The sundress?"

Lizette nodded.

"Did she ever wear it without a bra?"

"No," she answered in a whisper. "Why?"

"Maybe she just didn't wear one that night."

"No," Lizette's voice grew louder. "I have a dress just like it, you have to wear a bra."

I didn't look at her as I went on to my next question right away. I asked her if there were any strangers, new people in the neighborhood.

Lizette didn't answer. She stood up and took a step in my direction and declared, "You didn't find her bra?"

I didn't answer her for a moment as she stared right into my eyes. Then I nodded as I stepped around her and sat on the edge of the bed. I told her about Marie and Teresa and the missing brassieres.

"We're still not positive," I added. "No one can be positive they were all wearing bras, but it appears so."

Then I told her that only Mark and I and the murderer knew that secret, until now.

"You mean the other policemen don't know?"

"They only see our daily reports, only my partner and I figured it out so far. The others are too busy with other things." Then I told her how important it was to keep it a secret, and how it was a secret we and the killer shared and how it might bring us together one day. And as I told her, she sat heavily at the other end of the bed and her hands were shaking.

"Are you all right?"

"Yes," she said as she slowly lay back on the bed.

I got up and asked if I could get her anything. "Some ice water?" I asked.

"No, I'll be fine. I just want to lie down a moment." She closed her eyes.

I told her again how important it was to keep the bra information a secret. She didn't answer me. I watched as she lay on the bed, watched as her chest rose and fell in soft regular breaths. I took my notebook and Lynette's address book and walked down the long staircase.

As I stepped up to the front door, she called down to me, "What's your name?"

I looked up at her. Lizette was leaning on the top railing, staring down at me with those eyes.

"Detective LaStanza," I answered. "Dino LaStanza." I took a business card out of my coat pocket and left it on the table next to the front door.

•

He was still tired, even after sleeping all day. Jerome was so tired, he felt as if he were drained. His arms felt like lead against his sides as he sat on the chair by the tiny table in his room. He was still naked as he sat sweating from the heat of the room, but he would not open the window. He never unlocked the window. Instead, he turned on the small black electric fan and placed it in front of him. Then he rubbed his eyes as hard as he could and thought about her again.

There was so much blood. He remembered how pretty she was in the park with the yellow dress and the long dark hair. She was so pretty. She was like all the other girls with pretty faces at the university. She had a nice smile but didn't smile at him as she walked past the library that night. Pretty girls never smiled at him. They smiled at all the other men, but never Jerome. They didn't even look at him, like he wasn't there, like he was invisible. When she passed him that night, she didn't even see him.

But she saw him later. He showed her. He showed her how powerful he was. She fought him hard in the park but he beat her. He overpowered her. He had stalked her from a distance, had crept through the park and waited for her by the small trees. And then he took her. And the more she struggled, the more powerful he became until she resisted no more.

But now, at the table, he was drained. He was falling apart. He had washed away all the blood and put away her bra with the others. He had masturbated twice already. But he did not feel any better. He felt worse.

So he rubbed his eyes because he always felt better after. Yet, when he finished rubbing, he felt no better. He looked around the dark room and caught sight of something on the night stand next to his mattress. He remembered then that he had an idea. He gathered up some paper and a pencil and his book about Jack the Ripper. Then he took out the picture from the *Times-Picayune* and sat back at the table. The picture was from Dauphine Street. He looked at the solitary figure of the detective with the notepad, and the naked legs of the nasty girl. He read the printing beneath the picture again and wrote down the detective's name on his paper, "Detective

Dino LaStanza." He took out another sheet of paper and started to write the detective a letter, just as Jack the Ripper had done.

He had read the Ripper book again and decided he would write letters to the police, not to a reporter. He would tell them his *real* name. He would call himself *Jack of the Night*. He began to feel better as he thought of how he had fooled them all. *They* thought he was Jerome, but he was Jack of the Night. He had a secret identity. And to them, he was invisible. He would show them.

•

In the night the dream came again. It crept up on Dino as he slept, when he was most vulnerable. It sat upon his chest, heavy and hot, and whispered in his ear. It told him it was back, that it wanted him, that it would never go away. Then it reminded him that he would never get away with what he had done. Like a beast in the night, the dream came. When the streets were still and darkness cloaked the land, it came and breathed its hideous breath in Dino's ear. It woke Dino and had him sitting up, his face buried in the palms of his hands.

Dino was always good at keeping secrets but this secret kept him from peace. He no longer possessed the secret, it possessed him. It haunted him, touched him whenever it needed to touch him. Like a jealous lover, the Harmony Street dream would come to fuck him whenever it felt the need.

Dino was a proper character in a proper novel. He had one tragic flaw, and inner secret that was ugly and possessive and would not go away.

*Chapter 6*
North Murat Street

There was an explosion in the media, the likes of which had never been seen before in New Orleans. It started the morning after the Exposition Boulevard Murder. The newspaper ran an electrifying headline that Saturday morning which read: *Co-ed Mutilated In Audubon Park*. Below the headline was a college yearbook picture of Lynette. It was the kind of neat headline that grabbed your attention. It was the worst news article I've ever read.

Mark saved it for me. He gave it to me at the office on the Monday morning after the murder. The article told a story of how a 'terror-filled young woman' was chased through the park as she vainly attempted to get home from a date. It told of how the killer had attacked her from behind and had slashed her back with a 'huge butcher knife' and then raped her. Then it made up the rest.

It told of how a weeping boyfriend had found her and called the police and how an exhaustive search of the park had surfaced no clues, and how the killer was still at large, 'Lurking in the city's shadows'. The article ended with the information that the police were holding Lynette's boyfriend for questioning.

"Where do they come up with this shit?" I asked Mark.

"The Science Fiction Hall of Fame," Mark responded, "Check out the article on page two."

I turned the page and there was a half-page layout on Lynette Anne Louvier, daughter of one of the leading families of New Orleans. The article had more college pictures of Lynette, with statements from classmates and friends and one interesting old neighbor who had heard howling at the time of the murder.

"You see that old bitch?" Mark pointed to the picture of the old-lady neighbor. "I woke her up on my canvass, she didn't hear shit, she's seen too many fuckin' werewolf movies."

Over the space of one weekend, the media had grabbed the city by the throat and choked it with gut-wrenching headlines. Not to be outdone, the television stations paraded somber anchor-person preaching about the plight of the city. And there were mini-cam reports from Audubon Park and Exposition Boulevard, where equally concerned reporters told and retold the grisly details of the murder, each time adding nothing to the story except misinformation.

The reports had an immediate effect on New Orleans. The City That Care Forgot did not suddenly start caring, it just went ballistic with worry, gripped in a vise of fear. The ever present, dutiful media played it to the hilt. They had a hot story, one of the hottest ever, and they milked it for all it was worth.

One enterprising television station sought out the opinion of the common person. On Monday morning, a little blue-haired lady was interviewed while leaving the D. H. Holmes Department Store on Canal Street. Mark and I watched her on the TV in Mason's office. We watched the woman tremble as she was interviewed by a pushy reporter.

"What do you think about the murder?" The reporter asked the blue-haired woman.

"Murder?"

"The co-ed mutilation murder, tell me, are you afraid to shop downtown?"

The old lady's bulging eyes blinked in the ogle-eyed camera lens as she answered through quivering lips, "Oh, yes, terrified."

It was a public service. The public had right to know. So with painstaking detail, the television stations reminded each and every woman in New Orleans that they might be next, that they were not safe in their own city, in their own homes – and the only way to learn more about this was to stay tuned for details following the next commercial. And then some cutie-looking girl came on the air, dressed in tight white shorts to sell the latest tampon product. Television was about as subtle as gonorrhea. While the girl in the white shorts was telling us that her tampon was so comfortable, the camera zoomed in on her ass and crotch as she climbed a tree, to *show* us that not only was the fucking tampon comfortable, nothing leaked. I'm not fuckin' kidding. That was the commercial.

Another television station made a personal plea to the killer to turn himself in and they would *guarantee* he would be treated fairly. Which meant that if he turned himself in to the police, he was in fucking trouble.

Another station hired a psychic, and a different station – not to be outdone – hired a retired police captain from Las Vegas to aid in the search for the killer. He showed up at the New Orleans International Airport on Sunday evening in a polyester leisure suit and held a press conference next to the baggage-claim area.

"What we need here is a coordinated effort, to bring the local jurisdictions together and get to the root of the problem." The *root* of the fucking problem was *the fucking maniac*.

But the topper came from the newspaper again. They didn't want to be outdone and so they had to package their product in a neat, catchy format. They gave the killer a name. In the Monday morning paper they called him *The Slasher* and in an instant, the mother fucker had a moniker to rival Jack the Ripper, Son of Sam, the Yorkshire Ripper, the Hillside Strangler, and all the other scumbags who preceded him into infamous stardom. He had a catchy name and a secret identity that all famous villains had since Doctor Doom fought the Fantastic Four and Doctor Octopus tangled with Spider Man.

*The Slasher*, catchy nickname. Only he wasn't a slasher. He was a fucking stabber. He was a plunger of knives. But I guess calling him *The Plunger* didn't have the proper romantic flair, nor did it stir up the frenzied fear that the word *Slasher* created.

That sensational headline brought forth an immediate result. On that same Monday following the Exposition Boulevard murder, the mayor called a press conference to announce the formation of a Task Force. We watched the conference on the twelve o'clock news in Mason's office. It looked like a fucking convention of assholes all patting themselves on the back and pontificating about how they were going to end this 'crime wave'.

Headed by an Assistant Chief of Police, with functional leadership from our beloved Lt. Gironde of Homicide, the Task Force was assembled with much fanfare. Detectives where to be taken from each section of the Bureau and combined with follow-up officers from every district and officers on loan from the Harbor Police, the Levee-Board Police, the Mississippi River Bridge Police, not to mention the special agents from the FBI, who pranced around like well-dressed Yankees at a gathering of carpet-baggers.

Men who never left off the 'g' at the end of fucking. Men who never actually said, "Fucking." They said, "Freaking."

•

The only break Mark and I had in the entire month of March was when Mason turned off that television and announced that he was giving Boudreaux to the Task Force. "Let Boudreaux fuck them up a while," Mason explained as he called Snowood in from the squad room.

Mason's lean jaw cut a mean profile as he spoke. "Close the door," he told Snowood as he entered. We all sat and waited for Mason, who looked more pissed off than I've ever seen him. "You guys are still the case officers. You work your cases and let the goddamn Task Force run around like a fucking circus," Mason explained as he pointed his index finger at Mark. "I'll run interference for you. We'll let those idiots run down all the bogus leads." He started rubbing his eyes very hard and then added, "With all this publicity, we're gonna get swamped with a shitload of bullshit leads, we'll feed it to the Force, let them run down the cuckoos."

It was agreed. And so we took out our case notes and went over the details of Dauphine Street and Exposition Boulevard. Mark and I made up another list of what we would handle next and Paul sat eagerly at the edge of his folding chair. "I'll be an assisting fool," Paul said. "Just let me know what I gotta do."

"Let's hope that's all you gotta do is assist," Mason finished up. "If our killer strikes again, she's yours, Country-Ass."

•

When the killings first started, after the butchery on Dauphine Street and Bayou St. John, all I wanted was to get it over with, to stop him. I didn't care if a railroad detective caught him, or even a goddamn school-crossing guard, so long as it all stopped. But that was until Lynette, until they assembled that damn Task Force. It was then that I knew I wanted him *personally*. I didn't want anyone else beating me to him, unless it was my padna.

I went over my case notes on Exposition Boulevard carefully as I laid out a game plan. I had already checked out the classmates and neighbors and was more than halfway through the license plate numbers. I spent Monday evening at home with more coffee, carefully going over all the license plate numbers from all thee murders, to make sure no care had been around more than once. Then I went over Lynette's address book carefully. I compiled a list of people I would talk to. I would personally interview everyone on the list. No phone interview would do, I wanted to talk to them in person, face to face. Then I would take on the people whose names were registered to the cares parked around Audubon Park on the night of the murder.

Before I turned in at three in the morning, I made note of my next step further down the line. I would have to get the records of all students and employees at Loyola and Tulane Universities.

•

We caught another Signal Thirty on Tuesday afternoon. A freshly buried body was found at a work-site along the river front in the Ninth Ward. Mark and I assisted Snowood at the scene.

The Ninth Ward was on the downtown side of the French Quarter, beyond the old Creole Faubourg Marigny and the lower class residential area known as Bywater. The body was found at a construction site next to the Industrial Canal, where a construction crew was driving pilings. The foreman found the body in a shallow grave. He was talking to a couple of uniformed officers when we pulled up.

I took a look at the body as it lay on its back, its arms and legs outstretched like a manikin in a permanent sitting position. It looked just like the bodies in Vietnam. In fact, the body was Vietnamese. I looked around at the work crew leaning against one of the warehouses, and most of them were Vietnamese.

"Remind you of anything?" Mark asked with a smirk on his face.

I looked over at the large frightened eyes of the workers and I was back in Bien Hua again, with Oriental eyes staring at me and Vietnamese jabbering in my ears as a couple of the workers started talking to Snowood.

"What the fuck they yakking about?" Mark asked me.

"I don't fuckin' know. All I learned in Nam was how to get home," I answered, summing up my tour in one sentence.

We watched Snowood or a minute before Mark started laughing. "Look at Country-Ass over there." Mark pointed to Paul, who stood towering above a shitload of yellow faces all jabbering at once. Mark's laughter turned into a roar as he continued looking at Snowood. "You sure look fuckin' silly!" Mark yelled to him.

Snowood glared at us and spit a wad of brown shit over the heads of the Vietnamese. "You boys know how much I hate fuckin' foreigners!" he yelled back.

Mark was holding his sides. "I know." Mark lasted another ten minutes, then took off and left me with Snowood who was glad to see him leave.

"Sometimes that boy is a fuckin' pain," Paul said as Mark drove off.

So we spent the entire day with the Vietnamese and with the foreman, who was not amused at all. I took names and addresses and as much information about the Southeast Asians as I could get, while Paul processed the scene. We waited around for an interpreter from Catholic Charities to arrive, but when the interpreter hadn't shown up by six o'clock, Paul and I dismissed everyone. Then we went and got a beer in a quiet, run-down dive on Urquhart Street.

I watched Paul drink his beer and spit out his brown shit simultaneously. "How the fuck you do that?" I had to ask.

"It's all in the lips," Paul answered. "You just keep the tobacco between your lip and gum and let the beer go down the throat. It's easy. Wanna try?"

"Fuck no."

"You should, make a different man outta ya."

"Fuck you."

Paul smiled that smart-ass cowboy smirk of his and leaned back in his chair. "I can drink and eat with it in and never fuck up," he claimed.

"Eat pussy with it?" I asked.

"Sure. That's how I got my wife to marry me. You ain't never ate pussy until you do it with a pinch between your cheek and gum."

"You ever listen to yourself?" I asked. "You sound just like a red-neck on steroids."

"I know," Paul agreed, "but I'm happy. I got me a good job, a good-looking wife and a kid looks like Huckleberry Finn." He took out his wallet and showed me pictures of his pretty bland wife and his carrot-headed son.

"He don't look like Huck Finn," I told Paul. "He looks like Tom Sawyer."

Old Snowood laughed so hard he mixed up his beer and brown shit and had to spit it all out.

•

When I got home that night, my phone was ringing. It was Fat Phil at the Bureau. "Have you solved it yet?" he asked me.

"Fuck you."

Phil cackled. "You better be nice to me, I got a message for you."

"Yeah?" I said. "Give it to me."

"Say 'please'," Phil teased.

"Fuck you, Phil."

"Okay, a girl named Lizette called you, said you know her number." Phil cackled again. "Tell me, is she a good lay?"

"About as good as your daughter," I answered.

"That ain't funny."

I hung up on the Fuck-head and put on some coffee before calling Lizette. She answered after the first ring.

"I'm sorry to bother you," she began, "but I would like to see you. Can I meet you somewhere?"

"Tonight?" I asked.

"If it's convenient."

I had too many beers and not enough to eat, but what else was new?

"Sure," I said, "You name it."

"Can you meet me at the Camellia Grill at ten o'clock?"

"Sure."

"Will you wait for me out front?" she asked.

"Sure."

That gave me time for a quick shower and time enough to pump some coffee in me and return to human form.

The Camellia Grill was a popular restaurant because it had good food and great service and because it stayed open late. It occupied a one-story white wooden building on Carrollton Avenue, a half-block up from St. Charles Avenue. It had four large ante-bellum columns in front, a long grill inside with a W-shaped counter that ran the length of the place, and the sharpest waiters in the city. It was an old fashioned grill where you had to sit on stools at the counter. There were no tables. It was a hangout for college students, uptown professionals and their fashion-conscious wives, and debutantes from the finest families of the city. It was also a hangout for Second District patrolmen and an occasional cop from the Sixth District. When I rode with Stan, we dropped by the grill often, even if it wasn't in our district. It had the some of the best food that you could get late at night in New Orleans.

It was raining when I pulled up at the grill. I waited out front, leaned against one of the columns and watched the cars hiss by on wet Carrollton Avenue. It just stopped raining as Lizette pulled up in a white BMW at about ten after. She drove by and looked for me, nodded when she saw me, then parked. I walked over to her car. As she climbed out, she apologized for making me wait.

"I wanted to make sure you were here before I got out." I understood.

We sat at the far end of the counter on the last two stools, away from the other people. A neat, tall black waiter walked up, placed menus and settings in front of us. "How are you tonight, Miss Louvier?" the waiter asked Lizette. There was a big smile on his face.

"Fine, Alfred," she answered. "And how are you?"

"Just fine, ma'am." Alfred responded. "Can I get y'all anything right away."

"Coffee," Lizette said. Alfred stepped away still smiling.

She wore that same perfume, the one that lingered in my senses for hours after I'd left her Sunday night. Eerie, because it wasn't a strong scent but it stayed with me. I looked at her as she sat silently on her stool. Under the bright fluorescent lighting in the grill, Lizette's face was white and smooth. Each time I saw her, I was amazed at how pretty she really was. She had a look about her, a glamour. Even in a baggy shirt and blue jean like tonight, she looked glamorous. Maybe it was the way she held her head or the smooth, easy way she walked, talked.

I looked down at her hands and could see they were shaking. She looked back at me with frightened, misty eyes. She shrugged and wiped the wetness from her eyes with a Kleenex and explained, "Alfred must not read the newspapers, he calls me 'Miss Louvier' because he can't tell Lynette and me apart." She almost lost it there for a moment. She choked on the last words, but hung in there and composed herself.

I thought to myself that Alfred must live on Mars. I looked outside as the rain returned, harder, pounding on the sidewalk and against the big front windows of the grill.

Alfred returned with tow coffees. "Can I get ya'll something else?" he inquired.

I looked back at Lizette and asked, "Would you like something to eat?"

She shook her head.

"Well," I said, "would you mind if I ate? I haven't eaten."

"No."

So I ordered a shrimp po-boy.

Lizette watched Alfred leave to get the order. She sat still and said nothing. I stared at her pouting lips, at the deep red lipstick on those serious lips. After a while she spoke. "I called you because I have to know how the investigation is progressing." Before I could answer she added, "I want to know exactly what you've done. I have to know." She looked back at me with those familiar sad eyes.

"Well, to start with, I've checked out Lynette's classmates and all your neighbors and come up with a big zero. Nobody knows nothing, anything," I corrected myself and continued, "I'm about halfway through the list of people whose cars were parked in the area, "

"The what?" she cut in.

"We wrote down all the license numbers from all the cars parked in the area, in case someone saw something, or in case the killer left his car behind. I'm comparing the numbers with the list of all the cars from the two previous cases, in case a car was at more than one scene, still zero so far."

"There were *two* previous cases?" she asked.

That's right, she had been out of town. "Yes, there was one on Dauphine Street and one at Bayou St. John. We're working on all three."

"Are you staking out the killer?" she asked.

"No. The new Task Fore is gonna handle that." Then I explained about the Task Force and how I was still the case officer on her sister's case.

She continued to stare at me. "What about Lynette's address book?" she asked.

"None of the names in the book hook up to any of the license registrations," I explained. "I've gone through the book, I've got some interviews to do."

"And what else are you doing?"

"Then I'll go through everyone at Loyola, and then Tulane."

She looked away for a moment and asked, "You mean there's nothing so far?"

I didn't answer. I sat there with the words 'Detective Useless' bouncing around in my head. I felt my stomach knotting up. I listened to the pounding rain outside as the silence grew.

"I'm sorry to bother you like this," she said finally. "I know this is your job, but I have to do something, I have to *do* something," she explained. "I have to get involved. Is there any way you can keep me advised of what's going on? I have to know."

I nodded before I answered, "Sure. I'll let you know."

"I mean I want you to tell me everything," she repeated. "I've *got* to know." She looked away again and faced the blank wall next to her for a moment before adding, "I'll do anything to catch him."

"So will I, and not because it's my job either," I went on. "You don't know me, but I don't give up. I'll never stop, never, until I get him. I don't care how long it takes or what it takes. I'm gonna get him. *Period.*"

She turned back to me and asked, "But will he get off, I mean in the courts?"

"I don't know. I just hope he makes the fatal error of having something in his hand when I catch him, anything in his hand," I said coolly, "because I'll just blow his brains out. *Period.*"

Those topaz eyes look into mine.

"That's not bravado. Every cop on this case will kill him if they get the chance."

Alfred picked that moment to step up with my shrimp sandwich and a bottle of red-hot Louisiana Tabasco sauce. "More coffee?" he asked.

"Yes," I answered and looked back at Lizette after Alfred left. Her eyes seemed even bigger as she stared at me. The familiar knot in my stomach took another twist. I looked away and said, "I'm sorry about that 'brains' stuff."

"Don't be sorry. That's exactly what I want you to do." She continued staring at me. "Just promise me you'll let me know everything that happens."

"I'll call you every night," I said.

She took out a piece of paper and wrote down a phone number on it. "This is my number in my room, call me there."

"Fine," I agreed. "I'll call you every night."

"Promise?"

"I've already told you about the bra thing, didn't I?"

She nodded and took her first sip of coffee. The rain continued to pound as I started in on the po-boy.

"Don't you have a home to eat at?" Lizette asked in a voice that had lost its earlier sadness.

"Not since my third wife left me."

"What?"

"Just kidding."

Lizette almost smiled. And for the first time since I'd known the girl, we spent several quiet, peaceful minutes together, with the sound of the rain in the background and my stomach slowly unwinding as I fed it shrimp and French bread. Fuck the Tabasco.

•

We waited for the rain to subside and then started for the door. A unformed cop stepped in the doorway and a familiar face looked over at me.

"Hey you!" the cop yelled, pointing his finger at me. Every eye in the place followed the finger. "Didn't I tell you to stay outta here!"

All I could do was shake my head as he took a menacing step forward, still pointing at me, "Didn't I tell you the next time I catch you playing with yourself, you're going to jail?"

After I managed to get Lizette outside, I didn't look back. I just continued to shake my head.

Lizette took a reluctant step away from the grill and asked, "Who was that policeman?"

"That was Stan, Officer Stanley Smith of the Sixth District, my old partner."

Lizette stopped walking. I turned back to her. "That's his way of, that's just his way." I shrugged.

She looked at me with those big gold eyes as her face broke into a broad grin. Then she started giggling and could not hold back the laughter.

"That's hysterical," she cried. "Boy, did he ever get you!"

Her laughter was contagious. "That's the story of my life." I let the laughter out and explained, "He's been doing that to me ever since I was a rookie."

Lizette laughed long and hard and had to lean on the BMW for a while before she was finally able to control herself. "Did you see the people's faces?" she asked. I kept laughing.

Before she climbed into her car, she made me promise again to call her the next night.

"I'll follow you," I said and I jumped into my own car and followed her home. I pulled up behind her and waited until she went inside the mansion. Then I headed straight back for the grill, but Stan was gone, the son of a bitch.

So I went home, packed it in for the night. But sleep would not come, so I picked up the phone and called Jessica. I needed to talk to her, needed to hear her familiar voice, needed to feel her there with me. I wanted to touch her, to run my fingers over her naked body, to feel the softness of her breasts and the hardness of her nipples and the warmth of her soft pubic hair. I needed to feel the tightness fade away from my thighs. And I wanted more – I wanted to hold her an talk to her an have her there when I woke up.

But all I felt was a sinking feeling in my chest as I lay there in the darkness, the unanswered ringing in my ear. I tell you, the empty nights have a way of piling up. Each night alone magnified what was missing. Each night alone, a little of what Jessica and I had, faded.

•

"I thought we were on the goddamn evening watch," Mark complained as he tossed another paper clip into the empty typewriter on his desk. No wonder he could never get the typewriter to work.

"We are," I assured him, "until tomorrow morning."

"Don't remind me," he moaned.

I continued. "Maybe our killer will turn himself in."

Mark ignored me.

Mason entered the squad room and walked over to my desk where I was going over my notes from Exposition Boulevard. He dropped a set of car keys on my notes. "Your car's ready," Mason announced as he tuned and headed back for his office. From over his shoulder he added, "Now you don't have to go everywhere with Landucci anymore."

"Who?"

Mason stopped outside his door and tuned back, "You mean you don't know?"

I shrugged my shoulders.

Mason nodded in Mark's direction. "His name isn't Land, it's Landucci. They changed it. Must have been afraid of the Mafia or something." Mason turned again and went back into his office.

I looked over at my partner. "I knew you were a wop, but I didn't know, Landucci, that's a nice, wop name."

"My grandfather changed it." Mark yawned and turned to look out the window. "I prefer Landucci actually. Maybe I'll change it back. Marco Landucci has a nice ring to it."

"Just like Dino LaStanza," I agreed. I glanced over at Mark for a moment and an old cliché ran through my mind, you learn something new every day.

"Why am I here in the morning?" Mark complained again. "My wife actually told me she *missed* me this morning. I never thought she'd ever say *that!*"

Snowood was supposed to call me after the autopsy of the Vietnamese victim, but he hadn't. So I continued working on my notes until Mark finally decided where we'd go to lunch.

On our way out of the Bureau we ran into Snowood by the elevator. He was mad as hell. "Goddamn fuckin' gooks!" he screamed as he left the elevator and stormed into the office. We followed him and watched as he started to throw thing around.

"So what happened?" I had to ask.

"It was a *natural*, a goddamn, rotten-assed, fuckin' *natural death!*" Paul roared. "The mother fucker died of a coronary," he huffed and kicked over his trash can. "Two whole days wasted on fuckin' gooks!" he yelled as Mason came out and stuck his chiseled chin into the conversation.

Mason took a puff from his cigarette and muttered from behind a cloud of smoke, "Tell me about it."

It was then I noticed a nice-sized brown stain on Paul's chest as he tried to calm himself and explain what happened at the same time. "It was a fuckin' natural," he repeated as he sat heavily in his chair. He glanced down at his chest and moaned, "Looked, I spit all over myself, fuckin' gooks." He glanced around at us and couldn't stop a grin from creeping across his face.

"I look real fuckin' silly, don't I?"

"No difference," Mark responded.

"Yeah." Snowood looked over at Mason and told us, "The gook had a coronary and after three solid hours with that moron interpreter from the Catholic Charities, I learned that they just buried him, right where he fell."

"Just like Nam," I added.

Paul nodded. "That's what they've always done. They fall over and die and they bury 'em right where they fall. Goddamn Foreigners!"

I waited for Paul to look my way. "They aren't gooks. Koreans are gooks. Vietnamese are zipper-heads or just zips."

•

We followed the adventures of the Task Force with great curiosity as they plodded along. We watched them parade around the Detective Bureau during the day shift, cluttering up the place with Federal Agents and other alleged detectives.

The FBI agents busied themselves compiling a psychological profile of the killer. The profile was gobbled up by a hungry media that was ravenous for anything. It was curious how the FBI leaked the profile to the media in bits and pieces. It took them a week to come to the same conclusion Mason had come to right after Bayou

St. John. The killer was an Abnormal Sex Killer. The media went bananas.

The Task Force continued to plod along, plunging headlong after every lead. They stumbled around like a blind man at Mardi Gras, bumping into everything and coming up with a big blank. Mason kept a close eye on their daily reports in case something of real value surfaced. But nothing did.

It didn't take long for Mason to point out that the Task Force was actually a blessing. They took some of the pressure off us. They set up patrols, put a shitload of men on the street every night, freeing us from long surveillances so that Mark and I could be selective in our follow-up investigations. They were even kind enough to answer all the kook calls that inundated Headquarters after the recent publicity. People began turning in their friends and neighbors and even husbands, "My husband didn't come home the night that girl was killed in Audubon Park." – "My neighbor sneaks out late at night and he's got a dog. I heard Son of Sam had a dong." – "I know my cousin is the killer because his eyes are crossed now and they weren't until that girl got killed."

But the most valuable service the Task Force did for us was decoying the media. In the Task Force and the media's zest for publicity, they clung together, following each other around like dogs in heat, while Mark and I quietly went about our business.

•

As for me, I kept plodding along also, through the interviews of Lynette's associates and all the people whose names were on the car registrations. At the end of the day, when I got home after midnight, I would call Lizette on the phone and talk to her, explain to her that I was doing my best, but it just wasn't good enough. She said she understood in that soft, sensual voice and asked me to call the next night. And I would call.

I also called Jessica again and again until I finally caught her at home. She told me that I shouldn't call her and hung up on me. I tell you, the empty nights have a way of piling up, the softness fades, but the desire does not.

Desire hides but never goes away. There are times when a man's need is much more than a voice on the phone, when a deep animal desire reaches up and grabs you and you lie awake at night dreaming of silky legs and firm nipples and sweet, soft pubic hair.

I closed my eyes and ran Lizette through my mind, bright golden eyes, sad pouting mouth, full sensuous lips, long dark hair flowing around me like strands of light, full round hips ascending stairs in front of me, her soft sensual voice whispering in my ear, whispering of a longing, of a desire.

Lizette, beautiful, rich uptown girl.

I dreamt that night, but not of full lips nor flowing dark hair. I dreamt of rich, uptown, French Creoles in new Orleans society and of old dago Italians. I dreamt of my grandfather pulling his fruit cart up Exposition Boulevard chanting, "I got ban – na – na. I got tan – ga – rine. I got water – melon!"

•

I'm a mid-city boy. I grew up in the shadows of City Park and the Canal Cemeteries in a two-story house at 612 North Bernadotte Street. The house was made of blond brick and wood, with twelve concrete steps out front. We lived on the second floor and I must have climbed those twelve steps a million times. The first floor was sealed up and used as a basement. When I was little, we used to play in the basement during bad weather, until my brother put in a pool table and started having parties in his teen-angel days.

I remember my mother sitting on the big front gallery, which ran the length of the front of our house. She would sit in a rocking chair, shelling *petit pois* for dinner, or peeling alligator pears for a salad, and talking to the neighbors. The houses in our block were built close together, with only narrow alleys between them. The houses were so close, my mother could talk to her friends without shouting. My earliest memories of that porch, sitting with my mother, waiting for my father to come home. I remember a vision of my father, tall and thin in his blue uniform, ascending the steps.

•

I was a pain-in-the-ass kid brother, followed my big brother Joe around everywhere he went. I would peek at him as he talked to girls, as he smoothly moved in on their innocent eyes. I would follow him as long as I could keep up with him. But he would lose me whenever he really wanted to. He *always* seemed to know *exactly* where I was and exactly how to lose me.

My brother and his friends used to play in the Canal Cemeteries at night. I would follow, except when they went into Odd Fellow's Rest. Joe told me that it was called Odd Fellow's Rest because that was where they buried all the odd fellows – the deformed people, the hunchbacks, the dwarfs and midgets, and crippled people. That was where monsters were buried like the vampires of the Canal Cemeteries and the werewolves of City Park.

I wouldn't go near the place, even in broad daylight – until one evening Joe talked me into climbing the back fence with him. Odd Fellow's was a small cemetery, a triangular graveyard at the corner of Canal Street and City Park Avenue. Joe and I sneaked into St. Patrick's Cemetery that night, then he helped me over the rear fence of Odd Fellow's Rest because I was so small. We stuck together, until Joe found the perfect moment to leave me in the middle of the place. Then he took off and I was, in the middle of Odd Fellow's, alone, except for the monsters.

I couldn't yell and found I could not move for a long, long time. I stood there, as still as the tombs, as still as those little concrete houses of death. After a while, I realized I could move my head and look around at the crumbling sepulchers. The large palm bushes that were nestled between the tombs cast spider shadows beneath the high street lights from City Park Avenue. I remember one sepulcher was wide open, its cement doors had crumbled and the tomb was open, and there were bones inside.

I climbed the rear fence like a cat chased by a bulldog. But I didn't go straight home. I hid and waited until it got late and my brother had to go look for me. I waited even longer and then suddenly appeared at our front door, crying and pointing at Joe, who got the hell beat out of him by my father.

•

Once summer a girl named Jennifer moved in next door. She had long dark hair and big brown eyes and quickly developed a serious crush on my big brother. Joe was a little older than her and never paid much attention to her.

I remember vividly the evening she really tried to get his attention. You see, her bedroom was directly across the narrow alley from Joe's bedroom, and one evening when I was rooting around in Joe's bedroom, because he was out and there were always neat things in Joe's room, she came home and undressed with her window shade up. Joe wasn't in, but I was. I sat on his bed in the dark room and watched that teen-age dream as she stripped, completely. She played it to the hilt, standing stark naked in her open window, brushing her long dark hair. I must have held my breath for five minutes, until she flipped off the lights and climbed into bed.

That was the first time I saw a girl, a woman, completely naked, breasts and pubic hair and the works. I didn't sleep at all that night, I was eight years old and I knew what I wanted to do for the rest of my life, look at naked women. I wasn't very successful. Jennifer was the only girl I saw naked until I was in high school.

She and her family moved away the following winter. I wonder whatever happened to her. She's just a memory now, but that sure was nice of her.

•

I told Joe the story about Jennifer years later. He didn't believe me. I told Joe the story again just before he died. He was in a quiet mood that day and after I told him, he looked at me and asked, "You really telling the truth?"

I swore I was.

Joe suddenly looked sad. He sat there in his police uniform, sergeant's stripes and all, staring glassy-eyed into, space. He looked like a little boy who had lost a favorite toy.

"She really did that?" he asked again.

"She sure did."

Then Joe was quiet for along time.

Later, with a smirk on my face I asked Joe, "You believed that story?"

He glared at me and roared, "You little bastard."

Then we went out and knocked down a few cold ones. That was the last night we spent together.

•

The dark streets of the fifties are gone now, and so are the sock hops of my youth, and so is the brother who used to play jokes on me. But my house is still there at 612 North Bernadotte. My parents still live there. One Sunday, following the Exposition

Street murder, I received orders from my mother to come to dinner. I hadn't been to dinner since my transfer to Homicide.

When I pulled up, my father was sitting out on the front gallery with the Sunday paper. I watched him for a minute as he sipped coffee from a large mug and scanned the paper. His hair was gray but still full and curly and his pencil-thin moustache was almost white. He was wearing his familiar tee shirt and Bermuda shorts. My father was the kind of guy who wore his baggy shorts below his pot belly and wore white socks with sandals.

He peeked at me from behind his *Times-Picayune* as I started up the front steps. "Well, well, look who showed up today," he chided, his face still buried in the Metro section. "Been reading about you lately," he added as I plopped down in the rocker next to his rocker.

I didn't say anything. I just waited for him to continue. After a moment, he did continue, "Looks like business is up. You got anything good on this Slasher fella?"

"Nope." I leaned back and closed my eyes, inhaling deeply the sweet familiar scents from the trees.

My father shuffled his paper and sighted. "Well, he'll fuck up sooner or late and you'll get him."

"That's a load off my mind."

I could feel my father's eyes staring at me. It was the same feeling I used to have when I was a kid and he would point those eyes at me and I would feel my stomach bottoming out. I felt those eyes again and opened my own eyes to look back. And I smiled. "So, how's it going, Pop?"

He didn't answer me, but looked away back at the Sports section.

"The Chief says 'hello'," I added as I rose from the rocker and headed through the front door.

Just as I stepped in the house my father asked over his shoulder, "By the way, how's Jessica?"

I stopped for a second and said, "We broke up."

I found my mother in the kitchen and gave her a big hug. She held me an extra second before pulling back and looking me up and down. "Dino," she exclaimed, "you look tired, son. Have you been taking care of yourself?"

"Sure."

She looked behind me and asked, "Is Jessica with you?"

"We broke up."

My mother gave me her sad-eyed look. God, I hate it when she feels sorry for me. She shook her head, sighed, and tried a half-smile on me before returning to her cooking. She put the finishing touches on her lasagna and started telling me the neighborhood news, as if I cared about the people who occupied the houses around their house. I didn't listen. I just watched he move around the kitchen in that easy way of hers.

She moved as she had all my life, not wasting any movements. She looked the same as she had all my life, except for her eyes. The sadness within her eyes was a familiar look, one I'd seen many times in the past. It was a permanent look now, since Joe's death.

It was over my mother's lasagna that my father picked up or conversation about Exposition Boulevard. "Was the murder near a big old house that looks like a castle?" he asked.

"Castle?" I shrugged.

"Yeah. On Exposition Boulevard. I remember there was a house that looked like a castle, not too far from St. Charles Avenue," he explained with a curious look on his face.

"I don't remember any castle," I answered, glancing over at my mother who smiled and rolled her eyes.

"No gray brick house with ramparts?" he asked.

"No."

My father chuckled to himself and looked up across the table as if he were looking, far away. "When I was a boy," he started, "I used to spend weekends at my cousin Angelo's on Magazine Street." He looked over at my mother and added, "You remember Angelo, looked like a chimpanzee." He looked back at me as he hung his arms at his side and explained, "Angelo had real long arms and was all hair."

My mother cut in at that point. "Angelo was from the better-looking side of the LaStanza family."

"Ha!" my father roared. "I always knew your mother had the hots for old Angelo." He dismissed my mother with a wave of his hand. "Anyway, he's dead now. Got his head squashed in a elevator on Canal Street."

"What?" I had to ask.

"Don't interrupt your father," my father snapped as he continued his story. "When I was a kid I used to stay at Angelo's and we would play baseball in Audubon Park. Angelo was a couple years older than me and he told me about a prince who lived in the house that looked like a castle on Exposition Boulevard. We had me bow down every time I passed that castle, because if I didn't then the prince's guards would come out and chop off my head. So I did."

My father didn't stop or breath as he went right on, "I bowed every time I passed that place. Once, we were in a group of boys and I bowed, and when the boys asked me I told them, they laughed their asses off. Damn Angelo." My father paused for another bite of lasagna, then added, "Never did like Anglo."

"So that's it?" I asked. "That's the whole story? What about the elevator?'

My mother answered, "Angelo got his head caught in an elevator and died."

"He didn't die right away," my father added, "he lived about a month after that."

"And for a month he was the smartest LaStanza I've ever known," my mother announced.

I got a kick out of that one. She got my Pop again. But he just huffed it off. "Never did like Angelo," he repeated, looking over at me and asking again, "You sure there isn't a house that looks like a big castle on Exposition Boulevard?"

"Not near St. Charles."

My father slapped his forehead – an innate Italian gesture. "Damn. It wasn't near St. Charles. It was down by Magazine." He shook his head. "I'm getting old."

•

On my way home that evening I thought again about the pressure cooker of police work and about humor. My father knew it well and so did my mother. She was a veteran of many a long, lonely night wondering if someone would come home or not. And she could cut a joke with the best of us.

After Joe died, I thought there was no humor left in the world for a long time. We almost lost it there, but eventually the humor came back and a Sunday dinner could be almost nice again.

I only wish my parents wouldn't feel so guilty about me, about me not being their favorite son. Our family's story is the story of a family whose favorite member has died. Joe was my father's favorite. He was also my mother's favorite. I don't blame them for that. Joe was *my* favorite member of the family. He was the center of our family, its driving force, its unifying force. Only, we never knew that until he was gone and there was such emptiness. Sure they loved Joe more, but so did I. I just wish they wouldn't feel so guilty about it.

So now my parents let the pressure out with jokes, but I wonder if they relive Joe in their minds as I do. Sometimes I turn on that tape recorder in my mind and Joe is there with me, messing up my hair or cruising around City Park in his old Buick. My brother had this big white Buick with huge rear fins. It looked like a land-shark. Joe had the name of the car hand painted on its sides. It was called *The White Weenie*. I remember the day Joe put another sign on the truck of the car which read, "Don't laugh – your daughter might be in the back seat."

•

I'm a mid-city boy. I grew up on North Bernadotte Street, grew up riding the Canal Cemeteries streetcar downtown and going to Catholic Schools, St. Anthony of Padua and then Holy Rosary and then Archbishop Rummel High School. And now that I am grown, I still live by City Park in a small bungalow on North Murat Street with evergreens lining the narrow street and the tall, haunting oaks of City Park a half-block away.

I live alone in a one-story pale-green stucco bungalow with a red tile roof and a front door that is round at the top. It's the only house I've ever known that was built with one bedroom. My mother visited once and called it a dungeon. The name stuck. I've tried to buy the place but my little old landlady won't sell. The land's too valuable.

The Dungeon was built in the twenties and still has its original fixtures and a solid white kitchen that can blind you with the flick of a light switch, I love the place because its small and out of place, nestled behind the huge houses on City Park Avenue. In New Orleans, it didn't matter what neighborhood you lived in as much as what house you lived in. Even in the finest uptown neighborhoods, there were small wooden shotgun houses sandwiched between mansions, just like my bungalow behind the larger houses on City Park Avenue.

•

When I returned to the Dungeon that Sunday after dinner, I sat on my sofa and stared out the picture window of my living room. I started running the facts of the case through my mind again, and again come up with nothing but frustration. I crawled back in the pressure cooker again, beating my head against the walls.

I felt helpless and useless. And somewhere along in there, I felt a foreboding, a chill running across my face. I felt I *had* to do something. I felt he was out there, that night, that very night, he was on the prowl. So I prowled. I grabbed my .357 Magnum and climbed into my unmarked unit and prowled the city like a lone wolf, a predator just waiting for the moment.

I cruised the Quarter and then drove by Bayou St. John before pulling up at Audubon Park.

I took my place in the gazebo across the way from the Louvier mansion and waited for him. In old movies, the killer always returned to the scene of the crime. I waited for him to return that night, the night I felt the foreboding. I wanted to catch him lurking in the foggy night, to catch him slithering between the trees, to point my Magnum at him and blow the fucker's head away.

In front of the grand jury I would be asked why I shot him six times. And I would answer, "Because all I had was six bullets in my gun."

So I waited. But nothing happened. No one lurked. No one slithered. I watched the sun creep up, and with it, the hot, humid dawn warmed the land and drove off the foreboding I felt. I took a stroll by the Louvier's on my way back to my car and was surprised to see the front door open before six in the morning. The maid stepped out and called to me, "Mr. Policeman, Miss Lizette sent me to ask if you want some coffee.

All I could do was remember I hadn't called Lizette that night.

"I just fixed some fresh," the maid announced. "You come on in here now."

She stepped back in and left the door open for me. I went in and found Lizette sitting at the dining room table. She was in a thick purple robe, her hair up in a bun. She had on only a hint of make-up, but she looked so good.

"You look beat," she told me as I sat down heavily across from her. "Where you out there all night?"

I nodded and laughed. "Pretty much."

"What were you doing?"

"I just, I just, I was prowling last night. If he can prowl, so can I."

"Did something happen last night?" she asked, her big eyes round like golden saucers.

"No, I just had a feeling." Nothing had happened. If it would have, I'd have heard it on my little fucking radio.

The maid brought us coffee and it was good and strong. I was updating Lizette on the case when Mr. Louvier came down the stairs, also wearing robe. He stepped into the dining room and almost jumped when he saw me. He gave me a quick look, a look that said, "What are you doing here with my daughter?" He didn't have to ask, it was in his eyes.

Lizette saw it too, because she got right up and kissed him on the cheek and explained that I had been out all night, watching the house and how it was only polite to ask me in for coffee. Mr. Louvier said he understood. That was white of him.

I finished my coffee and rose to leave. I didn't get any argument. Lizette did walk me to the out the dining room, suggested I get some sleep. "Will you call me tonight after work?" she asked.

"Of course."

Lizette led me into the library and let me stand in front of the portrait and stare at the girl in the white gown, at the alabaster skin and the wide eyes that stared right back at me. I felt the pressure building inside me again. I could feel it, could feel my hands shaking ever so slightly. I didn't want Lizette to see it, so I left. She gave me a curious look, but I was too tired to read it.

I drove straight home and tried not to think about Lizette and that curious look, tried not to even think about Lynette. I wound up thinking about Mr. Louvier and the look he had given me. It was a look that said I wasn't good enough. Maybe I was good enough to work on a daughter's murder, good enough to guard a house all night, good enough to get down and dirty with the dead – but don't touch the living. Lizette was beyond reach, period.

I already knew that.

•

He was *The Slasher*. That was better than Jack of the Night. He would have to rewrite the letters to the police now. He would sign them *Slasher*.

Jerome Hemmel sat in his room after the newspaper came out with his new name and read the article over and over. He missed work Monday and didn't want to go in on Tuesday, but he did, and no one knew who he was. He walked around the university and looked into faces and they didn't even know he was the Slasher. He was invisible to them. All they saw was Jerome Hemmel.

During the nights that followed, he locked his door and made sure his window was bolted shut before he took out the brassieres. Lining up the three bras one after the other, he ran his fingers over the silk. He took each of the, one at a time, and held them against his face, smelling them and then slowly licking them. With his free hand he rubbed between his legs until her exploded.

Then he put away the bras and the new articles and sat up in his bed and shook as he stared at his front door, waiting for the detectives to come. But they never came. With each night that passed, he grew less and less afraid and thought that maybe they weren't ever going to catch him.

And soon the time came when he could stand it no more being Jerome Hemmel.

On that lazy Sunday night, he took out the long-bladed knife and hid it under his coat. He waited until it was good and dark, making sure no one saw him leave his apartment. He climbed into his car and left Urquhart Street and Jerome Hemmel behind. The farther away he drove, the better he felt. And slowly, the power came back to him, because he was now the Slasher. Jerome never felt that power.

When he stopped at a stop sign, a girl crossed in front of his car. He watched her walk away down the sidewalk. And when he turned the corner there was a parking place waiting for him, waiting for the Slasher. So he parked and jumped out and followed the girl.

She could not hear him as he approached because the Slasher wore sneakers. But he knew that if she turned around, she would see him. To his victims, the Slasher was never invisible. He stalked her quietly and quickly until he was right behind her, his hand on the handle of the long-bladed knife. He would fuck her good!

The girl seemed to sense something and turned quickly to look at him. She stopped and so did he. She didn't seem afraid at all. And as he looked into her face he saw that she was ugly.

There was a long moment with a hand on a handle and two sets of eyes looking back and forth. Then there was a smile that crossed the girl's face as she turned and walked away.

The Slasher did not kill her, because she was ugly. The Slasher actually felt sorry for ugly girls. They missed so much. But pretty girls had everything, beauty, attention, and those cruel smiles that ever came his way. The Slasher wanted to fuck pretty girls. Nobody felt sorry for dead ugly girls but *everyone* felt sorry for beautiful young girls who died. So fuck them. Fuck them all!

•

There was a Signal Thirty reported at the corner of Carrollton Avenue and Tulane, a man shot dead while standing at a bus stop at one o'clock in the morning. I was still out cruising and heard Mason heading over there, so I turned around and joined him.

"What are you doing ere?" Mason asked me. "Don't you have a girl friend?"

"Not anymore," I told him. "She said I liked autopsies better than I liked her."

Mason chuckled. "Welcome to the big league."

"So" – I changed the subject – "what happened to him?"

"Got himself shot in the head," Mason answered as he looked at his watch. "If he would have waited and hour, it would have been the other platoon's problem."

"Fucking inconsiderate, I'd say."

"Yeah," Mason agreed as he put away his humor and started processing the scene with the crime lab technician. I lent a hand by canvassing the area. There wasn't a fucking soul around. When I finished my canvass I found myself across Tulane Avenue, watching Mason.

A curious feeling came upon me as I stood there. I began to wonder how many times the dead man had passed the intersection of Tulane and Carrollton. I must have passed there a thousand time myself.

I wondered if he ever knew he would die there. Had he ever felt a chill when he passed? I wondered if he ever looked over an saw a figure standing in the shadows, a hooded figure with a skull face carrying a scythe. I wondered if he knew that figure waiting for him at Carrollton and Tulane.

I felt a chill myself standing there, felt that same creeping fear I had felt long ago in Odd Fellow's Rest. I looked around quickly for the hooded figure, but he was not there. And I knew why I could not see the Grim Reaper, because if I had a mirror and looked into it I would see that skull face looking back at me.

O'NEIL DE NOUX

*Chapter 7*
Cucullu Street

Paul Snowood was lucky. On his way to work one day, a car in front of him swerved and missed his car by inches before slamming into a telephone pole. Being a detective instead a traffic cop, Paul tried to drive off before anyone figured out he was a policeman. He could see that the driver of the other car wasn't hurt, but Paul was stuck in traffic, so he resigned himself to staying on the scene and doing whatever a good Mr. Policeman should.

Paul got out of his care with his little fucking radio in hand, his badge clipped to his belt, and called in an auto accident to Headquarters. As he stood behind the car that was resting against the telephone pole, the driver alighted from the vehicle carrying a beer can.

"Fuck me," Paul said to himself as the man approached. The man was smiling and exclaimed in a loud voice, "Officer, this is your lucky day!" The man stepped up to Paul and added, "I just killed my wife. She's in the car."

Paul hesitated a minute and then walked over to the car, keeping one eye on the man with the beer can. He glanced inside and sure enough there was a woman slumped on the floor of the front passenger seat. A check of vital signs revealed she was dead and still warm.

"I strangled her," the man confessed as he stepped up behind Paul. "I just got fuckin' fed up."

After he'd handcuffed the man, called for the coroner and the crime lab, Snowood had one question for the man with the beer can, "How'd you know I was Homicide?"

•

Paul Snowood was lucky. After the Exposition Boulevard Murder, Snowood was up for the next case. But he was off on the night the man was shot at Tulane and Carrollton. Paul was taking his pretty blond wife and kid who looked like Huck Finn, or was it Tom Sawyer, to the circus. So Mason got stuck with the dead man at the bus stop, which turned into a real fucking mystery. The dead man went unidentified for a week, until Mason dug up a frightened

**137**

teen-age girl at a halfway house who admitted the dead man was her father and that her ex-boyfriend had shot him. It took Mason a week to solve the case, a week of sixteen-hour shifts.

Snowood took less than one shift to complete the entire casework on the Telephone Pole Murder. And then he was no longer up for the next case. He was so fucking lucky. He had been in Homicide for two years and never caught a whodunit. He would always catch a suicide when he was up, or a misdemeanor murder, or a barroom killing, or someone would just walk up to him and say, "Officer, this is your lucky day!"

•

The FBI came up with a more detailed profile of the Slasher, Mason read it to us just prior to its release to the hungry media. He called Mark and Paul and I into his cubicle of an office and told us to pay attention as he read.

"He is an adult make between the ages of twenty and thirty. He is younger than forty because the urge to commit a brutal sex murder surfaces at an early age," Mason read as he kicked up his feet on his desk. There was a small hole in the bottom of his left penny-loafer. I looked down at my own shoes that were in dire need of a good shine and laughed at myself. Show me a detective with spotless shoes and I'll show you a detective who works in Burglary.

Mason continued, "He is a paranoid schizophrenic. He is probably a virgin who cannot sustain a lasting relationship with any woman. Since he is unable to have an interpersonal relationship with women in life, he will conquer them in death."

The usual smart-ass comments were conspicuously missing as our sergeant continued, "Statistics show the majority of such killers come from broken homes, and he probably lives alone now."

"Fuckin' where?" Mark interrupted.

"That's what *we* gotta find out," Mason responded, in a voice that was in no mood for joking. Before continuing, he glanced at each of us to show that he was serious. "Since none of the bodies were covered up or hidden in any way, the killer feels no remorse."

The picture of an unfeeling Jack the Ripper came to mind. The mother fucker didn't even feel bad about it.

"By leaving the bodies in exhibitionist poses in the open, it is unlikely the killer knew his victims."

That put the knock on my theory that the killer knew the girls, or was at least in some way connected to them.

"Except for the murders, no one knows he is alive," Mason read.

"What's that?" Mark asked, "a fuckin' challenge?"

"That's exactly what it is," Mason calmly replied. "It's a challenge for his real identity to surface and assert itself and maybe make itself known. It's the subtle approach. What do you expect from the FBI?"

There was no further comment, so Mason went on reading, "The chance that a man could commit a number of such murders in one area over many years without being caught is slim."

"Now, wait a minute," Mark interrupted, "are they trying to scare him out of town with that?"

"I don't know," Mason answered. "Maybe."

"At least he won't be our problem anymore," Paul commented.

"The fuck he won't," I argued. "I don't want him going anywhere. I wanna catch that Fuck-head. Period."

Mason waited for the ruckus to die down before concluding the profile with the usual FBI disclaimer that psychological profiles were subject to some error.

The media gobbled up the new psychological profile with a ravenous hunger and then spit it out at the public in bits and pieces. A barrage of stories spewed from the hallowed halls of the newspapers and television stations. They each took to the streets to educate the public about the frightened neighborhoods of New Orleans. And where they found no obvious fear, they instilled it, with stories of futile police efforts to apprehend the Slasher. The news media began to beat the drums of chaos. Competing one against the other for the latest scoop, they fanned the fires of fear that raged up and down the city streets.

The most curious reactions came from the television news anchors, who each in turn pleaded with the killer to give himself up, to the them. Each wanted to be the one to get him in. Maybe they planned to give him air time for a personal interview before reluctantly turning him over to the inept authorities.

And so it continued, with anchor persons pleading for a surrender, while street reporters popped up all over New Orleans with bad guesses about the Slasher's identity. One enterprising reporter went on television on three successive nights, speculating where the Slasher would strike next. This sandy-haired reporter with a northeastern accent would pop up on a certain street and declare that a computer study revealed that this particular street was 'highly likely' to be the location of the next murder, while terrified residents peeked out from behind venetian blinds.

What a fucking circus.

Not to be outdone by the media, the Task Force focused their efforts on blanketing the city streets with unmarked cars manned by eager, unmarked cops with fingers as itchy as mine were to blow the Fuck-head away.

Lt. Gironde contributed his own little two-step act by polygraphing and re-polygraphing his two prime suspects, the poor black fella I'd surfaced at Bayou St. John, and Cesar Rodrigues Corona, the husband of the second victim. I don't know what was more futile, the blondie reporter popping up on street corners declaring, "This is the next spot" or Lt. Gironde fucking with Corona and the mook, I'll bet the mook will never fuck a white woman near a murder scene again. The worst thing most fuckers can catch is VD when they fuck whores, but this fool caught a shitload of cops led by a lieutenant with a one-track mind.

Meanwhile, Cal Boudreaux came up with elaborate explanations about who did it. "I'll bet he's a cop," Boudreaux declared one afternoon while annoying us with his presence in the office.

Nobody answered him, but that never stopped Boudreaux. "I'll bet he's either a cop or a doctor. Jack the Ripper was a doctor."

I was about to remind Boudreaux that nobody knows who the fuck the Ripper was, but I knew better than to talk to him. The best thing to do with Boudreaux was ignore him.

"Could be a fireman," Boudreaux continued.

"They got nothing to do all day, unless there's a fire."

Mark had enough. He got up and moved toward Cal, roaring. "I'll bet you that no matter what he is, you'll never catch him because you couldn't catch syphilis in a fucking Bangkok whorehouse because you ain't got a dick. Your dickless mother fucker!" Mark was growling loud enough for the mayor to hear downtown. "Why don't you just get the fuck outta here and let real detectives work before I smash your fuckin' face in? Aren't you supposed to be with the Task Force, you needle-dick bug fucker!"

Boudreaux retreated until Mason stepped out and glared at them. Then Boudreaux added before leaving, "Well, I *was* going to tell you about my chief suspect, but not now."

"That boy has gotta go," Mark yelled. "Chief suspect, my ass! Who the fuck is he kidding? Who the fuck did he ever catch?"

Mason waited until Mark was finished before explaining that Boudreaux's suspect was a fifteen-year-old Hispanic boy who was recently arrested as a peeping Tom.

"He's fishing." Mason dismissed the theory with one sentence.

"He ain't fishing," Mark shouted. "He's out to fuckin' lunch!"

•

For a while my stomach felt better. Easting square meals helped. But it did not take long before the tension from the pressure cooker brought the knots back to twist even tighter. I felt tired all of the time, even after I woke up. I would sit in my bright white kitchen, pumping cup after cup of coffee-and-chicory inside but the caffeine did not good. I would leave, dragging ass to work.

I had trouble falling asleep. When I did drop off, it was a restless sleep filled with dreams in which I was banging around in the pressure cooker, stewing overnight with Dauphine Street and Bayou St. John and Exposition Boulevard running over and over in the recesses of my mind. At least I didn't dream of Harmony Street. I guess I had enough troubles so that Harmony didn't have to come a-haunting.

•

We caught another Homicide at a pool hall on Chef Menteur Highway, way the hell over in New Orleans East, halfway to fucking Mississippi. It was right before knocking off time again and Mason sent Mark and I across town. Mark was up for the next murder so he said nothing. He just piled into the car and sat brooding in the passenger seat as I drove over the High Rise Bridge across the lovely Industrial Canal.

I could hear Mark mumbling under his breath as I drove, but he never said anything audible. When we arrived at the scene, Mark jumped from the car and took out his Magnum as he stepped toward the bar.

"Whoa," I called out to him, "What do you need that for?" I could see a crowd of people standing outside the bar, all staring at us.

"Because if that fuckin' K-9 is here, I'm gonna shoot him," Mark growled, "and you write it up."

"Justifiable Homicide," I agreed.

"Fuckin' A!"

The Pool Hall Murder was just a typical barroom killing, a couple stupid white boys got pissed off at one another and one thing led to another and then one ended up dead. Paperwork, that was all it was, paperwork. Hours processing the crime scene, followed by the inevitable bloody autopsy, followed by a cursory search for the killer who took off and left town, followed by the inevitable arrest warrant and listing of the killer's name in the NCIC, the National Crime Information Center computer. He was on the lam, following in the proud footsteps of all those fellas who modeled themselves after Cagney and Bogart characters, only forgetting to remember that when the director said "cut," Bogie went home to Lauren Bacall and never worried about the real police.

•

Later Mark asked me, "How are you getting along with the Princess?"

"What?"

"The Louvier sister. I hear you been seeing her on the side. Am I right?" He asked as if he knew something secret about me.

"No, I haven't been seeing her at all."

"What about those nightly calls?"

"Business," I answered in a voice that even I didn't believe.

"Yeah. Well, I don't believe it for a minute. You better watch yourself, padna."

I looked at Mark's grizzly-bear face as he smiled at me from behind his moustache. "And what's that suppose to mean?" I asked.

"She's a princess who lives in a mansion and you're a peasant."

"That's it?"

"It sure is," Mark explained. "She comes from *society*, a debutante, one of those little rich girls who have breakfast at Brennan's, lunch at Galatorie's and dinner at Antoine's. You ever been to any of those places?"

"I've been to Antoine's" I answered.

"How many times?"

"Once."

"See what I mean?" Mark continued. "She's probably a regular, probably knows the waiters by name." Alfred, the waiter at Camellia Grill, came to mind as Mark went right on. "This girl grew up with maids and servants. How many servants did you have around your dad's house?"

I shook my head and laughed. "Go on," I urged him.

"The Louviers are the kind of people where the men grow up to be Mardi Gras Kings and the girls are all Princesses of Rex and Comus and all those Krewes that we gotta stand out and guard every goddamn year. They are probably typical, rich, uptown Tulane-Newcomb Jewish snobs."

"You know, Mark," I cut in, "You almost sounded same for a moment there, but *Louvier* is French, they're Catholic, Loyola Jesuit-Catholic."

"So I got the wrong religion," Mark chuckled. "But I'm telling you to watch out."

"Why are you suddenly interested in my social life?" I asked.

"'Cause you're my padna and you don't look so good lately since you broke up with Jack Blanc's daughter."

I took a long look at him and could see he meant every word he said. I hadn't realized he could read me so well. I hadn't realized a lot of things.

•

We caught another murder the next night. This one was black on black at the edge of the St. Thomas Housing Project. By the time we arrived, the scene looked like a mini Mardi Gras parade with screaming men and wailing women and kids all trying to get a view of the body sprawled out on the front stoop. It took over an hour just to clear away the people before we started in on the scene. At least the killer was nice enough to remain behind to turn himself in. The woman who had the murder weapons was also nice, she turned it over to us after she was finished using it to carve up spareribs in the kitchen.

It was a story worth re-telling. The killer's name was Alfred, no relation to Alfred of the Camellia Grill. Alfred had a woman named Paula who had a boyfriend named Lemoine. It seems that Alfred was passing up the street and spotted Paula talking to Lemoine out on Paula's front stoop. Alfred stopped walking and told Lemoine to leave. Lemoine refused. Alfred then told Lemoine to wait on the stoop while he went inside Paula's house. Apparently, Lemoine didn't have much sense, because he waited there on the stoop.

Meanwhile, Alfred walked back to the kitchen and asked Paula's sister if he cold use one of her butcher knives. The sister handed Alfred the largest butcher knife in the house, which she was using to crave up some ribs. She told him to bring it right back. Alfred said he would.

Ole Lemoine hadn't moved and still didn't move as Alfred stepped back out on the porch. Paula started giving Alfred a piece of her mind just as Alfred reached over and plunged the butcher knife into Lemoine's chest. Alfred pulled the knife out as Lemoine fell. Then Alfred returned the knife to Paula's sister as Paula ran off screaming down the street. The sister returned to cutting the ribs after she rinsed off the knife. She told me she had "no idea."

New Orleans, what a fucking city.

•

We finished with the Sparerib Butcher Knife Murder in time to meet at Café DuMonde for a couple relaxing cups of café au lait before knocking off. I told the story to Mason and Snowood, and even Mason laughed. Mark said he was pissed because Paula's sister didn't offer him any ribs.

As we sat joking at our tale, with our little fucking radios in front of us and the sounds of boat whistles from the Mississippi in the background, a tall back man approached us. He took a long look at us before asking Snowood, "Say, you the poleee?"

"No."

The fella looked as if he had brain damage to begin with and Snowood had to give him a trick answer. But the fella wasn't as ignorant as he looked. He figured we were lying so he stayed and waited until he gathered enough mind power to announce, "I gots a *hypocritical situation*."

Mark started laughing, which made the rest of us laugh. The black fella was patient and waited for the laughter to die down before continuing, "Wha' if a dude come home and finds anudda dude fuckin' his old lady, and wha' if da dude laughs and say he's been fuckin' my old lady for years, can I kill him?"

"Sure," Snowood answered.

"Well, good – dat's what I did," said the back fella as he handed a small caliber pistol to Snowood. Even the boat whistles wet silent.

It turned out that every fucking word was true. The black fella led us to his house, to the body. Mark refused to believe it, even *after* he saw the body.

Mason was beside himself. "I've never seen anything like this." Only Snowood seemed unfazed by it. Of course, he was no longer up for the next murder, again. As for me, I just don't understand how the fella knew we were in Homicide.

•

We were on a roll. We caught two suicides the following night. Mark took the first one. An old lady shot herself because the 'Monitors' were coming to get her. She put it in her suicide note. She was afraid they would take liberties with her so she sat on her toilet, placed her ex-husband's .45 caliber automatic under her chin and blew a huge hole out of the top of her head.

I caught the second suicide. A fifteen-year-old boy shot himself with his father's .38 caliber revolver. He left a brief note explaining that life wasn't worth living. I had to process that scene, in a house full of weeping women, two priests, and a father who looked as if he was about to blow his own brains out. I've never heard a man cry that hard before. It was pitiful.

•

We were on a roll. We went to so many goddamn autopsies, the pathologist was about to put us on the payroll. I watched again as the sharp razor knives lay open flesh in long smooth strokes, watched organs pulled out and dissected, watched faces pulled down to expose naked skulls, listened to the grinding of the skull-saw as mozzarella-cheese-brains were brought out for viewing, watched the inevitable tossing of the organs back into chest cavities and the sewing up with the thick black thread. It was truly pitiful.

As I stood there watching, I felt the pressure building around me. I felt myself stewing in the center of the relentless police pressure cooker. And there was nothing I could do to stop it.

*And the fucking Slasher was still out there.*

•

It was hot. Even at night, the heat would press against your face, filling your lungs with stifling humidity and turn neatly pressed clothes into wet rags. I was felling the heat crawling across my face as Mark drove us through the dark city streets on another haunted Friday night. I was staring out at the passing lights while Mark complained about our new twelve-hour shifts that were more like sixteen-hour shifts.

I tried to ignore him, but there was not ignoring Mark when he griped. After a while, when he didn't get an answer, he popped a good one on me, "Seen the Princess lately?"

I huffed and thought about not answering, but that would only make him try harder. "As a matter of fact, I haven't," I told him. I hadn't even called Lizette the last night. Made the mistake of telling Mark that.

"Suppose we go see what she's up to?" He swung our unit down Broadway toward St. Charles Avenue.

"Don't go over there," I told him.

"Why not?"

I rolled my eyes at him and just shook my head No. But that didn't stop him. It didn't even slow him down as he pulled up across from Loyola and parked the car. "I'm gonna take a walk down Exposition Boulevard," Mark goaded me. "Coming?"

"No," I answered. But before he disappeared up the boulevard, I stepped out and followed. The lights were on all over the Louvier mansion. As we approached I could see people standing on the gallery.

"Ain't that the Princess?" Mark asked as we got closer.

It was. Lizette was standing at the edge of a group of people dressed in formal evening wear. She was in a dark evening gown, her long hair straight and shiny beneath the bright porch light.

"I think she's with a hard-leg," Mark added as I stopped and turned around quickly to get the hell out of there.

"Hey," Mark called out to me loud enough to wake up the lions in the zoo, "where ya going?"

I got couple steps away when I heard her call out. I was going to pretend I didn't hear, but there was something in her voice that made me turn and walk back. She was at the gate of the wrought-iron fence by the time I arrived. Mark was leaning on the fence with a mischievous grin on his bear face.

"Hello," she said to me as I stepped up. Her perfume brushed across my face as those topaz eyes looked back at me. "You didn't call last night. Anything happen?"

"No," I answered. "We've been real busy. Case work, but nothing important. Nothing to tell you."

"Oh." She seemed relieved.

There was a moment of awkward silence that Mark quickly took advantage of. "We came by tonight because he wanted to ask you something."

I glared at him as Lizette asked me what it was. I looked away from those golden eyes. Out of the corner of my eye I spotted a tall blond fella on the gallery staring at us. He was inching toward the steps and looked as if he wasn't going to stop.

"He's kinda shy," Mark added. "You see he really wants to ask you out but he doesn't know how."

Lizette turned to Mark and almost smiled. "Dino is not shy and he knows exactly how to ask. And if you think you're going to *make* him ask with juvenile jokes, it won't work."

Mark threw his head back and roared, "Hey, I like her!"

She looked back at me and added, "I'm glad you came by. We've got some people over, can you stay a while?" She opened the gate for us to enter.

Just then the blond fella arrived, put an very friendly hand on Lizette's shoulder and smiled at me smugly. "Who are your friends, dear?" he asked Lizette.

"Take your hand off my shoulder, please," Lizette told blondie without looking at him.

When he hesitated a moment, Mark leaned over and growled, "Take your hand off her before I pull your arm outta its socket!"

The blond slowly removed his hand and stammered, "Lizette, who are these guys?"

"We're the police," Mark snapped. "We're her bodyguards, so why don't you go back inside and play?"

The blond hesitated until Lizette told him to, "Go ahead."

He walked off reluctantly as Mark called out behind him, "And don't touch her again, we'll be watching."

I had my hand and over my eyes so I couldn't see, but I could hear. Lizette reached over and removed my hand and smiled at me. "Why don't you come in?"

I shook my head and rolled my eyes in Mark's direction. "I can't take him anywhere."

"Come on," Mark urged me, "let's go in."

Lizette turned to Mark and added in a sweet voice, "I think maybe you should wait in the car." I didn't stop laughing until Mr. Louvier called for Lizette to come in. Before she stepped away, she had me promise to call her when I got off later.

"I like that girl," Mark told me on the way back to the car. "She's got a lotta class, too much class for the likes of us." I was feeling good until he started talking again. "She's awful pretty," he went on, "too pretty. Not only is she beautiful, but she's rich." He looked over at me and added, "What the fuck does she see in you?"

I didn't answer, but that didn't stop him from continuing in the car, "Girls who look like that can get anybody they want, get anything they want. What the fuck does she need you for? Why settle for a cop? What can you give her except low pay and miserable hours, pain and misery."

"I wish you wouldn't sugar-coat it," I replied.

"Just trying to save you some misery." When I didn't respond, he asked another goddamn question, "You wanna know why I'm tryin' to save you some misery?"

I didn't answer.

"I'll tell you why, because the girl's falling in love with you, my boy, it's written all over that pretty face, a fuckin' blind man could see it." He reached over and shook me by the shoulder. "So why can't you see it?"

I didn't answer.

"I'll tell you why, because you're falling for her. And that's bad. Go ahead and fuck her, but don't fall for her. A policeman in love is a sickening sight."

After a while I asked in disgust, "Is there anything else about me you wanna add?"

"Sure," he came right back, "I'll bet she looks gorgeous naked. Wonder how many times blondie's seen her like that?"

I kept my mouth shut after that. I wasn't about to open it because I knew I'd say something I'd regret later. I wonder why my partners always give me so much fucking misery?

When I called her, Lizette asked me to come by the next night. She sounded troubled.

"Are you OK?"

She just sighed. I started to apologize about Mark and me and she interrupted, said there was nothing to apologize for.

I got there at about nine o'clock the following evening. She was waiting on the gallery, on the swing, reading a book as an unusual, almost cool, summer breeze danced across the oaks of Audubon Park and found its way to the porch. She wore a white shirt, tied at the waist, and a denim miniskirt. Her legs were crossed as she leaned back in the double swing. She smiled as I let myself in the gate and approached.

"What are you reading?"

"Flannery O'Connor. Short stories." She shook her head, letting the breeze flow through her long hair.

I didn't mention the book I'd been reading. *The Complete Jack The Ripper* by Donald Rumbelow, the only former police officer who ever wrote a book about the case. Mason's wife bought three copies for us.

"It's so nice out tonight," she said as I stepped up on the gallery. I looked into her eyes and could see something was bothering her. She looked away as I leaned against one of the large columns. She started telling me how her little brother had retuned home from staying with relatives. Then she told me how much she loved the park when there was a breeze.

Before I could say anything, she changed the subject quickly and asked, "You've been busy?"

I nodded.

"Working on the case?"

"Between all the other cases," I answered.

"Others?"

"No more Slasher cases." I heard myself calling him Slasher again. "We've had some other cases."

"You have to handle other cases?" She asked.

"Oh, yes. New Orleans never runs out of murders." Right away, I wished I hadn't said that. Her eyes reacted as a child's eyes when someone says, "Boo!" I looked into those eyes and added, "But Lynette is the last thing I think about before I fall asleep and the first thing when I wake up."

She stared real hard at me. Those eye reached into mine and held them motionless for several minutes. Then she looked away again and I thought she was going to cry. She held on a moment before adding, "Last night was terrible."

"I'm sorry," I said automatically.

She looked back at me with red eyes, "Why are you apologizing?"

I shrugged. She looked away again, back out at the Audubon darkness. "I didn't want to go last night," she whispered, "but there were family obligations and I, " She choked off a sob. She swallowed hard and continued, "It's hard, sometimes, I just don't understand why everything goes on, as if nothing happened. It's all different now, only the city doesn't know it, the streetcars still run, everything still goes on and it shouldn't." She looked up at me with pleading eyes. "It's all different now." She looked away quickly as the tears started down her face.

I wanted to say something profound, something about how the city doesn't give a damn, about how New Orleans is truly the City That Care Forgot, but there was nothing profound in me to say. I knew exactly how she felt. So I told her that. I stood there leaning against the column and told her how I knew. I told her how my brother was murdered and all the hard times that followed and how it's never really the same.

"But the city doesn't change one bit. It stays the same, like nothing happened. It doesn't care."

She went inside for some Kleenex and left me for a moment. I stared out at the dark park as a sound echoed in the breeze. It was a distant roar of a hungry animal. Lizette came out with her face free of tears and redness and said, "Sit down." I sat next to her on the double swing as the roar echoed again.

"They're feeding the lions," she said.

"That's was no lion," I argued. "That was King Kong."

"What?"

"When I was a little boy, my brother Joe told me that Kind Kong lived behind the levee next to the Audubon Zoo and sometimes at night you could hear him roar. That was King Kong," I nodded in the general direction of the zoo.

"Oh," she said with a hint of a smile on her face.

"He also told me about the vampires of the Canal Cemeteries and the werewolves of City Park."

"Werewolves?"

"Yeah." I laughed. "I was a real scaredy-cat when I was a kid."

"No wonder."

City Park and Audubon Park, Mid City and Uptown, across town and as different as day and night.

Lizette Marie Louvier was of the old Louviers who once lived in French Creole splendor on Esplanade Avenue long before the coming of the Yankees. The true Louisiana French Creole possessed a native instinct that told them Louisiana was theirs and all the rest of us were foreigners. They possessed a certain manner, a natural grace. They did not think themselves better than everyone else, they just knew they were special, unique in a land that was daily becoming more common. French Creoles were a faint nobility whose daughters possessed the sweet gentleness of slow-moving southern belles with a hint of New Orleans gaiety.

New Orleans has always been a French Creole city, even when ruled by the Spanish or dominated by the Americans. That is why New Orleans, once the largest city in the south, yielded its dominant positions to the likes of Atlanta, Money-Hungry Dallas and Boom-Town Houston. New Orleans cared not to compete, cared not to become a giant, cared not to change. The City That Care Forgot is possessed by a Creole spirit, to live life to its fullest and to hell with sacrifice and change and progress. It is the Big Easy City. Fuck the gross national product.

LaStanza is a common name in Sicily. My ancestors were dirt-poor farmers who left home for the American Dream. My grandfather actually arrived in New Orleans on a banana boat. My mother's family changed their last name twice to hide from the Mafia.

LaStanzas possess no grace or charm. No LaStanza has ever attended any college anywhere. None has ever stood out among other men. We are just common. In the old country we weren't even good farmers. The LaStanzas weren't even good enough to join the Mafia. In America we became fruit peddlers until my father became a policeman. If we had a family crest it would have a banana on it.

Now, you may think that none of this matters because we are all Americans now, all equal in the land of equality. But you don't know New Orleans.

Have you ever wanted something so badly it actually hurt? Have you ever seen a girl, maybe in passing, that wiped you away, a girl you wanted to know more than anything? I wanted Lizette because she was beautiful, because she was special, because she was so far above me. It was not that Lizette was unavailable as much as she was unattainable. And that made me want her more.

And so we sat there on the swing as King Kong roared in the background. I wanted to reach over and touch her, to reach over and kiss her but it was another moment lost, and I just sat there and listened as she told me how Exposition Boulevard got its name. "It was built as a walkway," she said, "a promenade for the Louisiana Cotton Exposition held in Audubon Park in 1884. Sometimes I can imagine what it was like," she went on, "ladies dressed up in long gowns, walking under parasols, escorted by mustachioed gentlemen with slick black hair."

The 1880's brought a different vision to my mind, the vision of Jack the Ripper in London's East End, Whitechapel, Spitalfields, 1888.

•

It took me a while but I found an eyewitness to the Exposition Boulevard Murder. She was a Loyola student. When she answered her front door that night I came knocking, she looked at me as if she'd seen a ghost.

"Are you Bonnie Carson?" I asked.

She nodded.

"I'm Detective LaStanza," I told her as I presented my credentials. "New Orleans Police, Homicide."

She nodded again and let me in. She was terrified.

•

I found her name among the countless names on the lists I got from the university. I had to get search warrants in order to secure the names of all the students and employees of Loyola and Tulane Universities. I didn't use a subpoena because the universities would have turned it over to their lawyers and there would have been hearings and all that legal crap before I got the lists. Mason tipped me off and helped me draw up the search warrants.

Then we just waltzed in and took the lists from uncooperative administrators who were more interested in protecting their school's reputations than in butchered women. I secured the names of all present students and employees and former students and employees for the past five years. It took me two days to get the lists.

"I got every name," I told Mason, "from the honor graduates to the fuckin' janitors."

"Now what are you gonna do with it?"

"Knock on doors." Because you never knew.

•

I found Bonnie Carson's name among the Loyola students who had class on the night of Lynette's murder. She lived in a small house in Gentilly Woods with her parents. She was a freshman at Loyola, a sixteen-year-old whiz kid who wore thick spectacles and braces.

After she let me in, she led me into the living room, sat down and stared at me with frightened eyes. I started slowly, asking about her night classes and then about *the* night. I retraced her steps through class and after class until she broke down. I turned on my tape recorder when she cried, "I saw him."

Bonnie's parents came in when the crying started and it took a while to get back on track, but later we all sat together as Bonnie told us her story in bits and pieces. I felt like a dentist pulling teeth.

Bonnie left class a little late that evening because she stayed behind to talk to her professor. When she arrived at the streetcar stop on St. Charles Avenue directly across from Loyola, no one was there. She waited alone for about ten minutes until the streetcar arrived.

"While I was waiting, I looked over at the park," she said through trembling lips

"Any particular reason?" I asked.

"No. Well, I don't know. I just looked over and saw him."

It took another five minutes to get it out of her. She saw a man running hunched-over away from the shelter. He ran parallel to St. Charles Avenue, away from Exposition Boulevard. Bonnie only saw him for a few moments as he ducked behind a tree and then disappeared in the Audubon darkness. She never saw his face. But she described him as a white male with dark hair, height uncertain because he was hunched over, but he was neither very tall or very small. He was 'heavyset', wore dark clothing and carried something white or shiny in his right hand. Bonnie thought it was a knife. I thought it may have been a brassiere.

The hunched man did not look around as he ran, he just crouched down and ran straight-away across the park. "I know it was him," she cried. "I know it." she looked at me with pleading eyes, "Will my name be in the newspaper now? Will he know I told you?"

"No way," I assured her. "Your identity is safe."

"But how can you protect me?"

I looked at her parents. "By not telling anybody," I answered. "You didn't see his face, so you can't testify in court or go to any line-ups. Nobody has to know about you."

"Then why bother to take any of this down?" Mr. Carson asked.

"Because Bonnie has helped us a great deal," I answered. "We know a lot more now. We know he's a white boy with dark hair, medium height, heavyset and probably right-handed."

I asked Bonnie some more questions, in case I missed anything, but I hadn't. I was sure she had seen the killer. The time was right for it to be our boy. And since he didn't seem to have seen her, I told her she was safe – but I could see she didn't believe me.

•

Mason was ecstatic.

"Damn that's good," he told me after listening to Bonnie's statement. "Don't worry about her name," he added. "I won't give it to *anybody* until after we catch the bastard." Mason handled the lead. He wrote a daily to the Task Force explaining that "highly reliable information" revealed our killer was "a white male with dark hair, medium height, heavyset and possibly right-handed."

I left Mason at the Bureau as he was typing the daily, and drove straight to Lizette's. When I told her, she became vey excited. "How did you find her?"

"Knocking on doors," I answered.

Lizette's little brother came down the stairs and walked up behind us as we stood in the foyer. He wrapped his arms around Lizette's waist. She hugged him back and said, "Come on in the dining room. I've just made some fresh coffee. You've got to tell me all about it."

When she stepped into the kitchen, she left her brother alone with me. He told me his name was Alexander Louvier III. It was quite a name for such a frail-looking boy of eight. "Are you one of the policeman who came that night?" he asked me.

I knew which night he meant all right, so I nodded.

"Are you a detective?"

I nodded again.

"Where's your gun?"

"On my ankle," I answered.

His eyes lit up as he stepped over to me. "Show me," he urged. I leaned down, pulled up my trouser leg and showed him my revolver in its black ankle-holster.

"Wow!" Can I see it?"

Thankfully, Lizette entered, and after some urging by Alexander III and some assurance from me that I would make it safe, she agreed. So I unloaded my stainless steel .357 Magnum and handed it to the curious boy.

"Wow!"

"Never point it at anyone, even if it's unloaded." I told him. He was too afraid to pick it up anyway. He just touched it.

Between answering Alexander's questions about the revolver, I managed to explain to Lizette about our eyewitness.

"Did you ever shoot anybody?" Alexander asked me.

"Ss a matter of fact I have, unfortunately."

"Wow! How'd it happen?"

Both were silent as I explained about the Mardi Gras Day years ago when a cop was killed at Lee Circle and about the man I had to shoot in the alley.

"He didn't give me a choice. It was either him or me," I explained as I looked away. A vision of Harmony Street crossed my mind. I quickly ran that vision away. I wouldn't even touch that story. In fact, I shouldn't have said anything about Lee Circle. As I sat there, I wondered what Lizette thought of me.

"Wow! Real life shoot-em-up!" Alexander exclaimed. "Tell me more."

"Now, Alex," Lizette cut in, "that's enough for now."

I looked over at Lizette's pouting lips and smiled. She smiled back. She was wearing a ponytail that night and another nice miniskirt. She looked great. During my second cup I heard Mason calling me on my LFR. I picked up my radio and answered, "Go ahead."

"Meet me at the Sixth District Station," Mason said.

"Ten-four," I responded.

Mason came right back, "You got your vest with you?"

"Ten-four. Am I gonna need it?"

"Ten-four. We're running papers in the Calliope." Mason answered.

"Ten-four."

I looked at Lizette and said, "I've got to go now." I loaded my weapon and put it back on my ankle before rising slowly.

"What did all that mean?" Alex asked as he pointed to my LFR.

"It means we're going to serve warrants in the Calliope Projects."

"Warrants?" he asked.

"Search warrants, arrest warrants." I explained.

Lizette moved next to me with a concerned look in her eyes, "What did he mean by your vest?"

"My bulletproof vest," I explained. "I keep it in my trunk. Put it on when we have warrants or have to go into the projects or places like that."

Lizette's eyes narrowed as she looked at me.

"Are you gonna shoot-em-up?" Alex asked excitedly.

"Naw." I laughed.

Lizette stepped even closer and asked, "Is it dangerous?"

"Not really. More cops get hurt handling family fights than search warrants. Anyway," I went on, "the Calliope's my old stomping ground."

"What?"

"I used to work in the Sixth District. I used to go in to the projects every night. No big deal. Really." I didn't mean it to sound cool, but it did.

"Bye," Alex called out to me as he ascended the stairs. "Will you tell me all about it next time?"

I nodded and turned to leave. Lizette hesitated before opening the front door. "Call me when you're finished," she said.

"Oh, it'll be too late," I told her. "We won't finish until three, four o'clock in the morning."

"Call me anyway."

There was a moment of silence between Lizette and me at the doorway. Her face was very close to mine and I wanted to just reach over and kiss her, but I let the moment slip away and all I could do was say, "All right."

As I started across the gallery I didn't hear the door close behind me, so I stopped, turned around and walked back. I reached in and put my hand on the back of her neck and pulled her to me. She came forward, her eyes flickering shut. I kissed those soft, pouting lips as they parted like the petals of a flower. It was a long, warm kiss. And when it ended, when I started to step away, Lizette leaned forward and kissed me again.

"Call me when you're finished," she whispered.

"Absolutely."

•

I was feeling *great* by the time I stepped into the Sixth District.

"What are you ginning about?" Mason asked.

"I just love the Calliope Projects," I answered.

Snowood spit in his cup and exclaimed, "This boy's got a problem."

Mark stepped up and tapped me on the shoulder.

"That's good work on the witness, padna." He grinned.

"Okay." Mason announced as he passed out the papers. "Here's where we're going."

I took one look at the address and started laughing. "I know this place," I announced. "I handled something there as a rookie. Girl got her cat stolen there."

"What?" Snowood asked.

"She got raped there."

"Oh."

•

He crept from his apartment long after midnight on a hot, muggy night. He slid behind the wheel of his car and drove away from Urquhart Street, across town. He was searching. His breathing was heavy and rapid as the seething grew within him. He rubbed his crotch with his free hand as he drove in no particular direction.

He found himself on Magazine Street heading toward Audubon Park. He wanted no more of the park so he slowed down to turn off Magazine when he spotted a girl. She had blond hair and was dressed in a dark wraparound dress that opened up in front as she walked, revealing the length of her legs almost to her panties. "The cunt," he said aloud as he watched her get into a small red car.

As he drove past, he got a good look at her and she was very pretty. She reminded him of the girls who waited on tables at the restaurants where he used to work as a janitor. She was a typical good-looking bitch who knew it and flaunted it and gave it only to good-looking guys. The cunt.

He followed her as she drove down Magazine to Jefferson Avenue where she took a right and headed up the four-lane avenue with its narrow, neutral ground. Past St. Charles Avenue, he followed her, his heart racing, his eyes leering into the dark car ahead, at the long yellow hair of the girl as she drove, oblivious to his presence. He was invisible to her right now because he still looked like Jerome, but she would see him soon. Later, she would see him and feel his power. She probably thought she was too good for him, thought she was beyond his reach – well, he would reach her and fuck her up good.

He stalked her as she drove up Jefferson Avenue. As the cars approached Claiborne Avenue, he saw something on the neutral ground ahead. It was another blonde with long hair, standing in a silver gown. And there was a photographer there too, flashing pictures of the girl as the cars passed. It made him even angrier to see that blond hair and the camera flashing, the gorgeous girl, the blond hair, just like the girl he was following. Fucking cunts.

He hated them so much now. He felt the tightening in his chest increase as the car in front turned right on a narrow, winding side street. The red car pulled up in the small driveway of a big house at the first corner. He hurried past, turned the block and jumped out of his car. He hid behind a large tree at the corner as the blonde in the wraparound dress walked to a side door and fumbled in her purse for her keys. He glanced around and there was no one looking, so he moved from behind the tree and tiptoed up behind her, his heart pounding so hard he thought she would hear it.

When she unlocked the door and started to open it, he pounced, shoved her inside and followed her in, stood over her with the long-bladed knife in his hand. She looked up at him as he smiled at her. She didn't look so pretty now. She looked scared, and he loved it. He felt a familiar rage rising in his throat as he moved toward her. She crawled back like a frightened kitten, back into her bedroom where she suddenly jumped up on the bed and reached across for, the telephone.

He plunged the knife in to her back as hard as he could and had trouble pulling it out. She made a gurgling sound as he turned her over on her back and began sticking her again and again. Her eyes were closed, as if she could shut him out, but he fucked her again and again.

There was no scream. She just squealed like a pig. And when she stopped squealing, he stopped plunging. He looked at her for a while before returning to her front door. He closed it and locked it. Then he went back to work on her. He took the point of the knife, stuck it in her cheek and started to slice up her face. The cunt.

•

I was sitting at my desk, going over my notes and trying not to think about Lizette's full lips and small round hips, when Mason stepped out of his cubicle. He walked up to me and tapped me on the shoulder as he passed, "Lets go." There was a look on his face that I never wanted to see again. That look told it all. I bowed my head and slowly put my notes away. I grabbed a fresh notepad as Mason called Mark and Snowood on the radio.

"Drive," was all he said to me until we were on Claiborne Avenue. He lit a cigarette and stared straight ahead with icy eyes. "This one's real bad," he began. "Found her in her own bedroom. Jesus fuckin' Christ!"

"Where?" I asked.

"Cucullu Street, 5100 block."

"That's off Jefferson Avenue," I said. It was in the Second District again, like Exposition Boulevard. Only I felt this would be a far worse scene because it was one o'clock in the afternoon, broad daylight. A million people would be there.

I was wrong and glad to be wrong. There was a shit-load of Second District and Sixth District patrolmen there all aright, but they had the entire area roped off in a two-block radius. Even Jefferson Avenue was blocked off. We had to park on Claiborne and hike two blocks down to Cucullu Street, where a Second District patrolman let us through the line.

My old partner Stan-The-Man of the lovely Sixth District was standing in the street in front of the victim's house. He looked like he was about to vomit. He had nothing to say as Mason and I stepped up. I've never known him to *ever* be at a loss for words. He just pointed to a Second District sergeant standing near the corner of Cucullu and Soniat Street.

Mason asked the questions. I took notes. The victim lived in a house at the corned of Cucullu and Soniat, a two-story brownstone double house, half-hidden from view by two huge oak trees in the front yard, trees so large that Cucullu Street twisted in a winding curve around them. There were two front doors to the house. A large double door faced Cucullu, where the owners of the house lived. A second, smaller door, recessed on the Soniat Street side, opened into a small downstairs apartment where our victim lived. The house was owned by Mr. and Mrs. Donald Cotton, an elderly couple who were waiting upstairs for us to come up.

According to the Second District sergeant, "We spoke to them briefly. They claim they didn't hear anything or see anything." Before walking up to the house, we waited a couple minutes for Snowood and Mark to arrive. We were starting for the side door when the sergeant said, "No, we haven't been inside yet. This way." He led us to a side window that faced Soniat Street. "In there," he said and signaled for us to take a look in the window.

Mason stepped up first, looked inside and became very still for a full five minutes. Then he backed away without a word, signaling for me to step up net. I noticed right away that the window was still locked as I leaned close to peer inside. It took a second for my eyes to adjust to the light, for that hideous scene to take shape in front of me. It was the most gruesome sight I've ever seen.

It was a bedroom, a bedroom covered in red, streaks of bloody red on the walls and dresser and tables and all over the floor. There was a bed in the center of the room and a body on it, or the remains of a body. She lay on her back, spread eagle, her legs slashed to the bone. Her torso was now a empty cavity with its organs removed. I could see her liver and kidneys on one of the end tables. Her heart and lungs lay on the other end table. Ribbons of intestines stretched from the bed across the floor.

My stomach flip-flopped and I felt the knot inside twist again. I closed my eyes a second, but it was all still there when I looked back.

Her head was propped up on a bloody pillow, her long blond hair pulled back, streaked with blood. Her face had been sliced away to leave a red skull staring directly at the window. Her eye lids had been cut away, white eyeballs protruded from the red skull, leering right at me. I don't think I'll ever forget that face.

My stomach twisted again, sending a deep pain through my gut as I stepped away from the window to let Snowood have his turn.

•

The victim of the Cucullu Street Murder was Carolina Essex. She had been a white female, twenty-five years old, who lived on Cucullu Street for six months, renting from the Cottons. When she was still young and beautiful, she worked at the Apple Vase Restaurant on Magazine Street as maître de'.

Caroline did not show up for work that day. Just before lunch time, a girl friend went by her apartment. Seeing Carolina's car in the driveway, the girl friend knocked on her door. When there was no answer to her repeated knocking, the friend went over to tap on Carolina's bedroom window. Then she looked inside.

•

On the day Snowood's luck ran out he was the only New Orleans policeman allowed in the Essex apartment while the FBI processed the scene. He had finally caught a whodunit. As he stepped into the apartment, he looked as disgusted as I felt. Mason sent Mark and I out to canvass the neighborhood while he went to talk to the Cottons upstairs.

I felt so lousy. We *all* felt lousy. The press was right all along. We were incompetent. Each one of us was Detective Useless. This all had to stop now. No matter what, this all had to stop before the mother fucker killed every woman in the goddamn city.

The canvass produced nothing. So I took it upon myself to write down the license numbers. It wasn't long before I found myself by the press line on Soniat Street.

"Officer! Officer!" several reporters called out to me.

"We saw you looking inside the window, what did it look like?"

I found myself staring into two large camera lenses. I just stared for a minute before saying, "A nightmare. It's the worst thing I've ever seen." I started to step away and added – while still looking into the cameras, probably into the houses of everyone in the goddamn city – "There won't be any need for an autopsy. He sliced her to pieces."

"Officer, what's your name?" came the shouts. "Who are you? Are you Homicide?"

I nodded to the last question as I walked back behind the safety of the police line. I asked a couple uniformed men to finish with the license numbers as I walked back to Cucullu Street. I should have kept my mouth shut. But I figured the people *should* know just how bad we fucked up. It was like going to confession, I guess. Looking for an absolution that would never come.

Snowood came out a while later, just before sunset. He had slipped on the bloody floor of the bedroom, fell ass-first in the gore.

"They really know what they're fuckin' doing," Snowood said of the FBI lab as he tried to clean up before rushing back inside.

The rest of us waited outside like useless detectives as the FBI spent hours collecting minute fiber evidence before cutting away floorboards that bore the killers bloody footprints. Then they took blood samples and scraped her fingernails before taking her fingerprints for comparison with any other prints found. They dusted the usual places for prints – smooth surfaces like glass and metal doorknobs – then sprayed the entire apartment with Dura-Print spray, a radical new process which could surface a fingerprint anywhere, including finger prints on human skin. The monster had to have touched her. Meanwhile, Mark and I found traces of blood in the grass outside, near Soniat Street, leading us to believe that our killer had parked there.

At seven o'clock in the morning, I watched the coroner's meat wagon take the body away. I stood out in the middle of Soniat Street and watched the wagon as it passed through the police line up Soniat. Then I turned around and looked down the block, in the directions of a cemetery about seven blocks away where Lynette Anne Louvier was entombed beneath a statue of Jesus. I tell you, the pressure was unrelenting in the Homicide Pressure Cooker.

Mason and I walked toward my car in silence, until we approached the police line on Jefferson Avenue where someone shouted out to me, "Detective LaStanza! Detective LaStanza!" It was one of the reporters who had been on Soniat Street earlier.

"You still here?" I asked as the lens moved in front of me.

"Yes sir, Detective. I understand you're the detective in charge of the Exposition Boulevard Murder, is that true?"

I looked at Mason who shrugged and said, "What the hell, go ahead."

I looked back at the camera and said, "I'm the case officer."

"Tell me Detective LaStanza, how do you feel about this latest murder?"

I didn't look at the reporter. I looked into the lens. "Terrible, I feel terrible."

"Do you feel that maybe it could have been prevented by better police work?"

I glanced at the reporter's narrow eyes. "Do you mean," I asked, "could it have been prevented if I was a better cop?"

"Could it have?"

I looked back at the lens. "I don't know," I said. "I wish I was a better detective. I'd give anything to catch this bastard. *Anything!*" I found my voice starting to crack.

"Do you have any leads at all?"

I shook my head.

"Do you have anything to tell the women of New Orleans who aren't safe even in their own homes?" he asked me.

I didn't know what to say. I thought about Lizette and Jessica and my mother and about those eyes staring at me from the bedroom on Cucullu Street. I didn't know what to say.

The reporter wasn't about to let me get away with not answering. He had another question ready, "How many more will have to die before you catch the Slasher?"

I bowed my head a moment, then looked back into the lens for a long time before Mason tugged at my elbow and led me away. The reporter tried to follower, unsuccessfully, as Mason and I walked up Jefferson Avenue. God, I wish I'd had an answer for that reporter. I wish I could have said something wise or even something sarcastic. But there was nothing I could say. There was nothing sarcastic left to be said.

Cucullu Street was the only crime scene I've ever been at where not a single joke was cracked.

## Chapter 8
## Urquhart Street

I am a grim reaper. I live in death. I am a professional witness to the agony of man. I am there when death comes suddenly, violently. I have seen all there is to be seen of death and yet there is always more. I have seen pools of dark blood at my feet, the life blood of someone who used to talk and live, just like me. I have witnessed enough autopsies, seen enough dismembering, to last ten lifetimes, and yet there is always more.

It is gruesome. It is terrible. It is my life. And it is the only thing in life that is inevitable.

I am like a vulture, waiting for someone to die. I am an avenging Angel of Death, waiting to be called to gather my weapons and hunt down a killer.

I live in death, I work long, long hours, but not for society, not for glory or rewards, not even for myself. I do it because it is the most important thing I will ever do.

I am a grim reaper. I live in death.

•

After leaving the scene on Cucullu Street, I went home and collapsed. I didn't wake up until that evening when Mark called me. "Sorry to wake you," he said in a voice that sounded as tired as I felt. "I guess you haven't heard the news."

"Do I wanna fuckin' hear it?"

Mark chuckled and added, "Come on now, wake up. The FBI lab found a Negroid hair on the Cuculla body."

"What?" I sat up and rubbed my eyes. "What was that about a Negro?"

"The FBI lab found a Negroid hair on the body," Mark repeated. "The Task Force has gone bananas and you've got three messages from the Princess."

"Where are you?"

"At the office, Sleepy-head. You coming to work?"

"No. I quit."

Mark laughed. "You quit? And let him get away with it?"

"Okay, I don't quit."

"Well, you don't have to come to work," he said, "At least not until tomorrow. Mason called a meeting for seven in the morning. Got it?"

"Yeah."

"So why don't you call the Princess? And let me know what she says. Okay Lover Boy?"

He was being cute again. Grizzly bears should never try to be cute.

"What the fuck you doing at the office?" I asked.

"I couldn't sleep," he answered. "you should see this place, Task Forces bouncing off the walls. They got it all figured out. It's a *Neegro*." He started laughing again, voice raspy from exhaustion.

"Where did they find the hair?"

"On the body. They had it analyzed and it was Negroid."

I thought about it a minute before muttering, "Maybe she had a black boyfriend."

"Maybe, but not anymore."

"Yeah, whatever, but or killer *sure* ain't black." I argued.

"I know that. And you know that. But you should see ole Gironde up here. He's got that mook you fond at Bayou St. John and he's sitting on him, real hard."

"Fuck! That fella's got nothing to do with it."

"I know that, too," Mark cut in. "He's just a typical black guy in the wrong place at the wrong time."

"Fuck, I'm calling the NAACP," I said.

"They're closed," Mark came right back. "It's ten at night."

"Then I'll call them in the morning. I'm serious. God, I wish I'd have run that guy up the street that night."

"When did you start feeling sorry for mooks?" Mark asked. "Anyway, don't worry. They ain't torturing him. The FBI's up here."

That didn't make me feel any better. "Well, get off the line so I can call Lizette."

"Let me know what she says in the morning, especially if it's nasty," he ordered. I hung up and dialed her number.

She answered after the first ring and sounded shook up. "I'm scared," she said.

"I know."

"I saw you on television. I didn't mean to call so many times, but I wanted to talk to you."

"I'm sorry I didn't call you," I told her. "It was just –" I gave her my home number right away. I don't know why I hadn't before.

"Tell me about it," she said. "Tell me about everything. I want to know." The fear was back in her voice again, that same shaky fear that had gripped her voice those first few days after Lynette's murder.

"Is it true, what you said on television, about her being cut up?"

"Yeah." I sighed and then slowly told her some of it. When I tapered off at the end, she asked me if I could come by the next night.

"I'll try." God, I felt terrible.

"Not tonight," she said. "My father has a board of director's meeting in the library and the place is full of wives too."

"Can we just talk?"

"Yeah."

We did but not about murder. She changed the subject right away, asked me what was my favorite type of music, my favorite books, my favorite movie.

"*The Godfather* movies. One and Two. It's one story." I said.

Hers was *To Kill a Mockingbird*. We talked about both movies for almost an hour. I think. Heroes Atticus Finch and Michael Corelone and Fredo and Sonny and Boo Radley and Tom Robinson.

She liked *The Godfather* as well because it was a period piece and wasn't really about the Mafia. Right. It was about family, fathers and sons, about brothers.

"Tom reminds me of Apollonia," Lizette said.

"Innocent," I said. "Caught up in death."

"Exactly." Then she asked if I'd seen *Ordinary People* and *On Golden Pond*.

I hadn't. Didn't want to tell her Jessica wanted to see both but I missed them. She went with friends.

"I saw *Raging Bull* but the best movie I saw in a while was *Atlantic City*," I said.

She hadn't seen that one, so I told her about Burt Lancaster and a radiant Susan Sarandon.

"The woman from *Pretty Baby*. Did you see it?"

"No." I'd heard about it, of course. Filmed in the city.

"Susan Sarandon has a topless scene," Lizette says. "Her boobs are," Lizette paused, then added, "Pretty magnificent."

"You're a connoisseur of boobs." I couldn't believe I'd just said that.

"I am actually. Mine are pretty spectacular, for such a small girl."

I liked the way this was going. It was then I realized I hadn't noticed Lynette's breasts, identical twin, except for the bite mark. They were no longer breasts to me, to any of us in the autopsy room. I envisioned Lizette instead.

"I'm a leg man," I heard myself say.

"My legs are even better than my boobs. You ought to see me in a miniskirt."

I sat up on the sofa now, more awake than I'd been in a while.

"I have seen you in a miniskirt."

"Those were just short skirts." Her voice dropped an octave. "I'm talking about a *mini*skirt. My legs in stockings. I've caused a few men to walk into things."

I laughed and she laughed lightly and it sounded so damn nice.

•

Our meeting was low key. Mark and I and Snowood crowded into Mason's office with Mason's ever present cigarette smoke, and listened to our sergeant as he filled us in on the fallout from Cucullu Street.

Picture a city clutched in fear. Picture a city possessed by a primal fear of the dark, a fear of an unknown heinous killer of women. Picture, if you can, the sheer terror that grabbed New Orleans by the throat after Cucullu Street. And then picture a vulture atop a star-and-crescent badge and you will picture me.

After going over the 'Negroid hair' lead, Mason told us they found semen in her vagina.

"How'd they find it?" Mark asked.

"With a swab."

**168**

"Not the semen," Mark growled. "how'd they find her vagina?"

Mason went on without comment. "The FBI got some good fingerprints that don't match the victim. The Task Force is running down her associates to compare prints. They're also running the prints through the magic FBI computers, but you know how effective that's gonna be."

Fingerprints are only good if you have someone else's to compare them to. You can't take a print and just pull a name out of a hat or a computer. But the FBI tried. Maybe our boy had a criminal record. But if our killer had never been fingerprinted, then the FBI could search their computers until doomsday and come up with nothing. But you never knew until you check.

"What about a bite mark? I asked.

"Her breasts were sliced off," Snowood told me.

Mason added, "They both had bite marks on them."

"Son of a bitch."

"So," Mark added, "what's our game plan?"

Mason blew out a gust of smoke before he spoke. "Paul's the case officer."

As he looked at his note, Snowood spit a wad of brown shit into the coffee cup he held in his right hand. "I'm gonna handle following up on her associates and boyfriends." He spit again before continuing, "I'm gonna need some help on a real thorough canvass."

"You got it."

•

I sat at my desk later with another strong cup of coffee and went over my notes from Exposition Boulevard again. I still had plenty to do with my lists of students and employees and license plate numbers. I took out the license numbers from Cucullu Street, grabbed my cup of coffee and moved over to the computer where I started running registrations.

An hour later, Mason came over and told me I had a phone call.

I picked up the phone next to the computer and answered, "LaStanza."

"Hi," she said. "I saw you on TV."

"Yeah?"

"You looked tired."

"I am tired," I sais as I leaned back in the chair.

"You want to come over tonight? I'm fixing lasagna."

"I can't," I answered. I closed my eyes and thought about Jessica's face as she spoke to me.

"You've got to eat."

"Not tonight," I answered.

"Oh. Well, I just want to see you. Lasagna's just an excuse."

"You home?" I asked.

"Of course."

"I'll call you right back. Okay?"

"Okay," she said.

I hung up and called Lizette, asked her if it was all right if I came by late. It was. Then I called Jessica right back and asked if I could come by early. It was. Then I leaned back again in the chair, closed my eyes and thought about what I'd just done.

I was losing it. Losing my fucking mind. Then again, maybe not.

•

The knot in my stomach gave me a good kick as I stepped up to Jessica's front door at six o'clock. I felt jittery as I waited for her to answer my knock. When she answered, she stepped forward and kissed me long and hard, then grabbed my hand and brought me inside for another kiss. "I've missed you," she sighed.

I didn't say anything. I wondered if my face looked as confused as I felt. She didn't seem to notice, or refused to acknowledge it. Her sharp green eyes looked at me, at my face, but avoided looking into my eyes. She held on to my hand as she led me into the dining room.

"Now just sit here," she said as she pulled out a chair for me at the table. I sat and watched her flutter back and forth, refusing any help, until the entire meal lay like a feast before me.

I dug in because it smelled wonderful.

Jessica was bubbly. I'd never know her to be bubbly before. She spoke as if nothing had happened between us, as if all those empty lost nights had never been, as if we were as we were before I went to Homicide. She talked of silly things, of new outfits and a book she'd been reading by a New Orleans writer called Effington or Effinger, about a lost planet in another galaxy. Then she spoke of herself – not of what she felt or thought – but about what she had been doing lately. She had been spending time with her girlfriends.

"Have you been hanging out with the boys?" she asked as she removed my empty salad plate and spooned up a heaping portion of lasagna for me.

"No," I answered.

"Been seeing any girls?" she asked in a voice an octave lower, her eyes riveted on the lasagna.

"A couple of butchered ones," I muttered as I took a bite of the very red lasagna.

"Any live ones?" she asked as she sat back down across from me and, for the first time, looked right into my eyes.

I couldn't stop the smile from creeping across my face.

"So that's it," I said. "Who told you?"

"I heard it. Cops talk, you know," she answered coyly.

It wasn't hard to figure, her father was a retired sergeant who spent more time at Headquarters since he retired than he ever did when he was working. I shook my head and sent some more lasagna to my confused stomach. The silence was deafening and lasted for several bites, until she finally said, "I've made a mistake, Dino."

"I know," I said coldly, surprised at just how cold it sounded.

He bottom lip began to tremble as I shut my eyes for a second and wished I could just dematerialize. I knew what was coming. I should have seen it. But being a dumb Wop, I walked right into it.

"I can't believe you've found someone else," she blurted out as the tears started.

What the fuck could I say? I didn't know what the fuck I had found lately, except maybe an ulcer that I was feeding lasagna.

She quickly wiped the tears from her face when I didn't answer. Then, in a shaky voice, she said, "I want to talk about it, Dino. Tonight. I want you to stay here and talk to me." She fought off the tears and then added, "I want you to make love to me."

God, did I want to fucking dematerialize. I'll say it now, *I'm a fucking moron.*

"I can't," I answered without looking at those pleading eyes.

"You can't make love to me?"

"That I can do. I just can't spend the night." Man that was cold.

"Why? You got a late date on Exposition Boulevard?" she snapped.

"Yes."

Her voice became noticeably chilly, "Are you going to spend the night there?"

"No," I answered, "I'm going to work after that."

"Work, work, work! Why let a little thing like love come between you and your precious work?" Her voice was rising now.

"Because I've got a butcher to fuckin' catch!" I snapped right back. I should have left then, but it wasn't over yet.

I should have left anyway.

"I never thought, " she mumbled in a calmer voice as she quieted down. "I never thought we would break up completely." Her chin sank to her chest as she added "I thought we were born for each other. We used to talk about when we would marry."

I felt a cold dagger slip into my heart and slowly begin to twist. For the next hour, a fuckin' *hour*, Jessica did all the talking. She replayed our entire love life for me, scene after scene. She reminded me of every promise I made, of every one I'd broken and even the few I'd kept. She remembered times and places and scenes that I'd forgotten until she pulled them from the cobwebs of my mind. And all the while, the dagger twisted, until I felt my whole insides would explode. I didn't know which felt worse, my stomach or my heart.

Jessica continued until she brought our love life up to date, concluding, in one fell swoop, with, "I can't believe it's all over. I thought we were *one*." And with that, the sobbing could not be stopped.

I didn't know what to say, so I said nothing. I just left. I couldn't take the guilt, and believe me, I felt so goddamn guilty. But I had a fucking maniac to catch. There was a man out there slicing women to pieces and I *had to get him!*

I got the mother fucker who killed my brother and I was gonna get the mother fucker who killed Lizette's sister, *personally*. I'd face the guilt later, just like I'd face Harmony Street one day. Fuck Jessica and fuck Harmony Street. Fuck the whole world! I had a fucking maniac to catch.

And I had to see Lizette.

•

I was late getting to Exposition Boulevard. Lizette opened the door before I knocked. I pulled her out and kissed her, with a long French kiss. And she kissed me back, open and soft and warm in the Orleanian night. And then we sat on the swing for a while and talked.

I told her to stop worrying, that she would drive herself crazy. I told her I would take care of everything. I didn't believe it, and she probably didn't either. But then, when I kissed her again, I didn't care.

"You're a great kisser," she told me.

"You're not so bad yourself."

She smiled and added, "I'll bet you've had plenty of practice."

"Yes, millions of girls."

She kissed me again.

"How did you get so good?" I asked.

"I'm French," she purred in my ear.

•

I spent another empty night in my bungalow, alone with my notes. But I couldn't concentrate. I kept thinking about Jessica. I tell you, the empty nights took their tool. It all piled up so fast. Every night alone, a little of it faded, a little of the feeling I had for Jessica, the softness faded. And there comes a time when nothing is left but the memories.

And then she wanted me to do it all over again.

•

On our way to Cucullu Street the following morning, Mark and I stopped by the Apple Vase Restaurant to pick up the list of employees and former employees for Snowood. There was a 'Help Wanted' sign in the front window of the restaurant. Mark pointed to it as we walked in. "Life goes on," he muttered.

The effeminate owner of the place handed me the list and went on and on about the tragedy. He was so concerned. Mark turned and started to walk out, with the owner close behind, and me a few steps behind them both. I looked over the list as Mark continued to walk and ignore the owner.

We left the owner on the sidewalk as Mark drove down Magazine Street toward Jefferson Avenue.

"Most of the time I don't hate fruits," Mark complained as he drove. "That one just set me off."

I said nothing as I continued to look over the list. The Apple Vase sure had a high turnover rate.

"Hey," Mark said o me, "you fucked the Princess yet?"

"Nope."

"What your waiting for?"

I didn't answer.

"You're taking your time, huh? Cultivating the pussy?"

I wouldn't answer.

"Well, when you get around to fucking her, you gotta let me know. You gotta tell me."

"Why?" I asked, like a dumb shit.

"Because I gotta know if her pussy is as pretty as she is. I figured she's got to have a beautiful little pussy. I'd be real disappointed if she didn't," Mark announced. "I just can't imagine her having one of those big flat pussy with all that pink skin hanging out." He smiled at me as he added, "I want you to tell me exactly how it looks, each hair. I gotta know."

If I closed my eyes, I'd swear I was still riding with Stan.

•

Mason and Snowood were waiting for us at the corner of Cucullu Street and Jefferson Avenue. They stepped out of their car as we pulled up and parked. We gathered at the corner as Mason started giving instructions, "We need a thorough canvass, so take your time."

"Here's your list," I told Snowood as I handed him the names from the Apple Vase.

"You keep it," Paul said as he spit a big brown wad of shit on the sidewalk. "You're our list man."

"Okay."

Mason told Paul to get rid of the brown shit, then assigned Mark and I to canvass Jefferson Avenue. Mason and Paul took Cucullu Street. Mark started telling Mason about the 'Help

Wanted' sign at the Apple Vase as I looked at the list one more time. There was something about it that bothered me.

"All right," Mason announced, "let's get going."

He and Paul moved of. I could see Mark start up Jefferson Avenue out of the corner of my eye, but my legs wouldn't move.

"You coming?" Mark called out to me.

"I think I've seen one of these names before," I exclaimed as my stomach did another flip-flop.

"What?"

"I've seen one of these names before!" I repeated excitedly.

Mark stepped up to me and asked, "Which one?"

"This one." I pointed to the name Jerome Hemmel. "I've seen it before, on one of my goddamn lists."

"Now calm down," Mark said. "Do you remember which list?"

"No, Dammit! The lists are in my desk in the Bureau."

"Okay, they're safe. We'll check it out after the canvass."

Mark started to move away again. I hesitated a moment and then ran up behind him. "I tell you, this name is on one of the list, the license plate lists or Tulane or Loyola."

"Okay," Mark grumbled. "We'll check it out later."

He sent me to the west side of the street. I started the canvass, but my mind wasn't there. I was running lists back and forth inside my head. The more I thought about it, the more it bothered me that I couldn't remember. I have no idea what anyone told me on my canvass. Thankfully, they knew nothing, so I missed nothing.

As I approached Willow Street, I toyed with the idea of just leaving and going straight for the Bureau, but I had a canvass to finish. And old woman with blue hair answered the next door I knocked on. She wore a green housecoat and asked to see my credentials twice before telling me she had *indeed* seen something that night.

"And I'm not a bit scared of the Slasher," she assured me. "If he comes around her, I'll beat the living shit outta him." She held up a broom handle.

"Well, what did you see?" I asked her.

I saw a photographer," she told me with a proud smile.

"You wanna tell me more?" I went one.

"Why, of course. Would you like some iced tea or lemonade?" she asked as she stepped back to let me in. A cool, air-conditioned breeze grazed my face as I stood in the doorway. "Tea would be nice," I said as I stepped in. "No lemon please," I added, to please my stomach.

She motioned that I should sit on the living room sofa, then hurried out back for the tea. A moment later, she returned with a tall, icy glass. "You want me to spice that up?" she asked as she held up a bottle of Scotch.

"No, ma'am," I said. "I'm on duty. But don't let that stop you."

"Don't worry, son," she said. "I won't." She poured herself a triple shot and then plopped into a love seat on the other side of the small room. "My names Louise Wiltz," she said, "and on the night that poor girl was killed I was sitting out on my front porch and I saw this fella taking pictures on the neutral ground."

"What fella? I asked as I took a gulp of tea.

"His name is Kurt Hudson and he lives in the green house right across the street. Corner of Jeff and Willow. He's a professional photographer. I've seen him before."

"Yes, ma'am."

"And he was shooting pictured of a blond floozy that night, right on the neutral ground. She had on a sliver gown and was leaning against one of the palm trees." Louise ran on without even taking a breath "She was a tramp. Hiked up her dress and I could see her white drawers from here. I seen her leave the next morning with Kurt. She had on cut-offs. He always goes out with tramps and whores. I thought she was gonna strip right there on the neutral ground," Louise huffed.

"What time was that?" I asked.

"About one o'clock in the morning," she answered.

"I know this may sound dumb to you Mrs. Wiltz, " I said. "It is Mrs. Wiltz?"

She nodded.

I went on, "Why were you sitting out at time in the morning?"

"I always sit out at night," she answered as if my question was stupid. I just wished she lived on Cucullu Street instead of Jefferson Avenue. She would have seen the whole fucking show.

"I'm a widow, you know," she explained. "Planted my Henry five years ago. He got killed out back," she said. "A plane killed him."

"A what?" I had never heard of any goddamn plane crash on Jefferson Avenue.

"A big goddamn model airplane. One of those propeller jobs," Louis told me. "Kid on Octavia Street was flying it and it got away and hit my Henry in the head while he was cutting grass in our backyard. I was out of town in Canada, visiting my sister Myrtle, when they called me. I still got the plane. Wanna see it?"

"No, ma'am – I, uh."

She cut me off. "I sued the shit outta the kid's rich-bastard family on Octavia. Got me a real bundle."

"Yes, ma'am, but getting back to the murder on Cucullu Street, was there anything else you wanted to add?"

"No, But if I was you, I'd go talk to Kurt Hudson. He might have seen something."

"Yes, ma'am."

So I left the woman whose husband was killed by a fucking airplane while cutting grass while she was in Canada visiting her sister Myrtle, and I walked across Jefferson Avenue to Kurt Hudson's house. Hudson answered the door after the first knock. He was a young fella with a protruding eyebrow, which reminded me of the Incredible Hulk. He was genuinely concerned about his murdered neighbor and remembered the night vividly.

"I had a date that night. Girl named Stephanie. I took some pictured of her on the neutral ground before we retired in here for the night. Would you like to see the pictures?"

"Sure. Did you see anybody else out that night or anything out of the ordinary?" I asked as he led me to a darkroom at the rear of the house.

"No, except for the old busybody across the street. I really wasn't looking at anything except Stephanie. I'll show you what I mean." He showed me several pictures of a tall blond girl in a silky silver gown, posed against one of the palm trees on the neutral ground. She was a real looker. No panty shots.

"You should see her with her clothes off," Kurt told me. He shook his head as he looked at the pictures. "She won't let me take any nudes, but she fucks like a mink."

I looked back at the pictures and noticed that in two of the photos there were cars passing by in the background. "Your flash picked up those license plates pretty easily," I said.

"Yeah, ruined the pictures. I shoulda been more careful."

I took out my pen to write down the plate numbers and explained that those people might have seen something.

"Take the pictures," Kurt told me. "I got extras."

"Thanks."

"You wanna see some good nudes? Other women. You'd be surprised how many New Orleans girls don't mind posing naked."

"Some other time," I told him. "I don't need an erection right now."

He got a kick out of that.

I tucked the pictures in my notepad and went on my way with my canvass. At least I wasn't still fidgeting about that name on the list anymore.

•

When we got back to the Bureau I didn't wait for the elevator. I shot up the stairs and tore into the lists. I went over them three times, but couldn't find the goddamn name. When Mason asked what I was doing, Mark answered him and explained about the name.

"Well, let me know tomorrow if he finds it," Mason said on his way out.

Snowood plopped down at his desk next to mine and started complaining how our luck had gone to shit and how canvasses were a fucking waste of time. Then he apologized for complaining so much and packed it in for the day.

"I'll see you tomorrow," he said on his way out.

I sat back, took a deep breath and started over again with my lists, this time going over them slowly. Mark brought me a cup of coffee and sat and watched from his desk.

The office was quiet for a few minutes as I worked, until Lt. Gironde led his entourage of Task Forcers in. I paid them as little attention as I could as Mark got up and talked to the good lieutenant.

"We got a suspect," the lieutenant declared.

"Yeah, who?" Mark asked.

"The man your partner found near the Bayou St. John murder scene," Gironde said. "He's having a hard time accounting for his whereabouts during some of the murders."

"I heard he was in jail for Dauphine Street," Mark said. Mark had checked on the mook right after Bayou St. John.

"We're not looking at Dauphine Street," said the lieutenant. "We're looking real hard a Bayou St. John and Cucullu Street."

"That's great, lieutenant," Mark said as he sat back down.

"You boys keep up the good work," Gironde added as he stepped into his office, followed by several Task Forcers. Mark waited for the lieutenant's door to close before he started laughing.

I sat motionless for a long time, holding my breath as my eyes rested on the name I was looking for. it was on the list of employees at Loyola.

"He's a fuckin' janitor at Loyola." I whispered. Mark rushed around the desk to take a look. I was up and bouncing around like a fucking idiot. "See! What'd I tell you? I told you I saw that name before!" I was sky high.

Mark shot me down fast. "So what? So he used to work at the Apple Vase and now he works at Loyola. What the fuck does that prove?"

"I don't fuckin' know," I yelled back. "Let me think a minute."

"Do you really think a goddamn janitor is going around killing girls?"

"Why fuckin' not?"

Mark smiled as he sat in my chair and played devil's advocate. Sometimes the bastard sounded just like Mason. "Now, calm down a minute and let's see what we got." He went over it again and he was right. All we had was a tiny link.

"He *could* be our killer, you know," I stammered.

"Sure. And we're gonna look at him real hard," Mark explained. "But we ain't got much to go on now, except maybe he knew two of our victims. That sure don't fit the profile of random killings."

"Fuck the profile."

"Somehow I knew you'd say that." Mark laughed. "But we ain't got no probable cause yet." He stood up and stretched. "But you did good. At least we got someone to look at."

Mark went over and packed up his briefcase, leaving me with my stomach doing jumping jacks. "Maybe," I said as calmly as I could, "maybe he *does* fit the profile. Maybe he's an Abnormal Style Killer who just happened to kill two girls he's slightly associated with." I was on a roll. "Maybe he doesn't even know the link. He just came upon each of them and doesn't know he's linked to them."

"You're a good detective," Mark quipped, "but not *that* good. Don't start sounding like Gironde now. Remember, this ain't science fiction."

"Where you going?" I asked Mark.

"Got a hot date tonight," he said as he started to walk out. "Taking the wife to the Saenger, gonna see *Camelot* with Richard Burton."

"You can't go," I yelled. "We gotta do something."

"What?" Mark stopped and glared at me. "You wanna go sit on the guy?"

"Why not? What if he *is* the killer and he goes hunting tonight?"

Mark hesitated on that one. "You're bugging me, man," he said to me. "Look, we'll pick it up first thing in the morning, all right? It'll be here in the morning." I could see it bothered him. And I knew he wanted to see Richard Burton real bad. Hell, even Mark's wife had been missing him lately. And I could be stretching things a little. But I had a gut feeling about this Jerome Hemmel.

I was gonna push it with Mark but decided I'd do more work first. I followed Mark toward the elevators and stopped by the computer to run Hemmel's name. Mark stopped before he got to the elevators and turned back. "You gonna stay on it?" he asked.

"Yeah."

"Look, if you come up with anything, call me after the play, around eleven o'clock. Okay?"

I nodded.

"I can always fuck my wife some other time," he added as he pushed the button.

Jerome Hemmel had no criminal record in the metropolitan area and no driving record. He did have a driver's license. He lived on Urquhart Street and drove a 1966 Ford Falcon.

Mark disappeared into the elevator as I took out Kurt Hudson's pictures and ran the first plate from the photos. It came back registered to the Ursuline Convent. I wondered what the good sisters were doing out at one in the morning. I ran the second plate and the computer screen's green print jumped out at me. Suddenly, I was in Odd Fellow's Rest again, paralyzed with fear as the spider monsters closed in on me. The second license plate was registered to a 1966 Ford Falcon, owned by one Jerome Hemmel.

I'll never forget that feeling, that hot sweaty chill that gripped me as I sat there staring at the screen. It was there in front of me, *the solution.* I knew it, I fuckin' knew. I sat there face to face with the computer screen and with the very name of the fuckin' murderer blinking at me. It was Jerome Fuckin' Hemmel.

I flew down the stairs and caught Mark pulling away in his car. I ran in front of him, waving my arms. He stopped and rolled down the window.

"It's him!" I screamed. *"I've got the mother fucker?"*

"Slow down," Mark said.

"I got him," I declared. "It's Jerome Hemmel." I turned and trotted back into the Bureau. Mark came in a minute after I'd sat back down at the computer. I pushed the command for a print-out as Mark stepped up behind me.

"You wanna tell me about it?" he asked.

I handed him the Hudson picture showing the car in the background with Hemmel's license plate clearly illuminated by the photoflash.

"Remember the time of death on Cucullu Street?" I asked Mark in a calmer voice.

"About one o'clock in the morning," Mark answered.

I pointed to the picture in his hand. "That was take at about one o'clock on Jefferson Avenue. And that," – I put my finger on the license plate – "That license plate belongs to Jerome Hemmel, our janitor at Loyola who used to work at the Apple Vase." I waited a second for it to sink in before exclaiming. "That puts him around the corner from the murder scene at exactly the right time. He was *there*. I can put him at the scene. He fuckin' did it. He's our boy!"

Mark looked at the picture and then at the computer screen and then back again before sitting down heavily in the empty chair next to me.

"You sure about the time?" he added "We're gonna need a statement from the photographer."

Mark picked up a phone and punched out a number. He told his wife that she would have to see Richard Burton without him. I could hear her yelling. I picked up anther phone and dialed Kurt Hudson's number. When he answered, I asked him exactly what time it was when he took the photos with the cars in the background.

"Around one o'clock," he answered.

"Are you sure?"

"Positive. Stephanie and I got home at exactly twelve-thirty. I gathered my gear and we went right out to get some night shots. When I got back in, I looked at the clock and it was one o'clock."

"Good," I said. "Are you gonna be home for a while this evening?"

"Yes."

"Good, I'm gonna need the negatives, the ones with the license plates. They're evidence," I said. "I'm gonna send someone around for them and for a quick statement from you."

"What for?" he asked.

"This is off the record," I answered, "but you just may have helped catch the fuckin' Slasher."

"Not shit?"

"No shit."

•

By the time Mason returned to the Bureau that evening, I was almost finished with the search warrant. He stood behind me and looked over my shoulder as I typed. When I finished, he sat down in Snowood's chair and looked the warrant over, using his familiar red pen to make corrections. He handed it back to me and said, "Let's retype this. Make it shorter. Just put enough in it to get the judge to sign it. Bare facts only. Don't give the defense anything to shoot at. And make out another warrant for his car."

"Right, Good thinking."

As I typed, I told Mason that Mark and I had decided we didn't have enough probable cause for an arrest warrant but we had more than enough PC for a search warrant. Mason agreed as I continued typing. Mark arrived at that point with Hudson's negatives and statement and showed them to Mason. Mark also gave me a quick description of Jerome Hemmel's apartment house for the warrant. He had made a quick fly-by and told me the Falcon was not there.

"Dammit," I cursed.

Mark continued, "If he's our boy, then there's go to be evidence in his apartment. Maybe the knife or the bras."

"The what?" Mason asked.

Mark sat down with a big grin on his face and told Mason and Snowood, who had just entered, about the missing brassieres.

"That's incredible," Mason said. "Who figured that out?"

Mark nodded toward me. "My junior padna over there. Figured it out way back at Bayou St. John. And he's the one come up with Jerome Hemmel, too."

Mason peeked at me with those beady eyes of and announced, "That's great fuckin' detective work, my boy. But don't let it go to your head. We ain't home yet."

"Would someone mind telling me what the fuck's going on?" Snowood asked.

"Sit down, Country-Ass," Mark exclaimed, "and let me tell you how Dino done solved it."

When I finished with the warrants, Mason approved them and sent me to the oldest judge in Orleans Parish to get them signed. "He's the only judge I know who'll sign 'em without questions and tell nobody about it," Mason added before Mark and I left.

By the time we returned to the Bureau, Mason had laid out a game plan. "I'm gonna stay here at the office. I'll back you up and run interference. Take a couple of uniform men with you," he instructed. "Park your cars a couple blocks away and if you find anything, call me on the radio and I'll get the arrest warrant and send the FBI lab."

"God, I hope he's there," I said as we pulled away from the Bureau. "Remember, Jack the Ripper killed *five*," I added.

"That's reassuring," Mark answered. We drove past Hemmel's apartment house and didn't see the Falcon. Then we parked around the corner and waited for Snowood to show up with the uniform men. It didn't take long for them to arrive as we relocated our cars two blocks away and walked toward the apartment house. We only got one uniform man, but that was all we needed.

As we approached the address, I suddenly had a flash of déjà vu.

"Wait a second," I said aloud, turning to Snowood. "We've been here before." I pointed down Urquhart to a bar in the opposite direction of Hemmel's house. "Remember that bar?"

Snowood turned and nodded as he spit on the sidewalk. "Sure do."

"Well, I'll be damned. We were *that* close."

"Mind telling me what the fuck you talking about?" Mark asked.

I turned and started walking back in the direction of Hemmel's house. "Paul and I had a couple beers there after the Vietnamese Natural Death Case."

"Son of a bitch."

•

We found the name. 'J. Hemmel' on an interior mailbox with 'Apartment 11' printed on the box. Apartment 11 was an attic apartment with a lone wooden door that took three Mark Land kicks to cave in. Actually, the door itself never gave way but the frame did, as it crashed to the floor. We left the uniform man outside Jerome's door to provide security and keep out curious residents who might want to know who was breaking into their neighbor's apartment. But no neighbors came out, even after the door crashed in. It was that kind of house.

It was a seedy apartment house with stained rugs in the halls and dim bulbs that cast little illumination on the dark walls. Jerome's apartment consisted of a lone room cloaked in darkness. I stood in the doorway and flicked on the light with my ball-point pen. I examined the room from the doorway. There was a lone mattress on the floor in the center of the room, with several semi white sheets and a plaid blanket strewn half on the mattress and half on the worn-looking tan carpet. There was no pillow.

There was a tiny sink in the corner of the room next to a small refrigerator. Next to the refrigerator was a small wooden table and two wooden chairs, painted bright blue. A hot plate rested atop the blue table. There was a lone dresser between the mattress and table, with a small television on top. The TV set was an old black and white model with aluminum foil twisted around its rabbit-ear antennas. There was a small end table next to the bed with a single lamp that had no shade, just a bare light bulb. The overhead light, which I had flicked on with my pen, consisted of two bare bulbs attached to a metal plate that dangled precariously from that ceiling above the mattress. There was an open closet on the far side of the bed, next to a closed door that led to the bathroom. There was one window, located next to the blue table. It was covered with a heavy army blanket.

Atop the end table, next to the mattress, I could see a stack of newspaper clippings. Mark and Paul remained in the doorway as I cautiously moved to the end table. Staring back at me was the front page of the *Times-Picayune* from the Cucullu Street murder. I told Mark.

"I don't believe this," Paul exclaimed.

"Believe it," I told him as I carefully pushed away the Cucullu Street headline with my pen. Beneath it, I found an envelope addressed to *me*.

"You're not gonna believe *this!*" I said, swallowing hard. "There's an envelope here addressed to me."

"What?"

"It's addressed to 'Detective LaStanza, New Orleans Police'," I said. "He misspelled 'Orleans,' but got my name right."

Mark moved in cautiously and poked around without touching anything. It took us a couple minutes to find the book on Jack the Ripper. When we found the knife in the sink, Mark sent Snowood back to the Bureau with enough information for Mason to complete the arrest warrant.

"At least he ain't out butchering," I told Mark as I looked down at the knife in the sink.

"Unless he has another knife," Mark pointed out.

When Mark found the loose board in the wall behind the mattress I held my breath and watched as he carefully poked inside and came out with a red-stained bra dangling from his ball-point pen.

I tried to call Mason on my LFR, but the reception was too poor. There was no phone in the room and the reception was no better on Mark's radio.

"I'll try outside," I said as I walked out of the room and headed downstairs. I couldn't wait to tell Mason.

As I started down the last flight of stairs I saw someone standing at the bottom. It was a stocky man with dark hair. He was staring up at me as I started down, his eyes glued to me every step of the way. By the time I was halfway down, I was sure who he was. A recognition passed between us. We knew each other, absolutely.

I didn't know if he was going to make a run for it or a run at me, with the second knife. If he did, I was a goner. He could slice me into strips before I could even get my weapon out of my ankle holster. I felt that Odd Fellow's feeling as I stopped halfway down and stared back into those peering eyes. I felt a sudden touch of fear creeping up my throat as I hesitated. I was at the very top of the pressure cooker, I could feel it, but I was the *police*. And he was mine.

I could see his hands dangling as his sides as I started to move down again. I pointed my LFR at him and said confidently, "Hello, Jerome. It's about time we met. I'm Detective LaStanza." I continued forward until I stopped the first step and added, "Homicide."

Jerome nodded slowly, and through trembling lips said, "I know." I could see his hands were shaking now, and his knees wobbled as a weak smile came over his face. "You got me," he said.

"Put your hands against the wall, Jerome," I ordered, still pointing at him with my LFR. Slowly, he turned and placed both hands on the wall. "Now, step back and spread your legs," I ordered again, "and put your nose against the wall."

As he obeyed, I reached down and dug out my weapon. For a moment, a thought raced through my mind as I felt the smoothness of my stainless steel magnum in my hand – a thought of just blowing him away right there. There would be no witnesses and he would be gone, forever. My heart was pounding as I thought of Joe and then Dauphine Street and Bayou St. John and Exposition Boulevard and Cucullu Street, and then Harmony Street, fucking Harmony Street.

I kicked his legs out further as I stepped up behind him. I leaned close, placed the muzzle of my gun against the side of his face and cocked the hammer. I could feel him shudder at the sound. "There was a struggle during the arrest," I could say later.

•

But I couldn't do it. Patrolman LaStanza may have been able to, but not Detective LaStanza. There was too much I still had to know about this man. And I want to know all of it.

"This is a .357 Magnum, Jerome." I told him. "I had the trigger filed down so it's a hair-trigger now. Don't move or I may go off and you'll be in hell before you know it." I searched him quickly and pulled each of his hands behind him, one at a time, and I handcuffed him and then double-locked the cuffs before pulling his face from the wall. I stood him upright and then tucked my gun into my waistband.

Jerome had tears in his eyes as he asked, "You're gonna kill me?"

"No," I answered, "I'm just gonna arrest you."

He smiled weakly at me and I could see the chipped tooth in front. I looked at him now. I *had* really caught him. I smiled back at the guilty bastard as I took out my Miranda card and began to read him his rights.

"Hey, Dino!" Mark called down to me from above before I started.

"What?" I answered.

"Tell Mason to send the FBI Lab over here, okay?" I could see him leaning down. "What's going on down there?" he asked.

"Mark," I called up to him, "Come down here and meet Jerome Hemmel. Jerome, that's my partner, Mark."

Jerome turned sideways and waved his fingers at Mark as he came rushing down the stairs in three bounds. He landed hard enough to send Jerome reeling against the wall. Mark glared at Jerome as I completed reading the Miranda card.

"You understand what I just said?" I asked Jerome.

"Yes, sir."

"You know you don't have to talk to me," I added.

"Yes, but I want to." He looked at me with eyes that were tearful again.

Mark pulled me aside and told me to take him directly to the Bureau and get Mason to help me interview him.

Jerome's eyes became progressively wetter until the tears flowed. He looked like a frightened mouse. When I stepped back up, I put a hand on his elbow and said, "It's gonna be okay, Jerome. Nobody's gonna hurt you. Understand?"

He nodded as his head sank.

"You know we gotta have a long talk," I told him.

"I know," he sobbed. "I wanna talk to you."

We left Mark with the scene and sent our own crime lab to help. Mason couldn't get hold of the FBI lab. They were out with Lt. Gironde, processing *his* arrest scene of a black fellow named Tyrone who was guilty of being at the wrong place at the wrong time.

Snowood arrived with the arrest warrant for Jerome as Jerome and I stepped outside. I introduced them. Paul glared at Jerome a minute, then started laughing as he told me about how Lt. Gironde, the Task Force, and a hundred FBI agents had just gone out to arrest the wrong man. I left Snowood with Mark to process the scene, interview Jerome's neighbors, and then search Jerome's car.

I put Jerome in the back seat of my car and drove straight to the Bureau. I would have smiled all the way, except I was thinking about the statements I was about to take. I knew that this would be the most important confession I'd ever take. But I did smile, secretly, to myself.

•

I took Jerome up the back stairs of Headquarters to the Detective Bureau. Mason was waiting and put us in a small interview room that had no windows. The room had one gray metal table, two chairs, a telephone, and nothing else except two unused electrical outlets. The fluorescent lights overhead cast a soft white glow on the bare white walls.

I sat in the cushioned chair with my back to the door. I put Jerome in the special folding chair alongside the table. I made sure I didn't put him across from me. I remembered my interview classes and how you never put a table or desk between you and the interviewee. You don't give him any shield. You keep him close, unprotected, with nothing between you and him. You keep him by your side, with his back to the wall to add that 'trapped rat' feeling.

The special folding chair Jerome sat on was a more subtle touch. Its front legs had been shaved down one-half inch, so without realizing it, the interviewee was leaning forward throughout the entire interview. Gradually, the uncomfortable position would wear away most resistance. In Homicide, we don't interrogate, we interview.

We were alone for a minute, just the Slasher and I, while Mason went for the tape recorders. I looked at him as he looked at me. Under the fluorescent light, he looked lot less sinister than he did as the bottom of the staircase. There sat the man who had terrorized New Orleans as it had never been terrorized before. There sat the man who had sliced all those girls to ribbons.

I had thought that when we found him he would be a bigger-than-life monster, a powerful evil presence, instead, I found a sniveling, cowardly, frightened wimp. The monster who sat next to me looked just like a janitor.

I took out a field arrest report and filled out the necessary details, finishing as Mason returned with a large reel-to-reel tape recorder with an eight-hour tape. He told Jerome that once it was tuned on, it stayed on until the interview was completed. Then Mason handed me a cassette recorder and several cartridges, reminding me to take separate statements for each incident. He didn't have to remind me. I knew that each murder required a separate confession. All we needed was to have some pain-in-the-ass judge get a wild hair up his ass and throw out a statement on a technicality, and *all* our confessions would go down the fucking tube.

Before Mason left, we turned on both recorders and I read Jerome his Miranda rights again, in Mason's presence. Jerome

189

dutifully answered yes to all the sections and then signed a waiver form, relinquishing his right to remain silent.

"I want to talk to you," he repeated aloud.

I handed Mason my gun as he left the room. "I'll keep you under wraps," Mason said as he went outside to run interference. The confession would be a one-on-one affair. If two officers were present, then the defense could play games picking at each detective's memory until minor discrepancies were blown all out of fucking proportions.

"Okay," I started, "the time is eight o'clock on the evening of May 6th. We are in the Detective Bureau, 715 South Broad Street in New Orleans, Louisiana. This is the voice of Detective Dino LaStanza of the New Orleans Police Homicide Division. I am conducting an interview of Jerome Hemmel." I listed Jerome's date of birth and address. "Now, Jerome," I said as I placed the cassette recorder on the table in front of me, "We'll start at the beginning. Tell me about yourself."

He was sniveling as he started. He told me he had no father, was raised by his mother, who died when he was nineteen. "My father is unknown. My mama never told me about him." He sank back in the folding chair and added, "On my birth certificate the space where my father's name should be is blank. I have no father.

"When my mama died she left me alone. Got an aunt, but she don't like me." His sniveling gave way to a smirk as he added, "My aunt's name is Hemmel, too. She's gonna be famous now."

Then he told me when he was a boy, he wanted to be a policeman. "I like the uniforms, all that blue." But he never applied. "They wouldn't want me."

"Why not?" I asked.

He looked up at me and answered calmly, "Cuz I'm the Slasher."

"Tell me about Dauphine Street," I said in a low voice.

His eyes darted around the room for a moment. Then he sat back and put his hands behind his head and spoke in a calm, steady voice.

"I saw her go in a bar on Bourbon Street, followed her. She looked pretty but she wouldn't look at me, so I followed her, caught her. She tried to get away so I cut her."

"Did you know her?"

"No."

I leaned close and asked in a admiring voice, "How did you do it? How did you sneak up on her?"

It was as if a light switch was thrown on inside those beady eyes. He sat up and told me how he stalked her, how he danced after her in his mating dance of death, how, like Jack the Ripper, he had fucked her good.

"And then I bit her titty, hard, and I spread her legs so you could see her nasty pussy and I left her there."

"Did you take anything?"

He shot a hard look at me and said, "Yes, I took her bra."

"Why?"

"So I could fuck it later."

Jesus Fuckin' Christ, Satan was sitting next to me and Mason had my gun in the other room. We finished the Dauphine Street statement at ten o'clock. He was bragging, and I kept playing up to him.

"You want some coffee?"

"Sure, Dino." He answered with a smile.

I opened the door and asked Mason for coffee. He brought in coffee and fresh donuts a few minutes later as I prepared to start in on Bayou St. John. I took out a fresh Miranda waiver and was starting to read it to Jerome when he reached over, took it out of my hand and read it aloud himself. He initialed each part of the warning and signed the bottom. He was so helpful, the fuckin' idiot.

"How did you pull off Bayou St. John ?" I asked.

Then I sat back and listened to the sickening description as he bragged about it, as he became a big man again right in front of me. By then I was his friend.

We even went to the bathroom together, at least we went into separate stalls. But I wouldn't let him out of my reach until it was all over. When we stepped back into the room, with the reel-to-reel still going, I pointed to the phone and told him he was free to use it at any time.

"I'll even leave the room, if you want privacy." I wasn't kidding.

"I don't want to call nobody."

"Okay," I said as we went through another Miranda waiver form and then started in on Exposition Boulevard. He claimed the killing was random, he had seen her in passing at Loyola that evening, just as he's seen Marie Sumner on Bourbon Street. But he claimed he was invisible. She wouldn't look at him, because they couldn't see him until he turned into the Slasher. "Then I fucked them up real good," he bragged.

All the psychiatrists on earth couldn't help this fool. Even a brain transplant from a chinchilla would do no good. I sat there listening to him and knowing in my heart that this creature should be eradicated from the universe, period.

The hardest thing I have ever done was to sit calmly as he told me how he dragged Lynette, kicking and screeching, and how he 'ripped her'. As we finished with Exposition Boulevard, I moved my chair around to his side of the table. We sat face to face as I started in on Cucullu Street.

"I hated her, she was too pretty in that nasty dress," he started out, telling me about how he was cruising and how he spotted her and followed her. I asked him to give me every detail, and, without being asked specifically, he told me about the blonde in the silver gown getting her picture taken on the neutral ground. He even went back to look for her after he cleaned up on Cucullu Street. Like Jack the Ripper, he wanted a double event.

"Only she was gone," Jerome explained. Lucky girl was inside Kurt Hudson's house getting banged the right way. Jesus Fuckin' Christ.

I let him tell me about Cucullu Street in his own words, but this time, he didn't go into detail. He told me about stabbing her and locking her door, but nothing else between then and when he left her place. When I asked, he said that one was all foggy to him.

So I cleared away the fucking fog for him. As I told him about how we found her, he claimed that someone had gone in after him and done the rest.

"Like who?" I asked "You're the Slasher."

"I know," he answered, his chin sinking. I inched my chair even closer. I leaned toward him and asked, "Do you remember what happened to Mary Kelly?"

He looked up at me and nodded with wet eyes. I was glad I'd done my reading on Jack the Ripper because Carolina Essex was a copy of the Mary Kelly killing. He knew it, and I knew it. I went on. "Remember how they described what Mary Kelly looked like?" I asked.

He nodded again.

"Well, the girl on Cucullu Street was worse."

Tears began to stream down his face as he nodded one more time and started crying. Before long, he was kneeling and praying aloud to Jesus Christ.

I pushed him on. "Tell Jesus what you did."

I fuckin' loved it. Satan was praying to Jesus and I was sipping coffee and feeling good, real good for the first time in a long, long time. When the big bad Slasher was finished crying, he sat back on his chair and used a shitload of the Kleenex Mason had brought in with our latest cups of coffee. He dried his eyes and then looked at me a long time before asking, "How did you catch me?"

I smiled at him and said, "I'm good. I'm very good. And you made a big mistake along the way."

"Yeah?"

"Yeah," I said, "You killed someone when I was on duty."

Jerome actually smiled at that one. I was smiling all along. Inside. I picked up the telephone and dialed a number as I looked at my watch. It was past four in the morning. The voice that answered was groggy.

"Phil?" I asked as Fat Phil answered his phone.

"Yeah, who's this?"

"This is LaStanza."

"What's the matter?" Phil asked. "What's going on?" I could hear him fumbling around. "It's four in the fuckin' morning."

"I know that. I just called to tell you caught him."

"What?"

"I caught the Slasher," I said. "Remember you kept asking me if I solved it yet? Well, I did. I fuckin' caught him!"

Fat Phil started screaming, "You mean you called me at this time in the morning to tell me – "

I hung up on him. I sat back and smiled. Even Jerome thought that was funny.

*Chapter 9*
Harmony Street

"We caught him," I told Lizette as I stood on her front gallery at six in the morning. It took a moment to sink in. I watched the pupils of her eyes grow until her eyes were completely black.

"Really?" she asked.

"Really." I answered.

She stepped up and hugged me, hard, then took my hand and led me through the house to the kitchen where she started up a pot of coffee, put milk in a sauce pan for café au lait. I watched as she moved about in her long, white silky robe. The early morning light streamed into the kitchen window and I could see she had no make-up on. She didn't need it. Her skin was smooth and clear and bright, her face truly beautiful.

As the coffee began to brew, she turned back to me and ran her fingers through her long. dark hair. "I want you to tell me all about it," she said, "after you get some coffee in you. You look so tired."

"I am tired." I agreed as I leaned on the kitchen counter. I had to fight off a yawn as I stood there. Lizette laughed and turned to check the coffee. As she turned, the folds of her robe opened, revealing the length of one beautiful leg. I could see all the way up to her small pink panties. That woke me up right away. Only she caught me looking and laughed again. She smiled as left the robe open a little.

"I thought you were tired."

"I'm never that tired," I said.

"Told you I have nice legs."

She moved over and placed her hand on the side of my face. Her eyes were no longer black, but dark gold once again. "I was worried last night when you didn't call," she whispered as she leaned forward and kissed me a long time. We weren't even close to stopping when Mr. Louvier walked in.

"Excuse me," he said as he walked past. He pulled the boiling pot of milk off the burner before turning to face me. I could see the *Times-Picayune* in his hand, and on its front page was a picture of Tyrone, the black man from Bayou St. John.

Lizette took a step toward her father and declared, "They've caught him."

"What?" He asked as he looked quickly at the paper. "But here it says, "

"Don't believe everything you read in the paper," I told him.

He gave me an odd look, raised the paper, explained the Task Force said Tyrone was a prime suspect, but no arrest had been made as yet.

"That's not the Slasher," I said, pointing to the newspaper. "We caught the Slasher last night. I just finished taking his confession."

He glanced at Lizette as she moved over to hug him. He laid his head on her shoulder for a moment before looking up and asking me, "How about some coffee, son?"

•

Over hot café au lait, I told Lizette and Mr. Louvier about Jerome. I told them everything – from Cucullu Street to the photographer on Jefferson Avenue to Urquhart Street, I told them about the evidence we found on Urquhart Street and the confessions that followed.

"He was a nobody who became somebody by killing people," I wound up.

"Well then, what's this about this black fella?" Mr. Louvier asked, pointing to the paper.

"I'm the one who found him too and he didn't do a damn thing."

"You found him?"

"Yes, sir. I found him near the scene at Bayou St. John. But he's innocent. I guess the media needed something, so the Task Force gave them Tyrone."

"That doesn't sound too good to me," Mr. Louvier added. "I wonder what Chief Rosata's going to think of all this," he said as he looked at the front page again.

"He'll blow his Sicilian top," I said. "You won't have to call him. Just open your door and you'll be able to hear him."

At that point, Mrs. Louvier came in to tell us there was news conference on television. "They caught him," she declared.

We went into the living room and watched as the Chief's familiar face fill the tube. He was announcing the capture of the Slasher. "The reign of terror is over," he said. "Members of the New Orleans Police regular Homicide Division effected capture of one, Jerome Hemmel, last night, and secured evidence beyond doubt that Hemmel is the Slasher." The Chief then declined to answer any further questions. He announced a press conference for four that afternoon when the detectives who broke the case would be present and all questions would be answered.

"Oh no!" I moaned

"You'd better get some sleep," Lizette told me.

"You look awfully tired, son," Mr. Louvier added.

I nodded as I rose to leave. Lizette walked me to the door, kissed me and said she'd be watching television at four. "I knew you'd catch him, Dino." She signed as I held her against me. "I'm glad it's over."

"Me, too," I said as I kissed her again. But I knew better. It had just begun. There was a hell of a trial ahead and I knew I was going to be the goddamn star witness.

I wanted no part of television. I took my phone off the hook when I got home. I thought of just sleeping through it all. But I knew if I didn't show up, someone would be at my door to get me. The rank doesn't take to it kindly when you refuse awards. So I set my alarm before jumping into bed.

I lay there trying to sleep, so dog-tired I couldn't figure out what was keeping me awake. But I stayed awake, running over it all again and again in my mind. It seemed like a century ago when I started that canvass on Jefferson Avenue. I kept thinking about Jerome and how scared he became when the confessions were finished and he had to go to jail.

"Where are you taking me?" he asked.

"Central Lockup," I told him.

"And then to Parish Prison," Mark added as he and Mason stepped into the small interview room. We handcuffed Jerome again and led him away through the crowded Homicide squad room full of staring eyes. Mason stopped us a moment as Lt. Gironde stepped up.

"Lieutenant," Mason announced, "I'd like you to meet Jerome Hemmel."

"Who the fuck is he?"

"The Slasher."

Jerome smiled at Gironde with that chipped tooth and you could see the good lieutenant's face grow paler by the instant. Mason gloated. He stayed behind to explain while Mark and I took Jerome downstairs to Central Lockup. As the jailer led him away, Jerome waved to me.

"He fuckin' loves you," Mark commented as we stepped away. "That's great. I think you've arrived, my boy. When you can get them to love you, they'll tell you anything."

"He already has."

•

The news conference was held in the Mayor's office with the Mayor and the Chief present and the FBI's Special-Agent-In-Charge of the New Orleans Field Office, as well as every politician who wanted to get his or her face on television. Mason and Mark and Snowood and I were ushered in and displayed alongside the knife and the scribbled letters Jerome had written, and never mailed, to me. The letters were copies, word-for-word, of letters Jack the Ripper had sent to the police in 1888, with such well know quotes as "my knife's so nice and sharp", "I love my work and want to start again", "you will soon hear from me and my funny little games."

Thankfully, we were told not to say anything. We just sat there like manikins as the Chief and Mayor answered the relentless questions, fending off those that "may jeopardize the prosecution." I almost fell asleep after a while, but I heard the Chief's concluding remark. He said, "This was the finest piece of detective work I've ever seen."

•

Back at the Bureau there was a call waiting for me.

"Congratulations," she said when I picked up.

"Thanks."

"I knew you'd get him," Jessica went on in that same sad voice that she'd come to possess lately. "I'm happy for you, Dino."

"Thanks."

She paused a second and then asked me, "Remember when we first started going out? Remember where I used to work?"

"No." I wondered what she was up to.

"I was a librarian, remember?"

"I think so," I answered as I thought of the moonlit night at Longue Vue Gardens a long time ago.

"I used to work at Loyola," she reminded me. "I was a librarian at Loyola University. Remember?"

Talk about freak me out. I had forgotten. I told her that, and she said, "I knew you forgot." Then she asked me to call her sometime. I said I would, but we both knew better.

Some endings are memorable in themselves, but this one was memorable because it was in the middle of so much. As I hang up the phone, my father pranced into the Bureau and bellowed, "Where's my boy?" The place erupted with back slapping and hand shaking and my father holding court among the young detectives who had all looked at retired Captain LaStanza with respect and some adoration.

Then Kurt Hudson called and congratulated me for being on television and told me how he would be on the *AM News Show* with his story of the pictures that broke the case. "Just remember we have a date in court," I told him before he got off the line.

Then I received my first call from Jerome. I took the call in Mason's office. Jerome congratulated me, too, "I just saw you on television."

"Where are you?" I asked.

"Parish Prison. I'm in a pod with a TV and a private room so they can't get to me."

"Who?" I asked.

"The other prisoners," Jerome explained. "The guards told me that they got some bad dudes in here that would kill me in a minute."

The day was becoming freakier by the second. I sat in my sergeant's office and listened to a mass murderer tell me how he had to be careful because there were 'bad dudes' in jail. God, I love America. Where else can a mass murderer get a private room and use of a telephone so he can call anybody he fucking pleases?

"Hey," I called out to Mason after Jerome hung up, "guess who just called me?"

"Johnny Carson, you're on tomorrow night." Mason laughed.

"No, Jerome called me. How the fuck did he get a phone?" I asked.

"They have pay phones at Parish Prison," Mason explained. "It's against their constitutional rights to keep them incommunicado."

"Well, I'll be damned."

•

It didn't take the FBI long to match Jerome's fingerprints to the latent prints taken from Cucullu Street. Of course, until we caught Jerome, they had no prints to compare. Jerome had never been printed before. Once you catch the suspect, crime labs can really earn their pay. They can find all sorts of physical evidence to link a murderer to the scene and make your case easier in court.

Of course, there was nothing simple about *this* court case, especially when the Assistant DA assigned to the case started complaining that Jerome wouldn't talk to him.

"He'll only talk to LaStanza," complained the Assistant DA.

"What's wrong with that?" Mason asked.

"I've go a million questions for him, not to mention all the psychiatrists who want to question him."

"Just give me the questions," Mason told him, "and I'll pass them on to LaStanza and – "

•

Jerome continued to call me, daily. Sometimes he'd call just to tell me what was going on in his life, like during the insanity hearings. Jerome refused to talk to the doctors, too. "I told them I'd only talk to you."

"Jerome, you have to talk to doctors, for Christ's sake," I explained.

"I don't trust them. Just like that lawyer they appointed for me. I won't talk to him, either."

"You *better* talk to him. He's the only friend you got," I explained. And that was the goddamn truth. Any lawyer would be happy to take the case and get all the free publicity. The lawyer can fuck up and lose and still come out on top. Jerome was guilty as hell. No one expected a lawyer to get him off. But if any lawyer did, his career was made for life.

Once, when Jerome called me, he sounded down. "Is it true they call the electric chair 'Gruesome Gertie' at Angola?" he asked.

"That's right," I answered.

"I'm scared." He moaned for a minute before asking, "Can I plead guilty and get a life sentence?"

"I don't think so, Jerome. You can't plead guilty to a capital offense. The jury decides if you get life or death."

"Oh."

•

Then I got a call from Jerome's court-appointed layer. He told me who he was and then ordered me to stop talking to his client.

"He calls me, Counselor," I advised.

"Nevertheless, I'm ordering you to sop talking to him."

I put the smug bastard on hold and called Mason over.

"Can he do that?" I asked after I told Mason what the lawyer said.

"He sure can," Mason advised me. "One he notifies us, we can't talk to your killer anymore."

"Fuck him."

"You'll fuck up the case," Mason warned.

I pushed the hold button again and said, "Counselor?"

"Yes,."

"This is LaStanza again and I understand. I'm also ordering you to never call me again. I'm a prosecution witness and if you call me again, I'll tell the judge on you." Then I hung up and shrugged at Mason. It wasn't much of a victory, but it was better than nothing.

Mason smirked and said, "He'll have his day when he gets you on the witness stand."

•

Jerome call me later that day as I sat at my desk studying my case notes for the upcoming preliminary hearing.

"I can't talk to you anymore," I explained.

He sounded pitiful. "Please, don't hang up. I've *got* to talk to you," he pleaded. "I don't care what my lawyer says."

"I know," I cut in, "but I *still* can't talk to you anymore. You gotta quit calling me."

Jerome started crying. "Please, don't hang up."

I hung up.

And I felt bad about it. I don't know why. That creature needed to be eradicated. Only, the way he cried –

Jerome didn't give up. He left messages for me constantly. But I refused to talk to him. I just went back to my usual routine of handling the occasional suicide and an occasional misdemeanor murder, and another paperwork murder in a bar. But mostly I studied my notes.

I hadn't seen Lizette since the arrest, although I called her nightly. I finally asked her out for the first time.

"How about dinner and a movie Saturday night?" I asked.

"Sure," she answered. "What are you doing tonight?"

"Studying."

"Can I come over?"

My bungalow was a fucking mess. I needed a shower from the day's heat. I didn't have a thing in the house that was edible. "Can you give me an hour?" I asked.

"Sure. Just give me your address and I'll bring dinner. Have you eaten?"

"No."

I spent the next fifty-five minutes doing me best imitation of the Road Runner, buzzing around and showering at a hundred miles an hour. By the time Lizette arrived, I was almost human and my house was almost presentable.

Lizette breezed in, trailing perfume from my living room into the kitchen where she warmed up the Chinese food she had picked up on her way over. She wore a loose cotton blouse and a tight white miniskirt, and Chinese food was not what I wanted to eat. I moved over and kissed her on the neck. She craned her head around and kissed me back. Then she pulled away and said, "Dessert will be served after dinner."

I don't know what the fuck I ate. She called it Moo Goo something. It tasted good but my mind was elsewhere. I couldn't stop watching her as we ate. Finally we moved into my living room to the sofa. I tried not to rush it, but I was so excited. I kissed her on her neck and then nibbled on her ear before moving to her open mouth. Slowly, she slid beneath me until I was completely upon her, her legs wrapped around me, my hand rubbing her breast, feeling the hard nipple beneath her blouse. As I began to move against her, as we began to pump in unison, Lizette pulled her mouth away and gasped for breath.

"Dino?" she cried.

I lifted my head and looked at her face. Those big golden eyes did all the talking. I could see the fear there, the uncertainty in her eyes. She just looked at me and I knew. After a moment, I smiled and shrugged and lifted myself off her.

"I'm sorry," she said as she curled up against me.

After I'd caught my breath, I told her I didn't mean to rush it. "I just got carried away."

"Me too," she said. Then she added, "I'm not on the pill right now, Dino." She uncurled herself and looked at me with those soft golden eyes and whispered. "But I'm going to be, because I can't push you away again."

•

The phone woke me at six in the morning. It was Mason. "Can you meet me at the morgue for an autopsy at seven?" he asked in a tired voice.

"Sure," I said as I yawned, "what's up?"

"We had a 29S last night. Jerome Hemmel hanged himself in his cell. You wanna come to the autopsy?"

I sat up quickly. "Are you fuckin' kidding?"

"No," he sounded beat. "I been up all night handling it. You wanna meet me there?"

"Yeah, absolutely."

I jumped out of bed and dressed in a hurry. I beat Mason to THE CHAMBER OF HORRORS. When I walked in, I pointed to the stack of black body bags and asked the attendant which one was Jerome Hemmel. He shrugged his huge shoulders. So I made the rounds, checking the tags. Jerome's body bag was by the door to the autopsy room. I asked the attendant to put it up on the table first. He did, without saying a word.

At a quarter to seven Mason came in with a crime lab technician. I told him that I'd made sure Jerome was first in line. "You want me to take the notes?" I asked.

"No," Mason shook his head. "I'll handle it."

And so I watched the final scene unfold in front of me, the final autopsy of the Slasher murders. Jerome had claimed his last victim. I watched as he was sliced open, as all the repetitious steps were taken, one after the other. The only difference this time was what they did with Jerome's brain. They took it out, put it in an orange refrigerated container and saved it for all the scientists who wanted to pick it apart.

As I stood watching in silence, I had that grim reaper feeling again, that feeling of being a perpetual witness to death. I felt like a vulture again, perched atop a star-and-crescent badge, leering at dead people. I watched the monster known as the Slasher dissected in front of me, his organs tossed back into his chest cavity before they sewed him up again.

I watched and truly felt nothing, not even hatred anymore or sadness or even relief. I felt nothing. At that moment, as I watched Jerome's autopsy, I realized that I had indeed become a grim reaper. I was a skull-faced, unfeeling phantom of the night, a dark Angel of Death, able to leave my emotions at home or with a pretty girl on Exposition Boulevard. I was now a Homicide Detective.

•

I went with Mason back to the Bureau and turned on his television while he typed out his daily. When his phone rang, I answered it. It was Jerome's court-appointed lawyer.

"Is it true?" he asked in agony. He was crushed. The most famous defendant he would ever defend was gone.

"It sure is," I told him.

"Oh, my God!" the lawyer cried out as all those dollars disappeared from his dreams.

"Counselor," I cut in.

It took him a while to gain his composure. "Yes?" he responded.

"Jerome left a message for you," I told him.

"Yes?"

"The message is, fuck you!" Then I hung up on the mother fucker.

Mason stopped typing and looked over at me, "Now, that no way to win friends."

"Fuck him!"

Mason smiled for the first time that morning and went back to typing. I sat down in front of there TV and watched the early morning news. There was nothing about Jerome yet, but there was something else.

It seems that an unidentified New Orleans policeman, who was in uniform but in his personal car, had saved a cat's life late the previous night. According to eyewitnesses, the policeman stopped his car on the Mississippi Rive Bridge, climbed a girder and took down a frightened cat.

I started laughing before I picked up the phone and had to calm myself when the operator at the television station answered. I asked for the news room and then gave them the name of the heroic officer who saved the cat. I told them I was Chief Rosata and gave them the number in the Bureau to call me back for confirmation.

"What's the matter with you?" I asked the news director. "Don't you recognize my voice?"

"Yes, sir."

"I want to see that on the air," I told him before I hung up. They never called me back for confirmation. They just put it on the air. I sat back and watched as the newsman announced that he had just received confirmation that the heroic officer who had saved the cat on the bridge was Patrolman Stan Smith of the Sixth District.

I almost fell to the floor. I started jumping around like a chimpanzee, pounding on the desks. "What's the matter with you?" Mason asked. I just pointed to the TV as the newsman repeated Stan's name for the whole fucking world to hear.

Mason asked me what was so funny.

"Stan *hates* cats!" I roared.

•

I took a while for me to calm down. God, I would have given anything to see the look on Stan's face when he found out. That had to rank among the best jokes I ever played on ole Stanley. Roll Calls at the Sixth District would be torture for him for weeks.

Finally, I calmed down enough to join Mason in his cubicle. I sat down and kicked my feet up on his desk. He continued typing his daily. I was feeling *so good*, I couldn't believe it. My stomach hadn't acted up in days, I was sleeping soundly at night, and eating much better. And there was Lizette to occupy my mind now. I was on top of the world.

That was, until I saw what my feet were on top of as they rested on Mason's desk. I reached over to move the folder from beneath my feet and saw it was the Homicide file on the Harmony Street Murder. I could feel the blood drain from my face as my breath caught. I tried to hide it from Mason, but there was no way to hide *anything* from Mason.

When he finished his daily, he turned around and picked up the Harmony file. He looked at me with those steely eyes and said, "I've been looking into this." He leaned back in his chair, his eyes never leaving mine. "You know, its the only murder I've never solved," he added.

"I didn't know that," I answered with a raspy voice. I coughed in a poor attempt at coving up.

"Yep," he went on, "I've been up here all these years and solved every case assigned to me, except this one."

I tried my best to hide it. But I knew, deep in my heart, that Mason knew exactly who the killer was. He continued to talk about the case, not questioning me, but calmly reviewing the facts in the unsolved murder of the man who just happened to be a prime suspect in the murder of my brother.

As he talked, it all came back to me in flashes, the dark wharf, the gun in my hand, the surgical gloves I'd warn so there would be no prints on the gun that I knew could never be traced to me, the way I sneaked into the wharf and found him, the way he knelt before me, and my final words to him as I stuck the revolver in his mouth.

"Suck this like it's your mama's tit," I said, then added, "Bye, fuck-head," and squeezed the trigger. I remember how the gun erupted in my hand and how the body flopped at my feet.

The Harmony Street killer sat across the desk from Mason and we both knew it. But neither said it. Mason talked in circles. He told me the case could only be solved if the murderer confessed. There were no witnesses. There was no physical evidence. Only the killer's mouth could convict him.

Then Mason looked away and announce that he'd finally solved the Harmony Street Murder. "The murderer opened his mouth," Mason declared. "And I solved it."

I held my breath as I felt the blood rush back into my neck and face. I felt flustered and overheated as I sat there with my fingers digging into the fabric of the chair arm.

"Do you know this guy?" Mason asked as he tossed a mug shot on the desk in front of me. Slowly, I looked down at the face in the mug shot, the black face of a man I'd never seen before.

I shook my head.

"His name was Joe Martin," Mason said, "a typical low-life from the Fifth District. He's dead now, got run over trying to cross the interstate a couple weeks ago." Mason paused to light up a cigarette before continuing. "I got a good statement from his girlfriend yesterday. She told me the whole story. Martin's our Harmony Street murderer. It was a drug rip-off. The girlfriend knew the whole story. So, now it's solved and we don't even have to go to trial. Just like Jerome."

Mason didn't look at me anymore. He didn't have to. We both knew.

On my way out the door he did add one more remark, "You know, Dino," he said to my back as I stopped in the doorway, "catching Jerome was the best piece of Homicide work I've ever seen."

I just nodded and walked out, exhaled for the first time in minutes and then picked up my briefcase and left. I went home and ran it all through my head again. And for the first time in years, I felt that big fucking monkey on my back was finally lifted.

I prayed that Harmony Street would never come to haunt me again.

•

Everything returned to normal the next day. We went back to our old shift again and Boudreaux rejoined the squad. It was a nice quiet Friday for the first time in months. No one died and we spent the day finishing paperwork around the office and taking a very long lunch. As we left the Bureau early, Mark grabbed my shoulder and asked me how Lizette and I were getting along.

"Fine," I answered waiting for him to ask about her pussy in front of Mason and everyone.

But he didn't. He just turned to Mason and said, "You know, this was the only case I ever heard of where a Homicide Detective fell in love with a victim and lived happily ever after."

•

Lizette and I decided to spend the entire day together Saturday. When I arrived at her house she was waiting for me on the swing. She was a sight to see, her face made up like a cover girl, her long hair billowing in the unusual summer breeze. She smiled as I approached, her bright eyes flashing at me. She wore a backless gold mesh blouse that tied around her neck, and a tight black miniskirt. Extra short. She walked over and met me at the front steps and hugged me, her familiar perfume filled my senses.

"Why don't we go pay a visit to King Kong?" she suggested. "It's such a pretty day." She was right. It was an odd New Orleans summer day, with an alien, cool breeze flowing through the old oaks. I looked into those golden eyes and smiled.

"Okay," I agreed.

"I'll go get my purse," she said as she turned and went inside. I followed her in and waited in the library. I opened the drapes and let the light stream in on the portrait above the mantelpiece. I stood before the portrait and stared at those eyes that stared back at me. Those eyes were still sad. I don't know why I thought they wouldn't be sad anymore. Lizette came up behind me as I stood there. I reached over and pulled her to me and we hugged, both looking up at the portrait.

Lizette spoke first in that soft, lazy, sensual voice of hers, "Sometimes, I don't know about you."

"Yes, you do," I answered. "You know everything about me. I'm not very complicated."

She pursed her full lips and then smiled. "You're right. I knew it the first time I saw you here in the library, that's why I ran out, I knew it then."

"It's a little frightening," I said.

"It still frightens me," Lizette added.

"There's no need to be afraid anymore." I kissed those full lips and held her close. I knew this was a important time in my life, a turning point, a putting away of past sadness and reaching for he promise in Lizette's bright eyes.

I looked back at the portrait again, and could see for the first time that those were Lynette's eyes staring back at me.

"Come on," Lizette said, "let's go see King Kong."

We stepped out together into the sunny day and walked across the Exposition Boulevard to the street next to the lagoon. As joggers passed and kids on bicycles rode by, we headed toward the zoo on that bright sunny Orleanian day.

A lazy patrol car drove by as I put my arm around Lizette. I recognized the number on the side of the car, but it was too late. A familiar voice came over the public address system of the patrol car, a booming voice that caught everyone's attention as it shouted, "Hey you! Didn't I tell you the next time I catch you playing with yourself, you're going to jail?"

## *THE END*

### *Note from the Publisher*
### BIG KISS PRODUCTIONS

If you found a typo or two in the book, please don't hold it against us. We are a small group of volunteers dedicated to presenting quality fiction from writers with genuine talent. We tried to make this book as perfect as possible, but we are human and make mistakes.

BIG KISS PRODUCTIONS and the author are proud to sell this book at as low a cost as possible. Even great fiction should be affordable.

For more information about the author go to
http://www.oneildenoux.net

**Also by the Author**
**Novels**
*The Big Kiss*
*Blue Orleans*
*Crescent City Kills*
*The Big Show*
*New Orleans Homicide*
*Mafia Aphrodite*
*Slick Time*
*John Raven Beau*
*Battle Kiss*
*Enamored*
*Bourbon Street*
*Mistik*
**Short Story Collections**
*LaStanza: New Orleans Police Stories*
*New Orleans Confidential*
*New Orleans Prime Evil*
*New Orleans Nocturnal*
*New Orleans Mysteries*
*New Orleans Irresistible*
*Hollow Point & The Mystery of Rochelle Marais*
*Backwash of the Milky Way*
**Screenplay**
*Waiting for Alaina*
**Non-Fiction**
*A Short Guide to Writing and Selling Fiction*
*Specific Intent*

•

"O'Neil De Noux ... No one writes New Orleans as well as he does." James Sallis

"… the author knows his stuff when it comes to the Big Easy." *Publisher's Weekly*, 3/13/06

O'Neil De Noux would like to hear from you. If you liked this book or have ANY comment, email him at denoux3124@yahoo.com

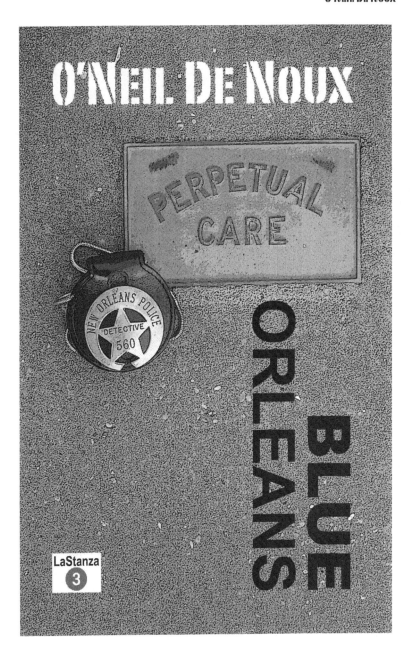

CRESCENT CITY KILLS

O'NEIL DE NOUX

NEW ORLEANS POLICE DETECTIVE 560

LaStanza 4

THE BIG
SHOW

LaStanza
5

O'NEIL DE NOUX

*don't miss the short story collection which begins when
Dino LaStanza is a patrolman –*

LaStanza Books by O'Neil De Noux
http://www.oneildenoux.net/dx/LASTANZA.html

More LaStanza novels coming –

OTHER BOOKS by O'Neil De Noux
http://www.oneildenoux.net

Made in the USA
Lexington, KY
31 May 2013